SEIDELMAN
& COMPANY

Bob Chinn

FLESH OF THE LOTUS

A Johnny Wadd Novel

**SEIDELMAN
& COMPANY**

Released by Publishing House
Seidelman & Company [Éditions Moustache]
Eintrachtstr. 41
52134 Herzogenrath
Germany

Copyright 2023 ©Bob Chinn
ISBN: 9783960346715
Cover Artwork: David Graham
Layout: Mirjam Pajakowski

Printed by Kindle Direct Publishing, Amazon.com Company
December 2023

First published by BearManor Media

Author's Preferred Text

SEIDELMAN & COMPANY:

Marco Siedelmann, Michael Gerhardt, Ewald Schulz, Mirjam Pajakowski,
Nadia Bruce-Rawlings, Tobias Gossen

Introduction

The fictional character Johnny Wadd was created purely by chance one day around forty years ago. This event came about after a tall, skinny fellow named John Curtis Holmes walked into my office looking for a job. At that time, I was only a few years out of film school and was working in the only field of the motion picture industry that had opened up to me.

This was the adult film business, which would later evolve into what subsequently be known as the porn industry. But these were the early days, the pioneering days, so to speak. I was working as a producer and a director, churning out extremely low-budget feature films that played the theaters that had the courage to play them, as well as the numerous storefront mini-theaters that had begun to pop up across the country.

These films were super-cheap productions, shot on 16mm film in one day with a total production budget of $750. We had only recently begun to really push the envelope with what we could show in regard to hardcore sex, and we were doing so with the belief that what we were doing was and should be protected by the First Amendment to the Constitution.

This was a moot point, however, because the local authorities were intent on shutting us down one way or another, primarily relying on outdated laws and ordinances. So we were forced to do what we were doing under constant threat of arrest and imprisonment. It was a hell of a way to make a living, but I had a wife and child to support, and aside from that, I really got off on striking my own little blow against censorship.

I have been adamantly opposed to censorship from the time I was in middle school, when I first learned, much to my surprise, that some of the books I wanted to read could not be obtained in this country because they had been banned. I found out that one way I would be able to read Henry Miller's *Sexus*, *Plexus*, and *Nexus* and J.P. Donleavy's *The Ginger Man* would be to mail order them from a source in Holland since they could not be legally sold in the United States.

I did this, and the source in Holland shipped them to me in two small parcels. One of the parcels made it through. The other was confiscated by U.S. Customs, and I was forced, under threat of prosecution, to go to the local post office and sign a Treasury Department form that authorized them to destroy it. The thought that the government of this free country, the greatest country in the world, was burning books made an impression on me that would eventually, for better or for worse, shape my future.

Along with the parcel that did get through came a long list of erotic literature that was banned and consequently not available for sale not only in the U.S.A. but in most of the English-speaking world. I was intrigued by these forbidden titles. The list included some of Henry Miller's banned and controversial earlier works, such as *Tropic of Cancer*, *Tropic of Capricorn*, and *Black Spring*, Lawrence Durrell's *The Black Book*, Vladimir Nabokov's *Lolita* and Terry Sothern's *Candy*. My youthful curiosity as well as my intellectual curiosity were aroused.

Of course, I ordered more books from overseas. Some of the packages that they came in got through to me. Others didn't. Eventually, the Treasury Department stopped making me go down to the post office by simply mailing me the destruction forms for me to sign. Not all of the books that I ordered could be considered literature, but I can say without shame that I enjoyed them all.

The graphic, sexually explicit passages fueled my imagination as they entertained me with their outrageousness and humor. I especially enjoyed the books by Akbar del Piombo, Alexander Trocchi, Marcus van Heller, and other creative and anonymous writers who churned out book after book for the pornography factory in Paris known as The Olympia Press.

Unfortunately, these packages sometimes took months to arrive, and the wait was always agonizing. Would the books I ordered make it through this time, or would U.S. Customs confiscate them once again? It was like playing a game of mail-order roulette. But when a package finally did arrive, bearing the postage stamps of the Netherlands or occasionally Germany, it was indeed an exciting occasion.

All those weeks and weeks of eager anticipation finally paid off when I unwrapped it and feasted my eyes on those innocent-appearing plain green paperback volumes bearing such interesting titles as *Skirts*, *Cosimo's Wife*, *Helen and Desire*, *Who Pushed Paula?*, *Sarabande for a Bitch*, and *How to Do It*.

It seemed to me that no one should be denied the pleasure of these books if they wanted to read them. Fortunately, a few years later, the Supreme Court of the United States of America made a decision that agreed with this, and they became legally available in this country for the first time. It is in the vein of these delightful works of once-forbidden erotica published in what was called *The Traveller's Companion* series that I have decided to base my Johnny Wadd novels.

As I said previously, John Curtis Holmes walked into the office looking for a job. One thing I have been asked many times, not only by the curious but also in various interviews on paper, in interviews that were taped, and in interviews that were filmed, is how I first came to meet John Holmes.

Since it now seems appropriate, I'll attempt to reconstruct this meeting now in a more or less definitive version: My business partner, Alain Patrick, and I worked out of a second-floor office that was situated in an old converted apartment building on Western Avenue, next to the Sunset Theater. The front room, which had been the living room, was an editing suite. What had once been the bedroom was the office area with the desk.

I was busy editing the trailer for our latest film when John walked in for an interview. We all went into the office, and John informed us that he had worked as a gaffer and was looking for a job on our film crew. Our film crew was pretty much set. Alain did the camera work, and our sound man was also the gaffer and the boom man. We didn't need and couldn't afford anyone else. Then John said he was also an actor.

I took one look at this tall, skinny white guy sporting an unruly Afro hairdo, which gave him a sort of goofy appearance. I didn't see a whole lot of potential there, so I went back to the front room to continue editing while Alain took the application and continued the interview. A few minutes later, Alain came into the room where I was busy editing and said, "Bob, you got to take a look at this guy's cock."

I looked up and told him that the last thing I wanted to do was to go into the office and look at some skinny guy's cock, but he was adamant, so I went in to have a look at it. You might say that I immediately realized the potential of John's sole, you might say outstanding attribute. We were scheduled to do another film in a couple of days, so we hired him on the spot.

We generally paid the male talent $50 for the day but John wanted $75. That extra $25 can mean a lot when your total production budget for the entire shoot is only $750. We hemmed and hawed then John said he would do three sex scenes and we thought well, we wouldn't need to have a third male actor, so we then agreed to his outrageous salary request.

I had always wanted to make a film with a sort of film noir type theme so I thought that this might be a good time to try this out. John would play a private dick with a big dick. I dashed of a quick script on the back of a legal-sized envelope. I was still having trouble coming up with a name for the private detective. We had been talking about the girls we were going to cast in the film and then the conversation came around to how much we disliked shooting those pull out and visibly shoot it all over climax scenes that theater owners insisted on, and then we were discussing the guy we had just hired and Alain casually remarked "God, the wad that guy must be able to shoot with a cock like that," and then I knew that we had it.

"Johnny Wadd," I said. "With two d's—we'll call him Johnny Wadd." It was a dumb name, but it worked. John showed up on the set a couple of days later wearing the one and only suit that he owned and also wearing a hat because we had told him that he was going to play a private detective.

He had also slicked back his hair with brilliantine, since I told him that the Afro had to go. The shoot went off pretty much as planned, except John wasn't really the stud he thought he was. By the time his third sex scene in eight hours rolled around, he was tired, but somehow, he managed to get through it.

We titled the film *Johnny Wadd* and released it without any fanfare. After all, it was just another piece of product for a market that was gobbling them up at the rate of one per week. A month or so passed before one of the theater owners called us up and asked, "Hey, when are you going to send us another one of those Johnny Wadd movies?" And then another called with the same question, and then another, and I realized that we might really have something going here.

The second Johnny Wadd film was titled *Flesh of the Lotus*. It was an immediate success, and the theater owners clamored for more. *Blonde in Black Lace* followed in rapid succession. Then the police began cracking down on porno shoots, and we decided to do the next Wadd movie out of town.

It was time for a vacation, so we all decided to go to Hawaii, where I managed to more or less improvise the fourth Johnny Wadd movie, which was titled *Tropic of Passion*. It was always interesting to see the reactions of the girls when they first got a look at John's oversized member. Some of these reactions were captured in some of the early films as well as a few of the later ones.

When we returned to Los Angeles, we found that the heat on the business had still not abated, so we went back to making softcore sex films and a few cheap low-budget mainstream exploitation features for awhile. I sold the outtake footage that was left over from the Hawaii shoot to a distributor named Manny Conde and gave him permission to work it into a softcore Johnny Wadd film that he subsequently released as *The Danish Connection*.

By that time, I felt as if I had gone as far as I wanted to with the series. It had reached the point where it no longer really interested me, and I just had to take some time off from it and do something else.

The next Johnny Wadd film would not be made until several years later. By 1975, my films were playing almost exclusively in the larger theaters that had begun to show adult fare as the old storefront minis began to slowly fade away or become adult bookstores and arcades. Even those early Johnny Wadd films, blown up from 16mm to 35mm, were playing some of the larger theaters.

By this time, budgets had gone up a bit, and the films could now be a little more elaborate. I hooked up with a producer who went by the name of Damon Christian and made the next series of Johnny Wadd movies for a company called Freeway Films. *Tell Them Johnny Wadd is Here* and *Liquid Lips* were both filmed back-to-back on location in Mexico and San Francisco, and both proved to be resounding successes at the large adult theater chain in California known as the Pussycat Theatres as well as other adult theatre boxoffices all across the country. The people, it seemed, remembered Johnny Wadd and wanted to see more of him.

We now had a little more money to work with, so we decided to invest it into teaming John with more beautiful girls and at least one name star. We had used Annette Haven in *Tell Them Johnny Wadd Is Here*, and it had proved to be a big selling point.

For the next production, we went back to San Francisco to film *The Jade Pussycat*, in which John appeared with Linda Wong and Georgina Spelvin. It was so successful that we made a sequel to it called *The China Cat*, which featured some of the most attractive newer girls of the time: Monti Stevens, Jennifer Richards, Christian Sarver, Eileen Welles, Kyoto Sun, and Desiree Cousteau. Then I licensed the Johnny Wadd character to Essex Distributing Company for one film, *Tapestry of Passion*, which was directed by my friend Alan Colberg.

The last Johnny Wadd movie that I directed was called *Blonde Fire*. It featured a newcomer named Seka as well as one of my favorite actresses, Jessie St. James, and had the somewhat exotic setting of South Africa. Of course, the budget constraints forced us to recreate this location at a warehouse in Oakland, which proved in itself to be an interesting challenge.

After *Blonde Fire*, I directed two more features that John starred in (*California Gigolo,* which featured the stripper Veri Knoty and an actual housewife who wanted to find out what it would be like to have sex with John named Vanessa Tibbs in her only role, and *Prisoner of Paradise* with Seka and Mai Lin), but by then he had become increasingly difficult to work with as well as a liability on the set because of his drug use.

It had reached the point where drugs had become more than simply an unhealthy obsession with him. I had always been able to control John on the set, but of course I had no control over his personal life. His cocaine addiction had begun to spiral way out of control, and when he began freebasing, I realized that I could no longer work with him, and I simply refused to do any more films with him from that time on. Of course, no one could predict the terrible tragedy that was to come, but in retrospect, it seems perhaps that it was probably inevitable.

Somehow I have been credited with fundamentally changing the Adult Film Industry with the Johnny Wadd series of movies, since it was the first time that adult films had been produced with a recurring character.

Of course, seen today, those shoestring productions of mine were, in all truth, pretty shoddy to say the least, and it would be a real stretch to try and justify them in spite of any idealistic intentions I may have had at the time. They can only be even remotely watchable if the viewer can accept them in the context of the time during which they were made, which makes them somewhat curious little historical artifacts and very little else.

To be known primarily as the creator of a private detective character with a foot-long schlong is a dubious distinction at best, but be that as it may, there never would have been a Johnny Wadd if a skinny young man named John Holmes had not walked into my office on that day in 1970. And John Holmes might probably never have become a household name if it hadn't been for a character called Johnny Wadd.

That name proved to be both a blessing and a curse for John. It made him into a major adult film star, but unfortunately, he was known and identified primarily by that fictitious name and not by his own. He made no secret of the fact that he was upset because people kept calling him Johnny Wadd rather than by his own name. He played many different roles in a good many of my films over the years that had nothing to do with the Johnny Wadd character, but that character still remains the role for which he is best known and nearly always identified.

I had not heard from John in many years, but one day, quite expectedly, he called me on the phone. He told me that he was terminally ill with cancer, but before he died, he wanted to make one more Johnny Wadd film. I had taken an early retirement from the business at that time and was living quietly in Hawaii. I really had no desire to make another one of those films, nor did I ever even want to work with him again, and I informed him of this. He then asked for permission to make one on his own, and I gave it to him and wished him good luck.

I have never seen the resulting production, which was titled *The Return of Johnny Wadd*, but from what I understand, it's a sad affair. I find it even more than sad that this dying man, who had somehow managed to get through the pure horror of a nightmarish downward spiral in his unfortunate and messed-up life, could only once again try to regain a small measure of his former self by making a final attempt at resuscitating the ghost of the particular character that had made him famous.

Of course, I say this just as I am attempting to resurrect that very same character in this novel, *Flesh of the Lotus*. The novel incorporates some of the framework of the one-day quickie mini-theater feature that I made back in 1971, but in actuality, it is nothing like it.

In this book, I have tried to depict the character as more or less as I had originally envisioned him and would have liked him to be, and the story is set in the very era in which he was created. It was the era of the Vietnam War when both our country and our society were in the beginning stages of undergoing a radical transformation.

It was the period before everyone had a cellular phone, and people still used phone booths and could smoke cigarettes inside of restaurants, airports, airplanes, or just about anywhere, for that matter. It was a time when handguns and car bumpers were made of metal instead of plastic. It was a period when our country was still in the grip of the Cold War and the threat of Communism appeared to loom large on the horizon.

We did not realize at the time, of course, that our politicians were cleverly manipulating the fear factor to justify war. The politicians of Red China were also using the fear factor in an attempt to consolidate and hold on to power in what became known as the Cultural Revolution. The end result in both these cases was the untold number of deaths of ordinary, innocent people—in our case from the result of war and in theirs as the result of politically motivated purges.

Sadly, the mindless paranoia of those times would be echoed once again when the Bush administration used the fear factor in a similar fashion to justify not only a needless war in Iraq but also to allow unprecedented government control over our basic liberties and right to privacy as well. If history teaches us anything, it is that we certainly do not learn from our past mistakes.

So let's go back to a time before the disease known as AIDS became a deadly international plague, a time before international terrorism and suicide bombing became an almost everyday occurrence in various parts of the world. It was a time that was a little more innocent than it is now, when people were becoming more aware of not only the vast and changing world around them but also of the true meaning of life, liberty, and the pursuit of not only happiness but pleasure as well.

Johnny Wadd, the private detective character that I have depicted in this book, was a part of that revolutionary era, and he should not be confused with John Holmes, the man, even though somehow they seem to have become almost inextricably linked by history into a single person.

—Bob Chinn

Chapter One

Los Angeles, California – Monday, December 18, 1972

The phone rang just after five in the morning, startling me awake from a deep and peaceful sleep, and I picked it up to hear the all too familiar voice of homicide detective George Lee. George and I went way back. In fact, we go all the way back to grade school, middle school, and high school in Santa Monica, where we were almost inseparable as best friends.

Good old Samo High, as we called it back then, and as they probably still call it now. Those were the days. But that was then, and now is now. George and I are no longer inseparable, and we're no longer best friends. And after only three hours of sleep, I really wasn't in the very best of moods.

"This better be fucking important, George," was all I could say as I struggled to open my eyes and clear the cobwebs of sleep from my head.

"It is," he said. "Come on down to the beach at the end of Washington Boulevard. I'll be there waiting for you."

Washington Boulevard was around a mile or so from my little one-bedroom house, which is a block from the beach near the edge of the inlet that separates the area of Los Angeles known as Venice from the area known as Marina Del Rey. So I decided that I was going to walk—notice I said walk and not jog—instead of taking the car. I used to jog a mile or two every day because I had believed that it was a healthy thing to do. I also had a friend who used to jog a mile or two every day because he thought it was the healthy thing to do. One day, while he was jogging, he had a heart attack and dropped dead right there on the spot.

He wasn't much older than me, so after that, I came to the conclusion that jogging just might possibly be somewhat dangerous to one's health. Walking, however, was a thing that I considered to be acceptable—acceptable, that is if you didn't overdo it.

Anyway, this particular day I reasoned that it would be a pleasant enough walk at this time of morning and, quite frankly, I needed the exercise. So after a quick shower, I brushed my teeth, gargled with Listerine to kill the germs and keep the plaque at bay, put on some casual clothes, and almost as an afterthought, grabbed my jacket and headed out to greet the day.

The night's darkness was beginning to make way for the coming of the dawn as I started out down the deserted walkway leading to the beach. I could see that the beach was shrouded with a low-lying haze that would probably begin to burn off with the welcome arrival of the sun.

The briny smell of the sea mingled with the early morning moisture in the air, and the appetizing aroma of freshly brewed coffee and frying bacon made its way from one of the anonymous nearby houses, where some poor soul had been forced to get up and prepare for an early day of work. The smell was making me hungry, and I began to wish that I'd at least made myself a cup of coffee before leaving the house.

The beach was pretty much deserted, and as I made my way down the boardwalk, I gradually became aware of the fact that I was really in crummy physical shape. I had only approached the halfway mark and was already starting to get winded. Way too many cigarettes and way too much booze was the only conclusion that made sense to me.

Even my feet were beginning to hurt, and it suddenly felt as if it would take me forever to traverse that half mile to where Washington Boulevard ends at the beach. I made a mental note to myself to start seriously thinking about changing my lifestyle.

I arrived on the scene with the sunrise as it tried valiantly to break through the low-lying fog. Even in Southern California, the early winter mornings can be very cold, and because of the winter storms that had blanketed the West Coast to the Rockies this past week, it happened to be especially cold on this particular one, which made me glad that I had decided to wear my coat. I buttoned it up as the wind whipped about with such force that I could feel the chill penetrating to my very bones.

There was a coroner's van parked near the beach, and several cops were standing around what appeared from the distance to be a dead body not far from the shoreline. Flashes of light periodically illuminated the scene as a police photographer went about his job of documenting what appeared probably to be the corpse and the surrounding area where it lay. As I moved closer, my initial suspicion was confirmed when I saw one of the cops leaving the van and heading toward the beach carrying an empty body bag.

There weren't too many gawkers about yet because it was so early, but some seagulls circled screeching overhead as they took in the strange scene of the humans milling about below them. From far away in the distance, the sound of a foghorn pierced the air.

As I drew closer, I noticed George Lee standing over the nude body of a female that had apparently washed ashore. George is easy to spot because he's usually one of the only cops who happens to be a Chinese-American standing around a crime scene. He was eating one of those greasy hamburgers that he loved to eat, and as I approached him, the smell of onions mingled with the strong and unpleasant odor of decomposed human flesh.

"How can you eat those things this early in the morning?" I asked.

He looked up and regarded me silently for a moment, but didn't answer. Then he took another bite of his burger and nodded his head toward the corpse lying there on the sand.

I followed his gaze down to the grotesque and grisly remains of what had once been a human life. "Looks like she's been in the water for some time," I managed to say as I struggled with the nausea I was feeling because of the sickening smell of rotting flesh and the stark, shocking sight of the discolored and bloated body. I had seen enough, and I turned away to look questioningly at George.

"So why did you get me out of bed to come here and see this?" I asked. I had seen more than my share of dead bodies in the course of my lifetime and wasn't really very enthusiastic about seeing another. "It's colder than a witch's tit out here this morning."

"Thirty-five degrees with the wind chill factor," George said. Then he made a motion with his head toward the corpse. "Take a good look at her."

"I already had a good look at her," I said with my teeth chattering.

"Look closer," George said before taking another big bite of his hamburger. And then, while chewing with his mouth full, "Recognize her?"

I squatted down and looked more closely, barely able to keep from gagging as the wind suddenly changed direction and blew the stench directly at my face. I was suddenly glad that I hadn't had a chance to partake of any breakfast or coffee. I could see that it was the body of a woman who must have been relatively young, probably in her middle or late twenties. She had reddish blonde hair and what had once been very fair skin, and she appeared to have had a pretty good figure.

As I examined the body more closely, I had the strange feeling that somehow she seemed familiar. I shifted my position to get a better look at what was left of the face, and I suddenly froze. A wave of nausea suddenly washed over me, and I felt as if I would be ill. I struggled to maintain control of both my equilibrium and the contents of my stomach.

The realization had dawned, in spite of the fact that a good deal of her face had been eaten away by crabs and countless other sea creatures, that I knew who this corpse was. There was a sinking feeling gripping the pit of my stomach as I hesitantly looked down at her right hip to see the small birthmark that confirmed my suspicion.

Totally taken aback, I stood up quickly, as if I'd seen a ghost, and backed away from the body, my face flushed and my head spinning, feeling somewhat dizzy and disoriented. I took a deep breath and struggled to overcome the shock of seeing her this way before I finally managed to gain control of myself. I turned around to see that George had been watching me.

"It's Sheila Ross, isn't it?" I said while at the same time still trying not to believe that it was, indeed, her or what was left of her.

George nodded. "Sort of a shock to see her like this, isn't it?"

Yes, it was a shock, but I couldn't find it in myself to dignify something so obvious with a spoken answer, so I only nodded in agreement.

"Probably been in the water a week or so," the coroner's investigator standing next to George said. "We'll know more after we do the autopsy." He took off his latex gloves, pulled a cigarette from his pocket, and lit it.

He continued, "It appears as if her throat has been slit, but I'm not so sure yet whether this was the cause of death or not. Sure looks like it, though." He had apparently finished his examination of the corpse because he motioned for the cop with the body bag over to bag the remains.

"When do you think they'll do the autopsy?" George asked him.

The coroner's investigator took a deep draw from the cigarette and exhaled the smoke, which blew past my face. At that moment, I had an extremely strong craving for a cigarette, but I realized that, unfortunately, I had left mine at home.

"I don't know how backed up the medical examiner is," the coroner's investigator was saying, "but this definitely looks like a homicide, so it'll be a priority."

What he said seemed to snap me out of my initial sense of shock. In its place, I felt a sense of outrage. "Who in the hell did this?" I suddenly blurted out with unrestrained anger.

George turned to me and calmly said, "I was thinking maybe you could tell me."

Ever since high school, George Lee and I have had a sort of love-hate thing going. But it's mostly hate. At one time, we were close friends, but that was a long time ago. A lot of water has passed under the bridge since then. One of the things we had a falling-out over was a girl, and that very girl was lying dead there on the beach, not more than a couple of feet away from us.

George tossed away the greasy hamburger wrapper, briefly littering the dirty sand, before a breeze picked it up and blew it off toward a wave that was crashing onto the shore. The wave picked it up, and the piece of yellow waxed paper slowly drifted out to sea.

He took a wooden toothpick out of his pocket, began picking his teeth with it, and said, "So what happened, John? You two get in a fight?"

"Come again?"

"I said, did you two get in a fight?"

I couldn't believe what I was hearing. "You think I killed her?" The emphasis was heavy on the word I.

George gave his sarcastic smirk. "I don't know, John. Did you?"

"Of course I didn't. You of all people should know that."

There was a dramatic pause while he chewed on the toothpick. He appeared deep in thought for a moment. Then he continued. "Her body washes up less than a mile from where you're living. She's your girlfriend. So what do you think?"

"She was my girlfriend ten years ago, George. When we were in high school and junior college, for Christ's sake! I haven't seen her in ten fucking years." I was getting a little hot under the collar by now, and he was watching me and enjoying it.

George continued chewing on the toothpick and smiling. "So you say, but I don't know that for a fact now, do I?" He spat the chewed-up toothpick out of his mouth. "Sure seems suspicious to me, John."

"That's bullshit, and you know it!" I had just about all I could take from George at this point. I turned around and started to walk off. My feelings were in turmoil with the shock and horror of seeing the corpse of someone I had once known and loved, and I had heard enough of his bullshit. If I hung around any longer, I didn't know what I'd do, but I knew that whatever I did happen to do would probably end me up in jail.

"Hey, wait a minute. I'm not through with you." George was beginning to sound pissed now, but I really didn't give a damn.

"Well, I'm through with you," I replied without turning back as I continued walking. There were some quick footsteps behind me, and suddenly I felt a hand on my back. I stopped and slowly turned around.

George was right there in my face, and he had one of those dead serious, threatening looks on his fat cop face. "Maybe you'd rather finish this up at the station."

"Are you putting me under arrest? Then read me my rights." He still had his greasy hand on my shoulder.

He considered his options for a moment, then suddenly smiled that shit-eating smile of his. "Just want to ask you a few questions, John, that's all."

"So ask."

"Did you kill her?"

"No."

"When was the last time you saw her?"

"Are you deaf? I already told you. Ten years ago. Now take your filthy fucking hand off my shoulder."

The frustration was building up inside me, and there was nothing that I could do about it. I could feel my face flushing red in spite of the cold wind blowing around us, and for a brief moment, I thought George might interpret this as a sign of guilt. But I didn't care because I knew that I was innocent. I just couldn't believe that he didn't think I was.

George hesitated, and then he complied by taking his hand off of me in a condescending manner while uttering that trite, silly standard cop line: "Just don't leave town, Wadd."

"I wasn't planning to," I stated emphatically, looking him straight in the eye. He looked as if he wanted to say something more to me, and he opened his mouth and started to, but I ignored him by turning away and walking off.

George had managed to stir up a lot of anger and resentment in me with his callous and snide innuendos, so I turned around, wanting only to get away from him as quickly as possible, and I couldn't help but cringe when I felt his greasy paw on my shoulder once again. I spun around to face him. At this point, I was getting much more than a little pissed off, and I wasn't thinking too carefully about what I said next.

"What is it with you that you can't keep your hands off me? Are you still bent out of shape because Sheila wanted to fuck me and not you? Is that it?"

I should have seen his fat fist coming, but I didn't, and I sure felt it as it crashed into the area between my stomach and my chest, exploding the wind out of my lungs and doubling me up with sudden and unexpected pain. My knees hit the ground, and I stayed there for a long agonizing moment before I was finally able to stand up. I struggled to recover while at the same time fighting the strong urge to strike back, which was just what George wanted me to do.

George and I were both the same age, thirty-two going on sixty. You might say that in the course of our years, we've both seen and experienced far too much of life, and by this, I mean mostly the bad side of life. We've both been through things that have aged us way beyond our years, things that are probably responsible for our warped mental outlook.

But whereas I was still relatively thin, he had given in to the tendency to put on more than a little extra weight. I suppose he just couldn't resist the siren call of all those sweet-glazed donuts and those artery-clogging, greasy hamburgers. It was more than evident that he was well on his way to becoming fat, and the prominent beer gut hanging over his belt showed it.

Physically, it was really no contest between us. He stood five foot eight inches, and I was six feet two. On the other hand, he was bulkier than me, and he weighed a lot more, but then again, most of that weight was just pure, unhealthy flab.

There was a time in the past when he used to work out, but that time was long past. Since he was basically lazy by nature, he'd given up on that particular struggle quite awhile back. Still, he could be vicious when provoked, and I'd never known him to back away from a fight.

He stood there, smiling and expectantly waiting, while studying my agonized expression as I held back my tightly clenched fist. I'm not particularly in any great shape myself, but I still knew that I could waste him right there and then. If anyone was more out of shape than I was, it would be George, no question about it. Besides, ever since we were kids, I could always cream his ass. He looked tough, but he really wasn't. I could very easily punch him out so that he'd be puking that greasy hamburger all over the beach.

But that was all I needed to do, I told myself. Hit a cop. That would be a one-way ticket to jail—do not pass go. And I knew that George would like nothing more than to see me in the slammer. Yeah, I just had to keep it under control, I thought to myself. Keep it under control. It took all the power that I possessed to restrain myself.

George was waiting, trying to anticipate my next move. I watched him just standing there and smiling, waiting for me to strike back at him. And believe me, I was really tempted to wipe that wise-ass smile off his face, but I didn't. Finally, he realized that I wasn't going to take a swing at him, and he laughed.

"I don't recall you being so chicken."

"Yeah, well, times change, I suppose."

"You got that right," he smirked. He started to say something else, but he didn't. He just stood there, smiling at me with that superior ass smile of his.

"Come to think of it, I don't recall you being such an asshole," I said, and the smile quickly disappeared off his face.

"Time has come for a few friendly words of warning, John. Watch out. Life's a meat grinder, and you can't stay out of it forever. It's only a matter of time before you fall in and get yourself all ground up."

Chapter Two

I thought about Sheila as I slowly walked down the beachfront promenade, heading for home. I remembered the first time I'd ever seen her, which was back in the third or fourth grade. She was a pretty, quiet little girl with dirty, stringy blonde hair who wore faded hand-me-down clothes that probably came from a thrift shop. George and I were best friends back then.

We were just a couple of wise-assed boys who took cruel delight in teasing the poor unfortunate girl, who always looked unwashed and walked around with her eyes downcast. One day we made her cry, and from that day on, we never teased her again.

We found out that she lived in a trailer park with her mother, who was an alcoholic. We had been in that trailer home once. It had reeked of years of stale cigarette smoke, cheap whiskey, and unwashed bedding. Her mother had never married, and Sheila never knew or found out who her father was. We realized what a sad life she had been forced to lead, and from that day on, we became her protectors.

Sheila's mother died young—this happened around the time we were in middle school—and Sheila went to live with an aunt. It was at this point that her life seemed to change for the better. The aunt worked in one of those large department stores on Wilshire Boulevard, and for the first time in her life, Sheila had nice clothes to wear and a decent place to live.

She began to blossom into a bright and attractive young woman. By the time high school rolled around, she was not only beautiful but very popular as well, and all the boys were after her. But I was the lucky one. It seemed as if she only had eyes for me.

We decided to go steady, and this put a crimp in both of our relationships with George. He was feeling left out, and especially so because he had some pretty strong romantic feelings for Sheila as well. I guess he just couldn't accept the fact that she didn't share a similar feeling for him. He started drifting apart from us at this point.

After high school, all three of us went on to attend Santa Monica City College, but by then, things were never the same between us. George had a deferment from the army, and he went on to begin his career with the Santa Monica Police Department.

Sheila and I briefly continued our relationship until I was drafted into the army and eventually sent to serve two tours of duty in Vietnam. We continued writing to each other for awhile, but by the time of my second tour, our letters had become fewer and further between, and then there were none.

I managed to survive through the war somehow and finished serving my military time. After I was discharged and returned to civilian life, I learned from mutual acquaintances that Sheila had been married and divorced and lived somewhere in the Hollywood Hills. But the past had become a chapter that was finally closed for good—for both of us. I suppose somehow things had changed and we all had just moved on with our lives. Sheila and I never got around to reconnecting.

Of course, I ran into George Lee a few times in the intervening years, occasionally on the street by chance or in a store or restaurant, and sometimes while I was pursuing an investigation, but we never got together again as friends, and we had never discussed either Sheila or our past relationship.

The first thing I did when I got home was light a cigarette to undo any good all of that healthy exercise had done for me. Then I started making coffee but decided to make myself a stiff drink instead. As the bourbon was warming and warring with my empty stomach, the phone rang. It was George Lee.

He said, "John, I was out of line. I'm sorry."

"That's okay."

Then, after a moment of silence: "Let's get together for a drink sometime."

"Sure."

I hung up the phone and finished the drink in my hand. It occurred to me that his apology had seemed sincere and that it meant more to me than I cared to admit. I heaved a heavy sigh and tried to ignore the uncomfortable feeling that I probably had what was going to be a long and unpleasant day ahead of me.

There were things that I knew I had to do, and the sooner I started doing them, then the sooner they would get done. I started by thumbing through the West Los Angeles phone book until I found that there was still a listing for Sheila's aunt.

After hesitating for a long and reflective moment, I dialed the number. After a few rings, an older yet unmistakably familiar voice answered. She was surprisd to hear from me, and when I told her that I had to see her, she invited me to come on over. I didn't have the heart to tell her about her niece over the phone.

Wilma Ross lived in one of those older apartment buildings that still lined the streets north of Wilshire, near where the city of Santa Monica bordered the area known as West Los Angeles.

Her crowded little two-bedroom apartment looked pretty much the same as it had all those many years ago. There was the familiar smell of furniture polish mingled with the absorbed remains of years and years of cigarette smoke and decades of food that had been fried or boiled in the small enclosed kitchen alcove just off the tiny living room.

It was like stepping into a time warp. The furniture was the same furniture in the exact same place as it had been all those many years before. Also in the exact same place were the now faded pictures on the wall. There were framed pictures of a young Sheila and her mother standing beside a much younger Wilma. There were a number of ancient photographs of people I had never known and never would know.

There was also Sheila's high school graduation portrait. I had a smaller print of that same portrait stored away with my own old personal possessions in a cardboard box somewhere in my bedroom closet.

Only the television set was different—a smaller, newer model as opposed to the big old wood-framed console that I remembered. Three Christmas cards had been placed on top of it, reminding me that the holiday season had indeed arrived, and this was doubly confirmed by a small artificial Christmas tree that stood lonely and forlorn beside it. There were no Christmas presents beneath it, and I made a mental note to remember to buy her one.

Wilma herself looked pretty much the same as before, just older. By now, she must be in her early or middle seventies. When I first arrived, I could tell that Wilma had been crying.

"George Lee called and told me about Sheila," she said.

I was glad that George had spared me the duty of having to tell her. She said that she would have to go down to the County Morgue to identify the body as the next-of-kin.

"I'll drive you down there," I said.

She looked up at me and smiled. "That's nice of you," she said, "but George said he'd come and pick me up." She was quiet for awhile, then we made some small talk about the unimportant things people speak of when they haven't seen each other in a long time before she continued.

"The last time I saw her was over two years ago. After the divorce, she came to live with me for a few weeks. Then she moved in with a friend who has a place over in Hollywood."

"Do you remember the name of her friend?"

"I have it written down in my address book. In case I had to get in touch with her for some reason."

She searched around for her address book, and after she found it, she copied down the name, address, and phone number for me. I thanked her, and as I started to leave, she said, "Sheila called me on my birthday last year. It was the last time I ever heard from her." Tears rolled down her eyes at this memory, and she hastily wiped them away.

I gave her my card. "If you need anything, please call me." She nodded.

Just before I walked out the door, I heard her say, "You know, Sheila was always very much in love with you."

I nodded but didn't turn around because the tears had begun to well up in my own eyes.

The address Wilma had written down led me to a small house on a small winding street in the Hollywood Hills. I didn't use the phone number to call ahead because I found that unexpected visits usually proved to be more effective. The name on the piece of paper said Billie Rae Chase, but there was no Billie Rae Chase at that address.

The current occupant was a young, brown-haired surfer-type dude who smelled of marijuana and Mennen Skin Bracer. He didn't know a thing about the previous occupant or anyone named Billie Rae Chase, but after a little prodding, cooperated somewhat by giving me the name and phone number of the landlord.

A phone call to the landlord confirmed that Billie Rae had indeed once lived in the house, but she had absconded, owing four months' rent and leaving the house a total wreck in the bargain. He complained about having to repaint the place, put in new carpeting, and replace broken furniture. After promising to let him know when I found her, he agreed to share any information that he had on her, which wasn't a whole lot.

Her rental application listed her job as 'actress,' and this could mean any number of things but usually meant anything from 'waitress' to 'hooker.' However, from the long experience I had trolling through the seamy underbelly of Hollywood, I knew something else it could also mean would be 'nude model' or someone who usually got jobs performing in skin flicks.

Most of the girls who flocked to Hollywood in pursuit of a serious acting career and movie stardom eventually ended up on this particular road, when their youthful, starry-eyed idealistic dream began turning into an unexpected and terrible nightmare—the nightmare for survival.

I had a strong gut feeling that Billie Rae was one of these girls. And the easiest way to check this particular theory out was to head for a popular modeling agency I knew about that occupied an old storefront on Santa Monica Boulevard in West Hollywood.

Hal Crane was a fatherly, middle-aged gray-haired man who called himself an agent but in reality was simply another bottom-feeder who made a sleazy living from the misfortunes of the young and talented and the young and not so talented girls who desperately wanted to be in motion pictures. Still, he was personable, friendly, and basically honest, and no one really spoke ill of him.

He was known for seriously trying to help those girls who really needed and wanted to work find work. He looked after those girls like a father, always stood up for them, and tried his best to protect them from the numerous unscrupulous operators that inhabited the entertainment industry.

By the same token, he was also a shrewd businessman, and as a shrewd businessman, he didn't hesitate to take his percentage of whatever salary they made because the bottom line for him was, of course, making money.

But what was generally not so well known was that if one of the girls he represented had absolutely no talent at all and really didn't have a snowball's chance in hell of making it in this town, he would take the money out of his own pocket and buy her a bus ticket back home. This was one of the reasons why I liked Hal.

Of course, Hal would never admit to being such a softie. Once, when I asked him about it, he replied by saying, "Hell, buying 'em a bus ticket is a lot cheaper than continually loaning 'em money for rent and food." But he knew only too well that girls in that position were just one step away from the streets.

Another reason why I liked Hal was because he didn't use or tolerate the use of drugs with his girls. It was a sad fact of life that drugs were really starting to become a serious problem in the local entertainment industry. But no one in the industry wanted to admit it. They just wanted to go on as if it was a problem that didn't exist.

As always, Hal was impeccably dressed in his somewhat out-of-style light blue suit and dark blue necktie as he sat behind his old-fashioned massive wooden desk and silently considered the question I had asked him before not answering it by asking a question of his own.

"Billie Rae Chase, huh? Why do you want to know about her?"

It was natural for him to be protective with regard to his clients, so I told him about Sheila and about her being Billie Rae's roommate. I explained that his client might be a possible connection that could help lead me to finding out what might have happened to cause her violent and untimely death.

A serious expression came across Hal's face when he heard this. He tapped his fingers on the desk while he thoughtfully considered what I had just told him. Then I could see by the look on his face that he had made the decision to tell me what he knew.

"Well, I dropped Billie Rae like a hot potato about six months ago," he finally said as he picked up his pencil and erased something on the piece of paper in front of him.

"Why did you drop her?"

"Why? She was way too heavy into the drug scene. She'd become unreliable, missing appointments, and constantly showing up late for work." He shook his head at the memory. "And then it got to the point when she didn't even show up for work at all, or when she did, she was usually so wasted that she couldn't remember her lines. I began getting a lot of complaints about her."

He paused for a moment and then leaned forward toward me and spoke softly, as if he were confiding a secret. "When I heard she was dealing on the set, well, that was just the icing on the cake. I told her to find another agent and took her out of my book."

This was all starting to get very interesting. It was beginning to appear that Sheila had switched gears to living her life in the fast lane, something that I would have believed to have been totally out of character for her. I found it difficult to reconcile this new Sheila that was emerging with the girl that I once knew.

"What kind of drugs are we talking about?"

"Cocaine," he said with undisguised disgust. "That seems to be the popular drug of choice now. It keeps 'em up feeling good and partying all night. Sure, they think that it's all innocent fun, but for some, like Billie Rae—well it really grabs a hold on them until it starts controlling their lives."

He shook his head at the memory and settled back in his chair. "It's really a shame because at one time she was a really nice girl—you know, the all-American girl type. She was a country girl, from North Carolina or somewhere, but it didn't even take her very long to lose the accent. She was young, fresh, and eager."

"Isn't that the way they all start out?"

"It is, but she was special. For awhile, there she was a hot commodity. She did print work for newspaper ads, a few television commercials, and, of course, the skin flicks. I had gotten her a lot of bookings over the years, until she fell apart. I really hated to lose her."

"You know where I can get hold of her?"

"Why would you want to? She's a lesbian, you know."

"I don't want to fuck her, Hal. I just want to ask her some questions."

"I'm just joking with you, John," he laughed. "But she is a stone lesbian, and that's a fact."

Hal went over to his file cabinet and pulled open a drawer. He rummaged through some files, muttering, "Chase…Billie Rae Chase," before slamming that drawer shut with a mumbled curse and pulling open another and rummaging through it.

It was taking him forever to find what he was looking for, and I was beginning to think that his filing system was even worse than mine when he finally pulled out a manila file folder and exclaimed with audible relief, "Here it is!"

He seated himself back at his desk, opened it up, and wrote down the last phone number and address he had on her. I glanced at her printed resume, which listed over a page and a half of credits. I also managed to get a look at her picture. She had long black hair and a dynamite body. Definitely an all-American girl type, like he said. Sort of ordinary in the face department, but not at all unattractive, and I thought silently to myself, too bad she's a lesbian.

Chapter Three

Billie Rae's small studio apartment on the second floor of the crumbling old building a few blocks south of Pico Boulevard in the Fairfax district was quite a comedown from the small house she once had in the Hollywood Hills.

The haggard woman with the cigarette in her mouth wearing a short, frayed, and slightly soiled terrycloth bathrobe who answered the door was also somewhat of a comedown from the picture I'd seen in Hal's folder. The drugs had really taken their toll. She looked me up and down appraisingly, blew a long stream of cigarette smoke in my face, and listlessly asked, "What do you want?"

"I just want to ask you a few questions."

"Not interested," she said, and began to close the door.

"It's about Sheila."

She hesitated. The name had penetrated the fog that enshrouded her mind and sent her brain some kind of signal. She looked me over again, and then, still somewhat suspicious, she cautiously opened the door just a little bit wider.

"Who did you say you were?"

"I didn't, but my name is Johnny Wadd."

She looked very closely at my face, and I in turn looked closely into hers, and I thought I could see some kind of light bulb turning on in her mind, and it suddenly seemed as if some kind of dim but slight recognition finally dawned in her eyes.

"Oh, yeah, you're the guy Sheila used to talk about. I remember your picture now." She opened the door wider. "Come on in."

As soon as I walked through the door, I could see that Billie Rae's place was a mess. Clothes were strewn about helter-skelter on the floor and on the sofa, and there was a pile of unwashed dishes in the sink.

There seemed to be about ten years worth of dust on everything, even on the partly opened portfolio near the sofa that held her model photographs and a small stack of the composite photo resumes that those in the motion picture and entertainment industries called head shots. Struggling actors and actresses saved their hard-earned dollars to get these printed up so they could hopefully get acting jobs, but the sad but true fact of life is that they usually ended up lining some casting director's trash can. One thing you could bet on for sure was that Billie Rae was not a great housekeeper.

There were some old, almost empty Chinese food takeout containers on the coffee table and a large abalone shell ashtray, along with a couple of dirty highball glasses which sat on a 33 1/3 rpm LP record that she apparently used for a coaster. There was also a half-empty wine bottle, which I had the feeling she'd been working on before I arrived, a half-eaten apple that had begun to turn brown, and a long flesh-colored double-ended dildo.

"Have a seat," she said as she moved aside a white bra and pair of pink panties to make a place on the sofa for me. I sat, and she sat next to me. Her robe parted in the front a little and revealed that she was naked beneath it.

Her lifestyle hadn't seemed to have affected her body, which still appeared to be in great shape. My eyes wandered to the dildo on the coffee table, and I wondered if she had been working on that before I arrived as well. She picked up the half-empty bottle.

"Want some wine?" she asked.

"I think I'll pass," I answered as she poured some into one of the dirty glasses.

She took a deep drink and then said, "I haven't seen Sheila for a couple of weeks now. How is she?"

I couldn't figure out any other way to break it to her than to say, "She's dead."

"Dead?" was all she said, and she said it not particularly as a question but more as if she didn't really believe me. She snuffed out her cigarette in the already overcrowded abalone shell ashtray and looked up at me as if she expected me to say more.

"They found her body this morning. It looks like a homicide. Her throat was slit."

The grim reality of what I was saying seemed to sink in, and she appeared to believe me now, and the puzzled and startled expression on Billie Rae's face told me that perhaps she really hadn't known. Then it seemed as if some kind of realization dawned in her befuddled mind, and her eyes darted from side to side, and she seemed scared. These all added up to a lot of expressions to come across a face in a very short span of time, and while they all appeared real, I had to remember that she considered herself to be an actress.

"You know something, don't you?" It was a statement as well as a question, and I waited for her answer.

Her hands were shaking as she quickly drained the glass of wine and poured herself another, then drained that one as well. Finally, she said, "I'm afraid, Johnny. I'm really afraid."

"What are you afraid of?"

"You really don't know, do you?"

"I do know that I hadn't seen Sheila for over ten years, until this morning when I saw what was left of her." I said.

Billie Rae shuddered. I continued. "What was going on with her? I know that you know, Billie Rae. Please tell me."

She poured herself the last drink in the bottle and quickly finished it off. Now it seemed as if she was ready to talk. "She was involved with some bad people—some really dangerous bad people."

"Did it have to do with drugs?" I asked, but I already knew the answer. She nodded and confirmed my suspicions.

"Did you get her involved with them? I know you're a dealer."

A look of stunned surprise came across her face. Then she laughed a short, bitter laugh. "You've got it ass backwards, cowboy. She's the one who was supplying me."

It was my turn to be stunned and surprised. My surprise must have shown because she went on, "There seems to be a lot you really don't know about Sheila."

"I suppose you're right. Like I said, I haven't seen her for ten years." I was still trying to process the startling revelations that were coming my way. "So tell me about her."

She was silent for a moment, as if she were considering my request. Her face was flushed from all the wine she had just chugged down, and I was hoping that all that wine would aid in loosening her tongue. But instead she said, "You want me to satisfy your curiosity, don't you? Well, what if I want you to satisfy mine?"

"What do you mean?"

She smiled and moved closer to me on the sofa. I could tell that she was a little more than slightly drunk. "You know, Sheila told me that you're really big—in that department." She indicated my crotch with a slight nod of her head. "Just how big are you?"

I was taken aback by her question but not totally unprepared. That question had been asked before, and I knew would continue to be asked again. We all have our cross to bear, I suppose.

I turned and nodded my head slightly toward the long double dildo on her coffee table and replied, "Bigger than that."

Billie Rae gave me a look that said she thought I was full of shit and she didn't believe me, but then again, she wasn't quite sure, so she said, "Well, then this I've just got to see."

She reached over, and before I could protest, she unzipped my fly. I felt a little embarrassed at being the object of a lesbian's curiosity, especially when she reached into my pants and pulled out my limp penis. She examined it with a critical eye.

"It's not so big," she said matter-of-factly.

"It gets a lot bigger," I said as I started to put it back into my pants. She reached over and stopped me.

"Well let's just see," she said before she took it in her mouth. You might say I was more than surprised. This was about the last thing I expected to happen. From the way she was handling the situation, I could tell that she'd done this before, and no doubt more than once. She was good. She was really good.

"I thought you were a lesbian."

She took my cock out of her mouth and looked up at me. "I am."

Then she put it back in her mouth and began sucking me like I'd never been sucked before. The blowjob she was giving me tran-scended the squalor of her gritty little apartment and made me feel as if I had suddenly been transported almost, but not quite, all the way to heaven.

Even though I hadn't really been in the mood for sex, Billie Rae's expert ministrations succeeded in making me hard within a matter of minutes, and when I say hard, I mean *really* hard. Billie Rae had turned into a virtual sucking machine, utilizing her capacious mouth and throat and both hands, which encircled me one above the other as well. Eventually she removed me from her mouth and, with wide and somewhat unbelieving eyes, surveyed her accomplishment.

"You're absolutely right," she said with a somewhat amazed smile. "It is bigger than my dildo." Emphasis, of course, was on the word is.

After saying that, she opened her robe, laid back on the sofa, spread her legs wide, and inserted me inside of her. She was very warm and very wet, and a quick gasp escaped her lips as it easily slid half of its length inside of her. After a moment, she said, "Push it in deeper." I pushed and felt it slowly sink in to the hilt, and she gave a long, low moan and said, "Now don't move."

What happened next was totally unexpected. She began rotating her hips, slowly at first—then faster and faster, screwing herself with my rock-hard erection, which was totally trapped inside of her. To say I was amazed is an understatement. First of all, I had never experienced anyone who could take all of me in this state, and she had indeed done that. I had absolutely no idea where it all went.

I had also never experienced what she was now doing to me. The sensations from being so totally engulfed inside of someone was so new and pleasurable that I was almost beside myself. And from the way she was moaning and groaning, she was obviously experiencing something new and pleasurable too.

"Oh, good," she murmured. "So good!" She raised her head up and kissed me. Her long tongue shot into my mouth, probing deeply inside of it while I probed deeply inside of her. Her breath smelled pleasantly of wine and apples, with a slight tinge of cigarette smoke.

She was panting hard now, and I could feel that she was working herself up to her climax. Suddenly she let out a little scream, and her hips stopped in mid-air. I felt a sudden hot rush of liquid engulf my entrenched penis, and as she tightened, then relaxed her vaginal muscles. I felt her juices slowly seeping out.

She opened her eyes and looked up at me. "Now fuck me, Johnny," she said. "Fuck me hard!"

I didn't need a second invitation. I began ramming into her hard and fast, just like I knew she wanted it. She was so well lubricated now that it went in and out easily, and each time I buried myself deep into the center of her warm, welcoming body, she let out a loud gasp of pure, unadulterated pleasure.

"Yes, that's it, that's it," she moaned as I continued to screw her with hard and deep. I felt as if I could keep going on for hours as I kept plunging in and out of her slippery orifice.

Occasionally, I've encountered women who are capable of really squirting out their orgasms, and it was apparent that Billie Rae was one of them. I could feel her muscles contracting as she began working herself up to another climax.

"Deeper," she said, "I want to feel you all the way deep, deep inside of me!" I began plowing into her now with a vengeance, which I guess is also exactly what she wanted because she began heaving up to meet my thrusts and uttering those quick staccato moans, and I felt myself grow even harder and bigger inside of her, and she moaned, "God, yes—oh God, yes." until finally I could control myself no longer, and I gave a final bone-jarring shove and felt my cock lodge deep, deep inside her as it exploded, sending burst after burst of scalding semen into her very depths.

I felt her vaginal muscles suddenly contract, gripping me hard inside of her. She opened her mouth, but not a sound came out, and suddenly her eyes went wide. I felt the violent gush of her own squirting orgasm against the tip of my cock, and then she expanded inside, going slack, which forced her copious juices to wash down the entire length of my distended organ.

"Oh my," she said breathlessly. "Oh my, oh my God!" and then she heaved a deep sigh, closed her eyes, and was quiet for a long moment. Sweat beaded her forehead and above her lip, which was still quivering. Slowly, her breathing began to return to normal.

Then she opened her eyes, looked up at me, and smiled. "You made me come twice."

"Is that a bad thing?"

"No. It's a good thing—a really good thing. No man has ever made me come before."

"Is that a fact?"

"I wouldn't lie to you. That's a fact."

"I guess I'll take that as a compliment, then." I reached over to the coffee table and helped myself to one of her cigarettes. It was menthol, but I lit it anyway and inhaled the cool smoke deep into my lungs. It proved to be more refreshing than I had expected it to be.

"So is your curiosity satisfied?" I asked, blowing a long stream of smoke across her breasts.

Billie Rae smiled and said, "Yes. I would say my curiosity is satisfied." She took the cigarette from my fingers, inhaled a long draw from it, then handed it back to me. "Actually, a lot more than my curiosity, I might add." She appeared to be relaxed and content as she exhaled the smoke.

I took another drag from the cigarette and said, "That's good, and I'm glad, but now it's time for you to keep your end of the bargain and satisfy my curiosity by telling me what I want to know."

There was a wary tone to her voice as she looked up at me and asked, "So what exactly is it that you want to know?"

"Do you know where Sheila was getting the cocaine that she was supplying you with?"

She looked at me as if I had just asked her the dumbest question anybody could possibly have asked and answered, "No, of course not. If I did, then why would I need Sheila?"

That made sense. "Well, what is it that you're afraid of, then?"

I handed her the cigarette, and she took a deep puff from it before answering. "I'm afraid because those guys that killed her must know that I used to live with her." I could see that there was real fear in her eyes as she said this. "What if they decide to come after me?"

"Why would they do that? Did you ever see any of them?"

"No..." She paused in deep thought for a moment while she snuffed the cigarette out in her ashtray, displacing a bunch of already snuffed-out cigarette butts that overflowed unceremoniously onto the coffee table.

"You didn't?"

"Well, yeah," she said somewhat cautiously, "maybe I did, just once. At Sheila's place a couple of weeks ago—the last time I saw her."

Now we were making a little progress. "You remember who it was or what he looked like?"

"He was Japanese—or he could have been Chinese, anyway, one of those Asian-type guys."

"So what did he look like?"

"Well, I guess he was kind of short. He wore a suit. He was a businessman-looking guy that came to the house that one time, real secretively, like, you know." She was straining her brain now, trying hard to recall the past. "I don't know who he was, but he brought something for Sheila."

"Did he bring her some cocaine?"

"No, I think he brought her some H."

"By H, do you mean heroin?"

"Yeah," she replied.

"So why do you think it was heroin?"

"Because after the guy left, I asked Sheila what she had, and she said that I wouldn't be interested in this stuff. She knew that I don't do H because I'm afraid I'll really get addicted to that stuff, and then it's so hard to quit."

She picked up a slightly used napkin from somewhere on the coffee table and dabbed at her nose, which had begun to run, before continuing. "I've got what you might call an addictive personality, and for me, that stuff would be really bad news."

"So Sheila was into heroin?"

"Yeah, that was her drug of choice." She thought about it for a moment, and then she added, "She got into using it after some kind of major family tragedy."

"You know what the major family tragedy was?"

"No, she never liked to talk about it."

It seemed as if I had asked her everything I could think to ask her. But then another thought occurred to me.

"Anything else you can remember about this Asian guy that you saw?"

She bit her lip nervously and looked up at me. "Yeah," and there was real fear in her voice as she said, "He saw me too."

Chapter Four

Billie Rae didn't satisfy my curiosity quite as much as I had satisfied hers, but she did give me an important name to follow up on. This would be the name of Sheila's ex-husband, who, it turned out, was someone else I had known a long time ago. Scott McGinnis was one of those guys who, in grade school, was known as a bully; in middle school was known as an asshole; and in high school, he was known as a football star. That is, until a bad leg injury sidelined him from his junior year on.

I hadn't seen him since the school years, but in the course of those years, I had experienced more than my share of run-ins with him. I wasn't looking forward to seeing him again, and I couldn't help but wonder what Sheila had seen in him and why she had married him. As I recall, she hated his guts in high school. Billie Rae also gave me the address of the house where she said that Sheila was living the last time she saw her, and I thought I should probably check that out first.

The small house was on a quiet street just south of Sunset Boulevard in a lower-middle-class residential area of Hollywood. There was a realtor's for sale sign in the front yard, and the lawn and landscaping were overgrown and not kept up. I parked my silver Porsche Audi a block away and walked up to the house.

Yellowing handbills, discarded fast food wrappings and other junk littered the small porch leading up to the front door. I knocked, and there was no response. I headed around back to scope the place out. There was a door leading to the kitchen from the empty driveway, and to my surprise, when I turned the doorknob, I found it to be unlocked.

I entered cautiously and silently, wondering if the police had already been here. The kitchen was neat and orderly. Some washed dishes and glasses were stacked in a plastic dish drainer. Attached to the refrigerator door with a small banana kitchen magnet was a small piece of notepaper with the names of two women on it. No phone numbers, just names. I pocketed the paper.

There was food in the refrigerator, including a couple of steaks that were well past their prime. A quick sniff confirmed that what was left in the carton of milk was spoiled. It appeared as if no one had been around for a long time. At least it seemed so—that is, until I heard the startling noise of a drawer being slammed shut in the next room.

It was at a time like this that I began wishing I had brought one of my guns. I have a license to carry, but I don't usually keep a gun on my person unless I feel that I'm going to be in a situation where I have to use it. I didn't know who was in the next room, but I also didn't want to take any chances. I picked up one of the kitchen knives and put it in my coat pocket before I made my move to confront whoever was there.

Whoever was in the bedroom, he was so totally engrossed in rummaging through the female undergarments in one of the dresser drawers that he didn't even notice me. "Excuse me," I said. "But who might you be?"

The man jumped a mile when he heard me, and I seriously thought he was going to have a heart attack right then and there.

"Jesus, you scared the hell out of me!" he finally managed to emphatically exclaim, his hand to his chest, as if he was amazed that he had just avoided having the big one.

"Sorry, I didn't mean to startle you like that, but I was just wondering what you were doing here. This is Sheila's place, right?"

I looked into his beady eyes and noticed that there was a somewhat guilty look on his face as he stammered out, "Uh, Sheila, yes, she lives here. Hey, uh, have you seen her?"

"I saw her this morning."

A look came across his face that showed that he didn't know whether to believe me or not to believe me. "Well, do me a favor. When you see her again, tell her she has to call me."

"Sure. Who is it you want me to tell her to call?"

"Oh, sorry, the name is Alex. Alex Eastman." He reached in and pulled a business card out of his shirt pocket and handed it to me. It was a realtor's card. And the name on it was Alex Eastman, like he said, and beside it was a small color photograph that confirmed the identification of same. "I've been letting Sheila rent this place month to month, but now I've got someone who wants to buy it. I've been trying to reach her for over a week. She hasn't answered her phone. So I thought I'd come check out the place. See what was going on."

"So that's why you're going through her things?"

For an uncomfortable moment, Alex seemed to be at a loss for words. "Well, she owes me two months' rent, you know. Doesn't look like she's been here for awhile, and I thought that maybe she'd skipped town."

"Why would she do that?"

"Why does anybody do anything?"

Having my question answered with a question was getting me nowhere. In fact, this whole conversation seemed to be getting me nowhere. By the time I had deduced this, Alex was looking anxiously at his watch.

"Hey, gotta run," he said, affecting a tone of urgency. "Have an important appointment with a client." He turned to leave, then turned back and said, "Don't forget. Tell Sheila to call me." He hesitated for a brief moment, as if he wanted to say something else, then turned around and hastily made his exit. I watched him leave, then I decided to nose around a bit myself.

I checked out the bureau drawers that Alex had gone through and found nothing of interest. Looking beneath the bed and rummaging through the nightstands produced similar results. There was just the expected personal stuff and nothing out of the ordinary.

But Alex had been looking for something. Was he looking to find the money for the rent that Sheila owed him? Did he think Sheila had a stash of drugs? Was he looking for something else? Whatever it was, he didn't find it. And if that whatever was still here, maybe I would find it.

I looked around very carefully but still could find nothing of any real interest. Nothing, that is, until I came across a white silk Chinese robe elaborately embroidered with a dragon that was hanging with the clothes in her closet. Hidden inside the pocket of the robe was a strange and exotic white gold pendant carved in the shape of a lotus flower, wrapped in a piece of white paper on which a woman's name and phone number had been written.

The woman's name was Suzy. I put the paper and the pendant in my pocket, left the knife back in the kitchen, and managed to sneak out of the place and get into my car just as the police pulled up in front of the house.

When I got home, I found that George Lee had left a message on my machine to give him a call. Knowing how late George usually worked, I figured he'd still be at the station, so I picked up the phone and gave him a call. "What's up, George?"

"I thought you'd want to know about the autopsy. Things were slow down there today, and it got pushed through. She was murdered, all right. Throat was slit, and she bled to death. There were some signs of torture, too. There were cigarette burns on her arms, and…" He almost choked when he said, "All of her fingers were broken, John."

There was a long silence, and then he regained his composure and continued. "The coroner said she would have suffered quite a bit." I could tell that he was really struggling to compose himself. "It was a terrible way to go."

This was disquieting news, to say the least, and I was almost at a loss for words, but I knew that I had to ask him the question that had been nagging at me. "They find any drugs in her system?"

There was a short silence, and then he said, "How did you know?" His question answered my question, so I answered his.

"I've been finding out a lot about Sheila lately."

"I figured you wouldn't be able to keep your nose out of this." Then he said, "Yes, they did find drugs in her system."

"Was it heroin?"

"No, what they found in her system was more exotic stuff—they think opium. They're running tests on it now."

"That's interesting. So she was into the high-end recreational stuff. Look, George. I just want to find out what happened to her. And why."

"Need I remind you that this is a homicide investigation?"

"I'm not going to get in your way."

"You better not, if you know what's good for you."

"Don't threaten me, George."

"I'm not threatening you, John. I'm telling you. Just because you carry that private investigator's badge doesn't mean you're a cop."

"Do we always have to end up in a pissing match? Look, remember, when we were kids, we made a pact. We promised we would always look out for Sheila, that we'd protect her and take care of her. Remember? Well, we didn't do such a great job of that, so we owe her, George. We owe her."

There was a long silence at the other end of the line. Then he said, "How about we have that drink?"

"I haven't eaten yet." I hadn't eaten all day, and I was beginning to feel somewhat dizzy and a little ill.

"Neither have I. You feel like beer and Mexican?"

That thought revived me. There's nothing like the thought of some tasty Mexican food to get the digestive juices flowing. "Sounds like a plan," I replied. I'll meet you at The Talpa in fifteen minutes."

The Talpa Restaurant on Pico Boulevard has always been one of our two favorite places for beer and Mexican food. The other is a small place about two blocks away on the same street known as Pancho's Family Restaurant. But tonight we were dining at The Talpa. The beer at The Talpa is always served at the perfect temperature, and the food that follows it is close to the best home-cooked authentic Mexican food in the city. It was as good a place as any to bury the hatchet once again.

George was waiting for me as I pulled up and parked in the small alley parking lot behind the restaurant. We both walked in the back door, nodded in silent greeting at some of the familiar faces, and shook hands with some of the even more familiar faces before we took our seats next to each other on the only two stools left at the crowded bar.

The place was buzzing with activity, and the television sets at each end of the bar were each tuned in to a different football game. A loud cheer went up from the other end of the bar, indicating that someone on the favored team had probably scored a touchdown.

The bar was right next to the kitchen, and the enticing aroma of the food that was being prepared wafted through the open door. My stomach was growling so loud in eager anticipation that I was sure it could be easily heard over all the surrounding noise and chatter. At least George must have heard it because he flashed me a sympathetic smile.

A few moments later, we were greeted by Andy the bartender, who placed an ice-cold bottle of Budweiser in front of George and an ice-cold bottle of Negro Modelo in front of me. "You guys eating tonight?" he asked, and we both nodded, and then he nodded because he knew exactly what we wanted to eat.

We always ordered the same thing, and he already knew what it was. He put the order in with the kitchen—four Tacos Dorados and an Enchilada de Pollo for George, and a Carne Asada plate for me—and then brought us a bowl of corn tortilla chips and the house's very famous and very spicy tomatillo salsa.

We drank the first beer in silence, and when we finished it, George gave the signal for another round. "Tonight's on me," George said. "I owe you one."

I wasn't about to argue because I always enjoyed a free meal much more than one I had to pay for, so I said, "Thanks. I appreciate it."

He took a swig of his fresh beer and turned to me. "We used to be friends."

"Yeah, I remember."

"I guess we just let something come between us."

"Something we shouldn't have, probably."

"Yeah." George dipped a chip into the salsa and popped it into his mouth. "So, what have you found out?"

"Did Wilma tell you about Billie Rae Chase?"

"The girl Sheila moved in with? Yeah, I was going to check her out tomorrow. The phone number we got on her is no longer in service."

"Neither is the address Wilma gave me. I had to chase this one down. She lives in one of those old apartment buildings on Fairfax, south of Pico."

"Is she Ethiopian?"

"I don't think so. She's white."

"That area is turning into an Ethiopian neighborhood, you know," George said knowingly. I didn't know if he was putting me on or not. It was hard to tell with George. "So you saw her today?"

"Yeah, she told me that Sheila was involved in the drug business with some heavy hitters. You might want to have a talk with her."

I had already warned Billie Rae that she might get a visit from the police. I told her that if I could find her, then they certainly could.

I also warned her not to mention her own involvement with selling drugs but told her to be completely honest about Sheila when they asked about her.

George had almost finished the bowl of chips, and he motioned for Andy to bring him another. "I'm hungry—haven't eaten since this morning," he said as if he needed an excuse for pigging out on the chips. I tried to chase the disturbing vision of George eating his hamburger next to the rotting corpse out of my head. "So tell me about this Billie Rae—what's her name?"

"Chase. Billie Rae Chase. She's an actress. She performs in skin flicks."

"Interesting," George sounded almost as if he were impressed. Then he had to go and add, "You tried her out?"

"She's a lesbian, George."

"Well, that shouldn't stop you."

"Yeah, I just go around banging anything I run into," I offered sarcastically.

"Sure you do," he laughed. "At least that's what I've heard, anyway." He looked up from the chips and called out, "Hey, how about a couple more beers over here, Andy?"

But he shouldn't have asked because Andy was already on the way with two more cold beers in hand. This guy is psychic when it comes to the serving of beer. He put down fresh napkins for coasters and set them in front of us, and we proceeded to go right to work on them. I was getting a good buzz now, and things were looking pretty rosy.

We continued to chit-chat about sex, life, baseball, football, and various other insignificant or sometimes somewhat earth-shaking philosophical things. We both seemed to be avoiding discussing the subject of Sheila, at least for the time being.

Finally, a couple of more beers arrived, this time with the food, and that managed to kill all conversation for awhile as we both ravenously dug in. I hadn't eaten a thing all day and not only really needed to refuel, but more importantly, get something in my stomach to sop up all the alcohol it was being inundated with.

After he cleared away the food dishes, Andy brought us a couple more beers, this time on the house, and George finally got around to asking me what else I had come up with in the course of my private investigation.

I told him, "Well, I found out that Sheila had been married to Scott McGinnis."

George, who had been taking a swig of beer when I said this, almost choked. "No, I don't believe it! She absolutely hated his ass." He shook his head in amazement. "You say that she actually married him?"

"That's what Billie Rae said."

"Did you go see him?"

"I've been trying to avoid doing that."

"I don't blame you. That guy's a major asshole." He shook his head again and uttered in a tone that still indicated total disbelief, "Scott McGinnis."

He took a pack of Viceroy's out of his pocket. George is the only person I've ever known whose brand of choice was Viceroy's. It had been ever since we had both experimented with smoking at the age of fourteen. After initially choking and coughing like hell, we finally got the hang of it, and before long, we were puffing away as if we'd been smokers all our lives.

He offered me one, which I accepted before he slipped one between his own lips and lit it up before he lit mine. He blew a long trail of smoke across the bar, then turned to me and asked, "You come up with anything else?"

"Well, Billie Rae also gave me the address of the house in Hollywood where Sheila had been living."

"I guess you went over there. Find anything?"

"Nothing much," I lied. "Just a couple of names I found on a piece of paper on Sheila's refrigerator. I'll run them down and let you know if anything pans out."

"Give—I'll run them down and let you know if anything pans out, sport." He shook his head. "You're just lucky that I'm not arresting your ass. You ever heard of tampering with evidence?"

Since he was the one who was paying for dinner and since I felt that he should at least be responsible for some of the work, I whined somewhat reluctantly, "Well, if that's the way you want to be."

He held out his hand. "That's the way I want to be."

I reached into my coat pocket and handed him the piece of paper with the two names, along with the address for Sheila's house that Billie Rae had written down for me, adding as almost an after-thought, "Oh, and by the way, here's that address of the house in

Hollywood where Sheila was living."

"We already have that, pal. We don't exactly just sit on our asses, you know." Something lit up in his eyes as if an important thought suddenly occurred to him, and he looked directly into mine and said, "And by the way, John, why don't you tell me why your finger-prints are all over that place as well as on a carving knife we found on the kitchen table?"

"Come on, George. I know you guys haven't had time to process all of the prints you found in that house yet."

George laughed. "You're pretty sharp, John; I'll give that to you." He snuffed out his cigarette in the ashtray, pulled a wooden tooth-pick out of his pocket, and began picking his teeth with it. "One of the guys from the Hollywood division thought they saw you near her place. I hope you didn't tamper with any more evidence."

"You know me better than that."

"Unfortunately, I'm afraid that I do," he said, almost as if he regretted that fact. Of course, I hadn't told him about either the lotus pendant I had pocketed or the phone number for Suzy that I had found at Sheila's place. I had to keep some cards close to my chest.

It was now my turn to make a move. "Ok, George. So far, there's been a whole lot of give and you know what? It's all been on my part. Now I think that it's time for a little take."

George gave me a wary look. He liked to play his cards close to his chest, too. From the look of his expression, I could tell that he was going to give me something, but he wasn't going to give me much. I waited, tapping my fingers on the bar with impatience.

Finally, he sighed and said, "All right. Here's something I'll bet you didn't know." He put another cigarette in his mouth and lit it. George really liked to draw things out.

"Well, what is it?"

"Sheila has a police record."

I was surprised to hear this, but I wasn't all that surprised. "You're right; I didn't know about that. You want to tell me about it?"

"Not particularly, but I will." He was still holding his cards close to his chest, but he was getting ready to show me one of them. "She was busted for possession of heroin and cocaine."

This was news, of course, but having learned what I'd learned about Sheila today, it didn't come as all that much of a shock. "When did this happen?"

"About three months ago."

"Did she do time?"

"It was her first offense, and she had a good lawyer, so she was just ordered to undergo rehab."

"Did you know about that all this time?"

"No, John. I just found out about it today. She was arrested in Hollywood. That's a little out of my jurisdiction, in case you didn't know."

We had already killed a dozen beers between us, and I, for one, was beyond buzzed and quite possibly more than a little drunk, so I drove home very, very carefully as I sullenly mulled over all the events of the day and wondered apprehensively what tomorrow might bring.

Chapter Five

The next morning brought with it one of those crummy morning-after beer hangovers and one hell of an equally crummy mood along with it. I drew open the living room curtain to be greeted by a dark and gloomy day obscured by dense clouds that promised rain. A thick, grayish mist hung ominously in the air. Resisting the urge to crawl back into bed, I bravely headed to the bathroom to brush my teeth, shower, and shave. This proved to be a painful ordeal, but somehow I managed to survive it.

Still feeling like crap, I groaned both inwardly and outwardly and attempted to minimize my suffering by making myself a Bloody Mary. Fortunately, I had just enough vodka left for a couple of drinks and the Tabasco sauce. I had no bitters, but I managed to find a bottle of Worchestershire Sauce—Lea & Perrins, the original.

Always go with the best, my father once had said, and of course I believed him. Inside the refrigerator, I found a very limp stick of celery left over from God knows how long ago. Unfortunately, I had to use V-8 juice instead of tomato, but that turned out to be all right.

The drink helped. I was beginning to feel almost human once again, so I made another, but before I could tear into the second drink, my phone rang. It was George Lee again, and he sounded bright and chipper. That guy never got a hangover, it seemed.

"What is it now, George?" The guy was starting to become a nuisance.

"I thought I'd tell you that we did find your fingerprints on the knife in Sheila's kitchen. Also found your prints on some things in her bedroom and living room."

"So I looked around a little. If I had wanted to hide the fact that I was there, I would have worn the pair of those surgical gloves you know I always carry with me. I picked up the knife as a defensive measure when I heard a noise in the other room."

"A noise?"

"Yeah, I snuck up on a real estate agent named Alex Eastman in Sheila's bedroom. He was going through her things."

"A real estate agent was at the house going through her things?" George was now beginning to sound more and more like an echo.

"That's what I said. His phone number is the same as the one on the sign on the front lawn. I'd give him a call and have a talk with him if I were you."

"What was he looking for?"

"He didn't tell me. He split before I could ask."

George was quiet for a moment, as if he were contemplating what I had just told him. "Is there anything else you're not telling me, John?"

"No, you know pretty much what I know at this point," I lied.

I could tell that George wasn't totally satisfied with what I had told him, but I thought—well, tough shit. I wasn't going to do all his work for him. It was his case, and he would get all the glory when it was solved. All I needed was the satisfaction that I had done whatever I could for Sheila because I felt that somehow this whole thing was crying out for some sort of closure.

In spite of all the things I had learned about her yesterday, I felt that there were many pieces of the puzzle that were still missing. I had a feeling that this girl Suzy, whose name was on the piece of paper that had been wrapped around the lotus pendant I found at Sheila's place, was one of those pieces. I decided to give her a call.

There was only a recorded message in a sweet British-accented female voice on the other end of the line that told me to leave Suzy a message, so I left her one. Then I decided that I could no longer put off going to see Scott McGinnis. If I wanted to delve into Sheila's past private life, I would just have to go on and delve. No matter how unpleasant the experience was going to be.

Like I said before, Scott and I went way back. We were always enemies and never friends. A couple of times when we fought, he totally beat the shit out of me. Only once did I manage to turn the tables around and beat the shit out of him, and as I recalled, I had to fight pretty dirty to do so. It also helped that he had been saddled with a broken right arm at the time. I don't know or remember what originally caused this perpetual enmity.

Scott McGinnis owned and operated a large and successful Cadillac dealership in Beverly Hills, a business he had inherited from his father, who had inherited it from his father before him. You might say that it was a family business because most employees were family. In spite of this, he treated them pretty much like dirt, if you believe the rumors that had gone around—and I did.

I knew for a fact that Scott was a cheapskate and a cheat. He was also ruthless and egotistical, and not beyond making a buck or two by breaking the law. Aside from that, the other thing that I really didn't like about him was the fact that he was extremely handsome—in a buff, California blonde, pretty-boy type of way. And he could also be very charming if the situation required it. The situation with me, of course, did not require it.

Scott was dressed in a stylish white designer suit—Armani, I think—and was wearing a blue shirt with a charcoal-colored tie, and he was standing looking down at a disemboweled engine in the dealership repair bay when I walked up to him. He ignored me and went on talking to the blonde-haired mechanic standing next to him.

Sure, and it is now if it isn't another relation, I thought, mainly because of the way that Scott was berating him. Finally, he got tired of cussing the poor guy out and turned to me. "Well, if it isn't the Pollack with the big dick. What brings you over to this side of town? Lose your way?"

"I suppose you heard about Sheila."

"Yeah, I heard about it. So what's it to me? I got nothing to do with her now. Ancient history, she is."

"You were married to her."

"Was married to her, like we're talking the past tense here, and that was an unfortunate mistake. I ended up with her after you'd stretched her all out of shape, you see."

I stifled the strong impulse to deck him then and there. To me, he had always been a worthless piece of shit. Instead, I made an attempt at diplomacy and said, "Look, McGinnis. I know you don't like me, and I don't particularly like you, but I'm hoping that you will help me. You know that Sheila and I were in love with each other, but that was a long time ago, and it seems that both she and I were different people back then. She's dead now, and I'm just trying to find out what happened. The woman they pulled out of Santa Monica Bay isn't the girl that I once knew."

"You're making me want to get out the violins now," he scoffed. "No, that girl you and I both once knew turned into a bitch and a junkie, and I put up with it for awhile until I had it up to here with her and couldn't wait to be rid of her."

"So you kicked her out of your life."

"More like she left me, and she did so of her own accord." He looked at me as if he were challenging me to challenge him. I didn't, and he went on. "Still, I provided her with a decent settlement, if it's any of your goddamn business."

He paused for a moment. Then looked me straight in the eye, suddenly turned serious, and came up with a totally unexpected confession. "You don't know this, John, but in high school—well, I was infatuated with her, you might say. I wanted her a lot, but she always ignored me because she was always with you."

I know it was difficult for him to admit this. And then he said, "I could never understand why." His meaning was plain. Look at you, then look at me. The choice should be obvious. He went on, "Sometimes when you really want something, it becomes an obsession. You might say that for me, Sheila became an obsession. So when I finally got the chance, well…"

I hated to ask, but I did. "Were you two happy?" And I was surprised when he answered.

"At first, we were. My dad passed on, and I inherited the dealership. I built it up to an even bigger business than it was before. Sheila became pregnant, and we had a son." He stopped, and I didn't think he would go on, but he did.

"We called him Sean. When he was two, he fell into the swimming pool and drowned. Sheila was never the same after that. She blamed herself, you see." There were the beginnings of tears in his eyes now, and he did nothing to try and wipe them away.

"I'm sorry, Scott. I didn't know."

"Well, you know now," he said. "Now get the hell out of my shop because I never want to see your ugly face here or anywhere else again."

Fortunately, that feeling was mutual. It was beginning to drizzle as I left the car dealership. My hangover had pretty much dissipated by now, and I was feeling hungry. I drove over to Pink's on La Brea and ordered a couple of their famous greasy and delicious chili dogs, something I either would or would not regret later.

During or after a hangover, my body seems to crave either chili dogs or a hot steaming bowl of rice congee called jook, something that the Chinese eat either as breakfast food or a late-night snack. Since I wasn't close enough to Chinatown, I settled for the chili dogs with lots of onions and a cream soda to wash them down. I hoped that I wouldn't be kissing anyone for at least a few hours.

I decided it was time to check and see if Suzy had returned my call, so I commandeered the nearest pay phone and tried to make an attempt to retrieve the messages from my answering machine. I say tried because I was never great at manipulating the intricacies of these newfangled electronics, so sometimes it worked and sometimes it didn't work. This time, it worked.

She hadn't called me back yet, so I decided to take another look at Sheila's place since I was still in the area. When I had been there the last time, I had to leave so quickly that I had neglected to check out her garage, which was located at the far end of the driveway that ran the length of the house and merged into a small concrete patio area beside and in front of it.

The slight rain that had been falling had let up by now, and the warming sun had finally managed to sneak out from behind the clouds to begin drying everything off. There was a welcome smell of freshness in the air, as if nature had briefly given the city an unexpected and much-needed reprieve by washing away the smog and grime that usually floated in the air.

The wooden garage door was one of those old swing-out affairs, and there was a rusty old padlock on it. Fortunately, it was one of those cheap padlocks that I could pick easily. It was apparent that Sheila had used the garage for storage and not as a shelter for her car.

Almost the entire space was packed with piles of boxes, discarded appliances, and dusty furniture. I decided to take a look in one of the boxes, which I found was packed full of paperback books, which I noticed were mostly fiction, primarily those big, thick novels that they make those blockbuster movies from, and a few scattered mysteries and romance novels.

The next box I looked in contained a haphazardly packed bunch of papers and letters. I noticed some of the letters were from me—letters I'd written to Sheila from Vietnam that she had never bothered to reply to. At least she had opened and read them, I thought. There were also a few letters from before that period that she had answered. I looked through these briefly and then came across some old photographs that she had apparently saved. As I looked through these, the memories came flooding back.

Suddenly, I was grabbed from behind, and my right arm was painfully twisted into a hammerlock as I was pushed forcefully and violently face first into the wall. I turned my head around to see two crew-cut gung-ho Marine types wearing dark suits and serious expressions.

The tall one was Caucasian. The thing that stood out the most about him was the fact that he had a face like a ferret. The short one was Asian, probably Asian-American. He was dressed in a navy blue blazer with bright brass buttons. He was moon-faced and had crazy-assed eyes. Both were chewing gum.

"Who the hell are you, and what are you doing here?" Ferret Face, the taller of the two, yelled in my ear in an overly rude and unfriendly manner. Then he banged me against the wall to facilitate my response.

"Hey, what the hell is this all about?" I managed to get out before the tall one spun me around and delivered a sharp blow to my solar plexus. For the second time in two days, the wind had been knocked out of me, and this time I was on my knees in pain on a dirty garage floor. A wave of nausea washed over me, and I fought to keep the chili dogs and cream soda down.

"In case you hadn't noticed, we're the ones asking the questions," the tall one informed me. I looked up at him. He had FBI written all over him. I looked at his buddy. His buddy smiled at me, then delivered a vicious kick to my ribs. He looked as if he enjoyed doing that.

The kick hurt like hell, and I was getting pissed. For a brief crazy moment, I thought about taking them both on, but rejected that half-baked insane plan almost immediately.

As some wise Oriental philosopher once said: 'There's a time to take action and a time not to take action.' I'm not really a coward, but I could definitely tell this was the time for the latter because the odds just weren't in my favor. So when I got my breath back, I managed to say, "Hey, was that really necessary?"

"I hear you talking, but I don't hear you answering my questions," the tall one continued. It was obvious that he was the guy in charge of this team.

The short one drew back as if he were going to kick me again, and I flinched and blurted out, "My name is Johnny Wadd, and I'm a private investigator. My ID and badge are in my coat pocket."

"Show us," the short one said. I noticed he was pointing a chrome 45-caliber Colt Gold Cup automatic pistol straight at my face.

"So he can talk," I said as I very carefully reached into my coat pocket to draw out my ID wallet. I flipped it open to reveal the badge, got up slowly, and handed it over to the tall one. He accepted it with his left hand, looked at it with mild curiosity, and then showed it to his buddy.

"That's an odd sort of surname—Wadd." The tall one looked at me as though he were examining some sort of strange specimen. "How on earth did you end up with a name like that?" I couldn't help but notice that he had a slight Southern accent, probably from Alabama. I also couldn't help but notice all the large flakes of dandruff on the shoulders of his black suit coat. It looked as if he'd been in a snowstorm.

"It's a long story."

"Make it a short one. I don't have a whole lot of patience."

"My grandfather emigrated here from Poland. The family name was Wadja, but the immigration official at Ellis Island didn't know how to spell it, so instead he wrote out Wadd."

"So that stupid name has managed to stick with you ever since, huh?" he said before he gave off with a silly little giggle. He opened his mouth and started to say something else, then stopped and sighed. Then he said, "Well then, that's already much more than I needed to know about you." He handed me back my badge wallet. Then he assumed his official, bullying air and got right up close and in my face.

"Now listen to this: You are to get your skinny private eye ass out of here and don't come back. This place is off-limits to you and whatever private investigation it is you are doing." I winced and drew back, not because of his threat but because of his bad breath. It was so bad that even the chewing gum couldn't mask it.

"I don't think so. Last time I checked, this was still a free country."

Before I could block it, he delivered a blow to the side of my face that nearly loosened a couple of teeth, knocking me down again in the process, and when I hit the ground, the short one delivered another hard and unwelcome kick to my ribs. This time it felt as if he might have broken something, and I couldn't help groaning from the intense pain.

"You don't get it, do you?" The tall one shook his head and looked down on me, and his face took on an expression as if he were addressing a retarded child.

I got it, all right. I got bruises that were going to leave me black and blue and make me ache for days. He continued, as if justifying all this needless violence, "You're disrupting a joint investigation between the Federal Bureau of Investigation and the Bureau of Narcotics and Dangerous Drugs. Your presence here is not wanted, and it won't be tolerated."

I rubbed the blood that was flowing out from inside my mouth and said, "I'm not trying to disrupt anything. And I thought that you guys were supposed to be the good guys." I started to rise, but the tall one held me down with his shoe on my chest.

"We are the good guys, pal. You're still alive, aren't you? If you want to stay alive, you better take my advice. It's so easy to get into some kind of fatal accident nowadays, you know." He smiled, and I got the feeling he was already visualizing my fatal accident.

It was as sincere a threat as any I had ever received, and government agents or not, I realized that they were fully capable of carrying such a threat out. I thought of responding with a wisecrack, but fortunately, my sense of self-preservation got the better of me.

The short one now spoke for the second time, and this time he said, "Do you understand?" There was a lot of menace in his voice, and I really didn't want to provoke another kick to my already damaged ribs.

"I'm reading you loud and clear," I replied in as cowardly a manner as I could.

"Good," the tall one reached down and picked me up and threw me bodily out of the garage. "End of discussion."

Chapter Six

I decided it was time to try and call the elusive and mysterious Suzy once again, so I stopped at the first phone booth I came to. The line rang for about ten times, and I was about to give up when a sweet voice with a slight British accent answered it. When I identified myself, she told me that she had been out of town for a couple of days and just got my message.

I told her once again that I was a friend of Sheila Ross and wanted to see her. She told me that her schedule was free for today and gave me her address, which was in an apartment building on Kings Road north of Sunset. I told her that I was not far away and would be there in a few minutes.

The apartment building was in a very upscale neighborhood, and it turned out to be one of those newer high-end luxury buildings where the rent undoubtedly cost more than a small fortune. It therefore came as no small surprise when it turned out that Suzy occupied the penthouse. I pressed the buzzer, identified myself, and was buzzed in.

The decadently elaborate foyer had an Oriental theme, complete with a small garden with several of those dwarf bonsai trees beside a bubbling little waterfall and a carp pond in which orange-colored fish swam around. I took the elevator to the penthouse and was met at the door by the most beautiful Asian woman I had ever seen, and having spent my share of time in the Far East, believe me, I've seen quite a few of them.

"I'm Suzy Huang, Mr. Wadd," she greeted me in her British-accented English. Still at a loss for words, I could only sort of grunt while noticing that Suzy seemed to radiate class from every pore. She was dressed in a beautiful and enticing red silk Chinese cheongsam dress, one with those sexy slits along the side that allowed you to see clear up to her thighs.

As I gazed at her appreciatively, the welcoming smile on her face suddenly turned into a questioning frown, and a look of concern came across her face. "You're bleeding," she said as she examined the side of my face. There was a quick moment of thought before she said, "Come with me."

Suzy led me to a large, luxurious bathroom painted in soft pastel colors that had a sunken tub and lots of tile and marble and had me sit on a small chair in front of the vanity area. Looking in the mirror, I saw that blood had dried and clotted around my lips, and the side of my face was bleeding from where it had scraped against the garage wall. In other words, I looked like shit.

"So what happened to you?" she asked while in the process of wetting some cotton with hydrogen peroxide.

"I had a run-in with a couple federal agents."

"Well, they weren't very nice to you." She raised the cotton to my face. "This is going to hurt a little," she said before cleaning my wounds, trying to be as gentle as possible. Still, it stung like hell, but I tried to bear up to it like a man.

Her face was near mine, her breath smelled sweet, and her skin gave off the faint scent of gardenias. "There," she said. "That wasn't so bad, now, was it?"

"No," I answered, feeling somewhat like a little boy who, after a fight, had just been given first aid by his mommy. "Thank you."

As I started to rise, a sudden, sharp pain in my ribs made me wince, which was something that she couldn't help but notice. She frowned again, then extended her slender fingers and gently felt my chest and ribs. Then she told me to take off my shirt.

The bruising around my ribs had become evident. "I don't think any are broken," she said, examining them with the skill of a nurse. "How do you feel?"

"Like I've been beaten up and kicked a few times in the ribs."

"I think you'll survive," she opined. "You appear to be pretty tough. Do you want to take a shower?"

"I had one this morning," I replied, thinking that she was being very hospitable to a total stranger.

"Then go ahead and take off your clothes."

Now that took me by surprise. "What?"

She handed me a large white bath towel. "Take off your clothes. You can wrap this towel around you. Then go in the bedroom and lie face down on the bed."

I was too alarmed to say anything, and before I could, she left the bathroom anyway, closing the door behind her. I decided to go along with the program and removed my pants, which were soiled, slightly torn, and a little worse for wear from the unexpected encounter with the filthy garage floor at Sheila's place. I hesitated for a moment before removing my underwear and then wrapping the large, soft bath towel around my hips.

The bedroom was an elaborate affair done in an extravagant and tasteful Oriental motif. It contained what appeared to be very expensive traditional Chinese antique wooden furniture. A large canopied bed occupied the center of the room. On each side of the bed, there was a beautiful wooden Tibetan cabinet elaborately hand-painted with the traditional representation of the Buddha, seated beatifically on the lotus.

On top of one of those tables, beside one of the matching table lamps fashioned out of colorfully painted old metal Chinese tea chests, was a Pan Books paperback copy of Nevil Shute's novel *In the Wet*, inside of which was a small Dutton's Bookstore bookmark placed about three quarters of the way through.

Beside the lamp on the other table was a beautifully carved teak wood box that could have been Burmese in origin. My curiosity got the better of me, and I opened it to find that it contained a small green box of imported Simon Arzt Egyptian cigarettes, a pack of matches, and a tiny porcelain ashtray.

Along the walls hung ancient scrolls and other colorful hangings, some of which were also embroidered with the lotus flower. There was also a large, framed black-and-white memorial photograph, probably taken in the late 40's or early 50's, of a very beautiful Chinese woman who looked a lot like Suzy.

My guess was that it was probably her mother. A small Buddhist altar was directly beneath it, and a thin stream of aromatic smoke wafted from the sticks of incense placed in the sand of the brass holder in front of it.

I followed Suzy's instructions to lie down on the bed on my stomach. It was only moments before Suzie entered the room, and she did so almost noiselessly. She was now dressed in a white dragon robe that could have been the identical twin to the one I had seen in Sheila's closet, and she was carrying a towel and two vials of liquid— an amber one and a clear one. I noticed that without her high heels, she was smaller than she had first appeared.

I felt her cool hands on my shoulders. "Relax," she said, "you're very tense." I made an effort to do as she said, but it was proving somewhat difficult under the circumstances. I couldn't help but wonder what this was all about. Suddenly there was the cold shock of the aromatic oil against my skin as she poured it on my back, immediately followed by the soft but firm feel of her hands as she slowly began rubbing it in while gently massaging me.

Her practiced fingers and palms gradually increased their pressure, working out all the kinks and, it seemed, all of the tension that had been building up inside of me over the course of years. It was a strange combination of pain and pleasure that combined itself into a sensual experience such as I had never felt before.

Her hands worked their magic all the way down to the small of my back. Then she moved down to my feet, massaging them with expert ease, before slowly and deliberately working her way up to my thighs and then on up to the base of my buttocks. When she reached my buttocks, she pulled off the towel before she began massaging them.

By now, I was not only totally relaxed, but I was beginning to feel very aroused. She finished with my buttocks, slapped one of the cheeks playfully, and said, "Turn around."

I did as I was told, and there was an audible gasp as my pulsing erection was revealed in all its naked and unashamed glory. Her hand reached over and touched it. "My goodness," she said. "I've never seen one this huge." Then she looked up at me and said, "I really don't know whether I should scream out and run, or pay you, or charge you double."

When she told me this, a light bulb went off in my head, and everything suddenly became crystal clear. Suzy was a call girl, and a high-class one at that. She apparently thought that her friend Sheila had sent her a client. I was beginning to wonder if I had enough cash on me to afford this. "Uh, just how much would double be?"

Suzy laughed. "Didn't Sheila tell you my fee?"

"I knew she forgot to tell me something."

"Don't worry about it," she said as she took me in her mouth.

She had a very small mouth but a very deep throat, and it wasn't long before I was groaning in ecstasy, and I seldom groan. Suzy undid her robe while she was doing this, and it slithered to the floor, revealing a pair of perfect little breasts on her slim and well-proportioned body.

She moved into the sixty-nine position, and one of her legs passed over my face as she positioned herself over me, revealing a tiny and very appetizing vagina. She lowered herself over my mouth so I wouldn't have to raise my head, and my tongue licked playfully at her clitoris. She lowered herself a little more, and I began munching in earnest. She smelled heavenly and tasted like some strange, exotic fruit.

I knew that I was starting to get to her because occasionally she would unwrap her mouth from my cock and moan. I spread her with my fingers. She was getting nice and wet, and I noticed that, like most Chinese women, her vaginal canal was not very deep. She was going to be a tight one. Nice 'n tight.

I began tonguing her clit faster now, getting her ready for me. I put two fingers inside of her, swirling them around until she was wet enough to take three. Then I felt her grab my cock with both hands and heard her say with some urgency, "I want to feel this inside of me now."

Suzy was ready, and so was I. She rose up and turned around to face me as she straddled my hips and guided herself onto my rigid and waiting cock. She gave a gasp of pleasure as she inserted it, and it slid in inch by inch until about half of it was engulfed inside of her. Then it would go no further.

She began panting as she began the up-and-down motion, slowly at first, then faster and faster. She was breathing heavily now, and I could feel her begin to work herself up to a climax. Then suddenly she slowed down, and I could tell she wanted to prolong her own pleasure as well as mine.

This went on for a while. She would alternate fast, deep strokes with slow, shallow ones. Gradually, she worked herself up into a frenzy of passion, and she began grinding herself into me with wild abandon, impaling herself as deeply as she could.

Then she abruptly stopped and gave a long, high-pitched moan, and I felt her already tight vagina contracting even tighter around my distended manhood, so tight that I felt she was going to squeeze that half of it that was inside of her clean off.

Finally, she relaxed and looked down at me. There were beads of sweat on her forehead and upper lip. She smiled and said, "That was good for me, but you haven't climaxed yet."

"That's all right," I said, even though I really didn't mean it.

"I'm sorry that I'm not very big down there. I know that it would feel better for you if you could get more of it inside of me. You're very big, but I think that I could take most of you up my ass."

"Are you serious?"

"Of course I'm serious. See how hard you are?" She held me with both of her hands as if to prove her point. In fact, it took both of her hands to navigate the circumference, and I had absolutely no idea how she thought it was possibly going to fit into the place she had mentioned. But she obviously had no doubt about the matter.

She turned around and placed herself in the doggie position, then lubricated her anus with the juices that had flowed copiously from her vagina during her climax. I took my position behind her, and she reached back with her hand and guided me to her waiting posterior.

"You're going to have to go easy at first," she said somewhat breathlessly as she struggled to insert me. She managed to work the head of it inside of her, then she said, "That's it, now push." Slowly, I pushed. Trying to be as gentle as possible, I managed to work a couple more inches inside of her.

In spite of her enthusiasm, it was proving to be a very tight fit. "Ahhh—stop for a second!" she suddenly exclaimed. I could feel her trying to relax her muscles, and when she had done so, she continued, "All right, now go on."

I obeyed and pushed, and much to my surprise, watched my cock slowly disappear inside of her until it stopped only two inches or so from the hilt. She gave a long, low moan as I touched bottom and then began moving her hips back and forth, expertly milking the entire length of me with the exquisite tightness of her anus.

The pleasurable feeling was so intense, I didn't know how much more I could take before I would shoot my pent-up climax into her. Her right hand was expertly manipulating her clitoris at the same time and in the same timing with her back and forth movements.

Everything I was seeing and feeling was really turning me on, and I felt myself start to lose control. I pushed to meet her thrusts, slamming myself inside of her as her own backward movements became faster and faster and loud exclamations erupted from her throat as her masturbating fingers kept pace with the thrusting action and she was moaning and panting as she said "Quickly, quickly," and then she said "Yes, now, together, together!" and suddenly I felt an orgasm well up from my balls and course through the entire length of my manhood and explode like molten lava from a volcano deep inside her most intimate depths while she shuddered and uncontrollably screamed out her own violent and intense climax at the same time.

Afterward, as we lay quietly next to each other, she finally broke the silence and said, "I feel as if my insides have been rearranged—and I'm really not sure whether I'll ever be able to take a crap again."

"Surely you exaggerate."

She laughed. "I'm not so sure."

We took a shower together, and then she had me lie down on the bed again, this time on my back. She said, "At times I noticed you were grimacing in pain from your injured ribs," as she picked up the vial of the clear liquid that was on the nightstand.

"This is a Chinese medicine. It's called Kwan Loong Oil. It will help to relieve the pain of your bruised ribs."

She poured some of the clear, fragrant liquid onto her hand and began gently rubbing it on my ribs and chest. There was an unexpected feeling of analgesic heat on my skin, and the pungent fumes from the oil seemed to open up my nasal passages and impart a light-headed feeling.

I wasn't sure how it was happening, but I could feel the strange medicine begin to work its healing magic. Either that or the fumes were making me so high that the pain no longer mattered. Whatever it was, all I knew was that I was beginning to feel better.

When she finished, she wiped her hands on a towel, leaned down, and kissed me on the lips. It was one of those long, lingering kisses, and when we finally broke it off so we could breathe again, she said, "You know something? I think you're quite a guy, Johnny Wadd."

"Well, I happen to think that you're quite a gal yourself, Suzy Huang."

She laughed and got up from the bed. She put on her white silk dragon robe and said, "I'll bet you're hungry."

"You bet right."

We went to the kitchen, which was large and impressive and sported an immaculate, highly polished birch wood floor. Almost dead center of it was a cooking island, which served as a preparation area. It had built-in gas stovetop burners and an oven, all finished in brushed aluminum and stainless steel. She went over to one of those large, expensive stainless steel refrigerators—the kind you find in restaurants—and peered inside.

After I finished looking around, I said, "Cool kitchen."

"I haven't had a chance to get to the market today, but I think I can throw something together," she said confidently as she critically examined the contents of the fridge.

"So you can cook too," I commented with proper amazement.

She retrieved some green leafy vegetables of the variety known as kai lan, another variety of green leafy vegetables that appeared to be Chinese mustard greens, half of a Chinese roasted duck, some ginger, green onions, and a few assorted other things. Then she opened her kitchen cabinet and pulled out some bottles and jars of assorted strange condiments and spices.

"I'm an excellent cook, Mr. Wadd. I hope you like duck."

"Call me Johnny. And I love duck."

She handed me a bottle of Baja California Cabernet to uncork while she put on the rice, began heating up some soup stock for the mustard greens, and began expertly chopping up the other vegetables and the duck with a large Chinese cleaver. I asked if I could help, but she said no, so I poured myself a glass of the Mexican wine, which turned out to be great, and quietly smoked one of her Egyptian cigarettes, which were unfiltered and very strong, while she casually went on with the preparation of an elaborate three-course Chinese feast. Occasionally, she would walk over to me and take a puff from my cigarette or a sip from my glass of wine.

I was truly impressed as I watched her tackle everything with the seemingly effortless ease of a professional chef. The room began to fill with the aroma of garlic, ginger, and other exotic spices as the oil spattered in the large cast-iron wok as she threw in some chopped garlic and ginger and then she began to stir-fry the vegetables with the duck while at the same time putting the finishing touches on two cold appetizer dishes.

Suzy hadn't lied when she said she was an excellent cook. What she had managed to put together from a bunch of leftovers went beyond even the finest Chinese home cooking. It was the best meal I'd had the pleasure to enjoy in a long time, and I told her so. This girl really knew what she was doing.

"You do this for all your customers?" I asked.

And she laughed, "No, you're actually the first one." True or not, what she said made me feel good.

After dinner, we retired to the quiet luxury of the sunken living room, which was also done in an elaborate Chinese motif. Dark lacquered wooden furniture with highly polished brass fittings. Beautifully hand-painted porcelain gods and goddesses stood alongside rare and expensive Ming dynasty vases, all tastefully and decoratively displayed.

One glass curio cabinet contained a large and varied collection of antique Chinese snuff bottles, while another held elaborately decorated, hand-painted Ch'ing dynasty plates and serving platters, the kind that once graced the homes of either the very wealthy or the aristocracy. A good portion of the polished hardwood floor was covered with an oversized traditional handwoven blue silk dragon carpet. It must have taken years to make one that size.

A larger glass display case sporting an old Chinese brass locking device contained an impressive array of ancient bronze weapons and terra-cotta artifacts that appeared to have come from the Sian excavations. I'm no expert, but everything looked so authentic that I felt like I was in a museum instead of a high-priced call girl's pad.

Suzy saw me looking around and said, "I might have gone a little overboard on the décor."

The next thing I noticed was a large, lifelike oil painting of Suzy herself hanging prominently above the fireplace. I noticed that in her hand she was holding a lotus flower, and that suddenly made me realize that I hadn't gotten around to talking to her about Sheila. I felt in my pocket and retrieved the white gold lotus pendant I had found at Sheila's place and handed it to her.

"Do you recognize this?" I asked her.

Surprise appeared on her face as she carefully examined the pendant. "Yes. It is the symbol of the lotus flower." Then she looked up at me and said, "The lotus grows out of the filthy chaos of a muddy swamp and yet remains resilient, strong, and pure. It is a symbol I identify with because I grew up in filth and poverty in the slums of Hong Kong. My mother was a drug addict and a prostitute, and she could barely support us. I have always been determined not to share the same fate." She gazed inquiringly into my eyes. "I gave this to Sheila. How did you get it?" I told her about Sheila, and she appeared horrified at the news.

"I wondered why I hadn't heard from her in so long. It's been almost two weeks now." She shook her head. "I still can't believe it. Are you absolutely sure it was her?"

I told her there was no doubt. Then she told me how it was that she came to know Sheila. She told me that she devoted some of her spare time to working at a drug rehabilitation clinic, which was where she had met Sheila, who had come there to try to get her life back together.

She also told me that Sheila had managed to succeed in shaking her addiction to heroin and that she had given her the necklace with the lotus pendant and a white silk Chinese robe like her own to celebrate the purity of her new life.

It was nearing dusk when I finally took my leave of Suzy. As I drove on the Santa Monica Freeway headed toward the beach and home, I marveled at the beautiful muted pastel colors that the sunset cast over the haze of the West Los Angeles cityscape. All the while, I was seriously contemplating everything that I had just experienced and all of the things that I had learned in the course of the last couple of days.

More pieces of the puzzle had finally come together, but there were still a lot of pieces that were missing. I had the uncomfortable feeling that I really didn't know where I was going with all this. I still didn't know why Sheila was killed. I didn't know where the FBI fit into all of this. If Sheila had managed to get clean from drugs, why was opium found in her system? There were too many questions without answers. But I knew that those answers were out there somewhere. It was just a matter of finding them.

By the time I got home, night had fallen. There were no messages on my answering machine. There was just an uneasy quiet and a strange stillness throughout the whole place. I thought about having a drink but decided not to. I turned on the television and put on the news just to hear the voices so I wouldn't seem to be so all alone. I sat down on the sofa and heard the drone of the voices coming from the television set, but my thoughts were elsewhere, distracted and unfocused.

I shook off the reverie to hear and see that something exciting was going on in the local newsroom. At first, I had a difficult time concentrating, but when I finally managed to do so, I learned that Apollo 17 had returned to earth after a successful moon landing nine days ago. That was the good news.

The news anchor then talked about the growing controversy over the resumption of bombing raids over North Vietnam, now called Operation Linebacker II, and after that, there was more speculation about whether President Nixon would survive the Watergate scandal. And then on the local front, there was another gang killing in South Central Los Angeles and a heartbreaking story about a five-year-old girl killed by a stray bullet during a drive-by shooting in East LA.

Finally, there was a brief mention of a mutilated body that had washed ashore on Venice Beach. The body was identified as a missing woman named Sheila McGinnis. The news anchor said that the police were actively pursuing an investigation into her death.

I turned off the television, sighed, thought to hell with it, and poured myself a water glass full of Jack Daniels Green Label, emptying the bottle in the process. I lifted the glass to my lips and breathed in the harsh, aromatic fumes of the straight Tennessee whiskey. The fumes seemed to sharpen my thoughts and clear my head.

As I drank and felt the burning warmth slide down my throat and into my guts, my thoughts went back in time to the pretty little girl with stringy blonde hair who wore soiled, ragged clothes and lived in a broken-down Santa Monica trailer park with a broken-down mother. In my mind's eye, I could see her looking up and smiling when I told her that she didn't have to worry anymore, that George and I would always look out for her.

And then my thoughts drifted to the quiet, lonely, black-haired little street urchin playing all by herself in the filthy alleys of Kowloon, dreaming that she would someday be beautiful and wealthy, while her mother tried to earn money for food in the waterfront bars of Tsimshatsui.

Chapter Seven

Wednesday, December 20, 1972

During the night, the rain had fallen. I knew it had because I vaguely remembered hearing the thunder and then the sound of the raindrops splashing against the bedroom window before I dropped off to sleep. The next morning, I woke up early to a bright and sunny day. Much to my surprise, my bruised and battered ribs weren't really all that sore. Suzy's Chinese medicine had really worked wonders.

Feeling somewhat renewed and energized, I took a long, hot shower, then made a pot of coffee and fried a leftover piece of Spam and two sunny side-up eggs for breakfast. I also made lots of heavily buttered toast to sop up the yolk with, even though the bread had grown slightly moldy. A little bit of penicillin never hurt anybody. I managed to get through breakfast without the phone ringing, but as I was gathering up the dishes, the doorbell rang.

Of course, who else would it be but George Lee. As he walked in I reminded him, "I don't see you for three years, and now I see you three times in three days. This has to be some kind of a record."

George ignored my sarcastic but nonetheless accurate comment, followed his nose into the kitchen, and poured himself a cup of coffee. Then he looked at me with that serious look of his and said, "I had to talk to you, John."

"You know there's such a thing as a telephone."

"Not any more. Yours might be bugged."

"No shit?" was all I could think to say as I tried to ignore the somewhat uncomfortable feeling that came over me.

He picked up a piece of toast and looked at it. "What are those dark spots?

"You don't want to know."

He regarded it suspiciously for a moment, then shrugged his

shoulders and began eating it. "There's something fishy going on." George was good at talking with his mouth full of food.

"I had that very same feeling. You know, I ran into a couple FBI guys yesterday. They gave me a warning to keep my nose out of this."

"I was wondering what happened to that ugly face of yours."

I'm not really ugly. But then again, I'm not particularly handsome, either. If you were kind, you might say that I have a rather ordinary but not too unpleasant face. The working over I got yesterday really didn't help it any. I countered his comment with one of my own. "Yeah, well, if only you could see what they did to my ribs."

"Beat you up pretty well, did they?"

"Some people just like to keep kicking a man when he's down."

He threw the half-eaten piece of toast back down on the plate. "Somebody went to the Chief, and he's ordered us to back off."

"Can they do that? Stop the investigation?"

He nodded. "The Feds even took whatever we had on the case, the murder book—everything. It's a shame because we really were starting to make some progress on this one." He opened one of my kitchen cabinets and made a quick examination of the canned goods inside of it before closing it again. "Apparently we were getting close to something sensitive because after they stormed in and took over, they told us to make like all of this never even happened."

"Now that is sort of fishy. So what are you going to do?"

"I don't know, John. I don't know if there's anything that I can do."

It was obvious that George was frustrated and angry at the turn of events. "It's not like you to allow yourself to be pushed around, even if it's by the Feds."

"I'm not going to let them push me around. But I'm not going to lose my job, either."

"I've got no job to lose."

George smiled and patted me on the shoulder. "And that's exactly why I'm here." Then he proceeded to fill me in on everything that they had come up with so far. Their investigation of Alex Eastman, the real estate guy, had hit a dead end, although George felt there was definitely something strange about him.

George said they'd been unable to come up with anything on the names of the two women I had given him. "Another dead end," he said. But I decided to continue to pursue it, so he gave me back the piece of paper with the names, and I told him that I'd try to track them down.

All in all, it wasn't much more than I already knew. That is, until he dropped the bomb. "The trail leads to Chinatown," he finally said, "to a triad outfit that calls itself the White Lotus Organization. It's run by a woman named Suzy Huang."

I couldn't keep the startled look of shock and surprise off my face, and the cop in George immediately picked up on that. "What? You know this woman."

I told him about going to see her yesterday at the penthouse apartment on Kings Road, leaving out the stuff about the sex, of course. I saw the questioning look on his face and decided to come clean, even about that. I spared him no details. After I had finished, he seemed lost in thought. Then he shook his head and said, almost incredulously, "In the ass, John? She wanted you to fuck her in the ass?"

"What can I say?" was all I could say.

"I've got to meet this woman," he said. Then he let loose with another bombshell. "She owns that apartment building on Kings Road, you know."

This was more surprising news. "I didn't know," I admitted.

"She also owns several other apartment buildings in various parts of the city and a big, opulent restaurant in Monterey Park, as well as interests in several relatively large businesses in Chinatown. From what we could find out, she must be a very wealthy woman."

All of this was news to me. "She hadn't mentioned anything about any of this. I thought that she was some sort of high-class call girl."

George gave a short, sarcastic laugh. "I don't think so. You know what the triads are up to, don't you?"

"Yeah, a lot of nasty stuff, as well as some nasty stuff that probably includes drugs."

George nodded and picked up the half-eaten piece of toast he had abandoned, shoved it in his mouth, and poured himself more coffee. He looked around the kitchen as if he were searching for something else. "You wouldn't happen to have any donuts, would you?" he asked.

"No."

"I didn't think so. Look, John, it was when we started to dig out information on this woman, Suzy Huang, that the Feds suddenly jumped into the picture." He paused for a moment to let that thought settle in.

"There's a lot more we could have learned about her, but we didn't get the chance. I have a hunch that she's the key to the whole thing. And for some reason, people high up the ladder don't want her investigated."

Intrigued, I asked, "How high up?"

He scratched his head, an indication that he was seriously contemplating something, before he said, "I get the feeling that it goes all the way to the very top."

George looked around for something else to eat, picked up and considered an overripe banana for a few seconds, then put it back down. He reached in his pocket and pulled out his pack of Viceroys, offering me one before he slipped one between his lips.

He lit the cigarette and continued, "Usually on a homicide case like this, the Feds let us work our angle, the murder, while they work theirs, which in a situation like this would be the drug angle. But this time they took us out of the picture completely. It takes someone with a hell of a lot of power to put the brakes on a murder investigation. I know for a fact that the chief wouldn't have given in easily."

What George was saying just didn't seem to make a whole lot of sense, but then again, in the light of everything that was happening, it did. If he was right, then this case would have taken a completely different turn. If all this was true, then who exactly was this woman who called herself Suzy Huang? She certainly didn't sound like the person that I met yesterday. But I knew well from past experience that people could easily be something other than what they seem.

I wondered if Suzy had been playing me. If so, she had played me well, but what was her purpose in doing so? I now had even more questions for which I had no answers. This was starting to become a nightmare. The more I found out, the more questions there were, and the more questions there were, the more the mystery kept growing deeper and deeper. Like they used to say when I was a small kid, you dig a hole deep enough and you end up in China.

I could tell that George had his thinking cap on because he really seemed to be going at it. Finally, he looked up at me. "Since you've got such a big in with her, why don't you see if you can find out more from this Suzy Huang?" This seemed to be a reasonable thing to do, so I nodded in agreement.

"Meantime," he continued, I'm going to nose around and see if I can find out who it is that got this investigation sidetracked. Like I said, John, there's something funny going on."

We were suddenly interrupted by the loud beeping of George's pager. He pulled it out of his pocket and looked at the number before turning to me and asking, "May I use your phone?"

I said, "Sure, be my guest," then indicated where it was by pointing my head toward the phone on the bar.

George made his call, during which he said, "Shit!" Then, "Are you absolutely sure that it's her," followed by a "Fuck!" and then, "Ok, I'm going over there now," before hanging up. There was a grim look on his face.

I already knew that something bad had happened, and George confirmed it when he came over to me and said, "We got a call from West Hollywood Division Homicide. It was about Billie Rae Chase. They just found her dead in her apartment. Her throat's been slit. I'm going over there."

He started out the door, and I said, "I'm going with you."

We took separate cars and proceeded to fight the tail end of the morning rush hour traffic. Avoiding the freeway, we both headed down Venice Boulevard toward Fairfax. Somehow we managed to arrive at Billie Rae's place at just about the same time. The homicide detective in charge recognized George and lifted up the yellow crime scene tape so we could go in.

"What's the scoop?" George asked him.

"Neighbor called 911. Said she heard a lot of scary yelling and screaming. The door to her apartment was unlocked, and the patrolmen who responded found her."

George nodded. "Thanks for calling me."

"I figured it might have something to do with your case over in Santa Monica. This one appears to be a very similar MO."

We headed on up to the second floor and the crime scene. Billie Rae's apartment looked just about the same as it had when I had left it two days ago, with the exception of the old take-out food containers, which were now in the sink with the dirty dishes, probably by this time breeding a variety of interesting and colorful mold cultures. I was too afraid to look.

The dildo was still there on the coffee table. The only other change

I noticed were a couple more empty wine bottles on the coffee table and more cigarette butts in the already overflowing abalone shell ashtray. Now there was also the unmistakable smell of death about the place.

Billie Rae was face down on the floor in a large, dark pool of dried blood. Her bare arms were extended as if she were trying to reach for something, and she still had on her tattered terrycloth bathrobe, from which her naked legs stuck out, spread wide apart in an almost obscene position. I moved in for a closer look and recoiled at the pungent, coppery smell of the blood.

"Throat slit, huh?" George inquired of the coroner's investigator, who was bent over her.

"Ear to ear," he replied without looking up. "Whoever did it had a real sharp knife and knew exactly what he was doing. Almost severed her head clean off."

"Just talked to her yesterday," George mused, "and today she's worm food."

"You think it might have had something to do with her talking to us?" I asked, realizing that it was a dumb question even as I asked it.

"Probably" was all he answered.

We both knew that it did, and I sensed that we were both feeling pretty bad about it. George always tried to hide behind a callous façade, but when push came to shove, he really did have some feelings. He bent over and looked curiously at her arms, which were scratched and bloody. Two fingernails of her right hand were broken off.

"Looks like she put up quite a fight," I observed. I noticed that George had taken out his pen and was gingerly poking around at the cigarette butts in the abalone shell ashtray. I also noticed that some of the newer ones in the ashtray weren't menthol.

He just nodded his head and agreed by saying, "Yeah, looks like it," before squatting down to examine the body a little closer. He reached over and examined the fingers on her right hand. From the expression on his face, I knew right away that they had all been broken.

I moved in and looked at the body a little closer myself and saw the numerous fresh cigarette burns on her arm.

He sighed, and then he stood up and addressed the coroner's investigator once again. "I hope you guys are going to go through this place with a fine-tooth comb. This girl's death directly links to a homicide case I have in Santa Monica."

The coroner's investigator nodded his head and said, "I'll keep you posted on what we find."

"Good enough," George said as he handed him his card. "This'll give you a direct line to me." He took another quick look around, then motioned to me for us to leave. Outside, he had a few words with the homicide detective in charge. Then we walked back toward our respective cars before he said a few words to me.

"I think they'll do a good job," he said as nodding his head back at the crime scene, "but just in case, after they leave, I think I'll go back and have my own look."

I nodded that I thought it was a good idea. "It's still pretty early in the morning, so I'm going to head up to Suzy Huang's place and see if I can catch her."

And George nodded back to me and said, "Sounds like a plan. I'll see you later."

As I got into my car, I looked cautiously around the neighborhood. There wasn't a single Ethiopian to be seen anywhere. In fact, the only signs of life around there were just a couple of old Jewish ladies standing on the stoop of a nearby apartment building, ignoring all of the police presence while casually shooting the shit in Yiddish.

The rush hour was over, and the mid-morning traffic wasn't all that bad as I headed north on Fairfax toward Suzie's apartment. I went over in my head all that I had learned that morning. What George said about Suzy had come as quite a shock, and I was still trying to process it all in my mind.

That, combined with Billie Rae's brutal murder, gave me a sort of uneasy feeling in the pit of my stomach. What if Suzy was involved in all this in some kind of sinister and dangerous way?

What if she herself was sinister and dangerous? She certainly hadn't seemed that way yesterday. I just couldn't reconcile these contradictory thoughts. I shook my head and looked out the car window at the bright and beautiful morning. The night rain had washed away the grime and smog, and the air was fresh and crisp. The sun was shining, and the birds were chirping happily in the trees as I pulled up in front of Suzy's apartment building and parked.

When Suzy opened the door, I could hear the beginning of the second movement of Schubert's *Trout Quintet* playing softly in the background. She looked up at me and smiled. She wore high platform heels, which made her seem taller, and she was dressed in a gray business suit, which gave her the appearance of a successful attorney or businesswoman. All in all, she gave off a look that was totally different from the first time I had seen her.

"Strange, I was just thinking about you," Suzie said as she opened the door wider and let me in. "We must be on the same wavelength." She ushered me into her living room and indicated for me to take a seat on the sofa.

"Would you like some tea, or maybe coffee?"

"I've already had some; thank you." I felt a little uneasy as I tried to figure out how to ask her the questions that I had to ask her. I decided that the direct approach would probably be the best.

"Suzie, I'm here because there are some questions that I have to ask you."

She seated herself next to me with a puzzled and questioning look on her face. "You seem to be troubled, John. Tell me, what it is that you are concerned about, and what can I do to help you?"

I looked directly into her eyes and told her, "You can tell me about your business, Suzy. Tell me about the White Lotus Organization."

The puzzled, questioning expression on her face had not changed and remained there for several moments before she smiled, nodded her head, and then whispered softly, "Come with me."

She led me into a room I had not yet seen. It was a large office, and two of the walls were lined with floor-to-ceiling dark wooden bookcases filled with books, both hardbound and paperbound, in English, French, and Chinese. There must have been at least two thousand books on those shelves. On another wall hung an ancient, large red silk Tibetan temple tapestry embroidered with golden thread with various prayers and religious mantras and symbols.

In the center of the room, prominently placed in front of a large circular window, was a beautiful, hand-carved antique Chinese desk elaborately inlaid with mother-of-pearl. On top of the desk was stacked a profusion of account books, papers, and what appeared to be various business contracts. There was also a copy of King Hussein of Jordan's autobiography *Uneasy Lies the Head*. I picked the book up and looked at it. I was somewhat taken aback to see that it was inscribed to her and signed.

On the wall near the entryway opposite her desk hung diplomas from a Hong Kong community college and the London School of Economics, along with a number of framed photographs of Suzy, who was smiling and standing alongside a virtual who's who of Asian, British, French, and American celebrities and politicians.

As I quickly scanned the wall, my eyes wandered to a photograph of Suzy and the current governor of California, one of her with the mayor of Los Angeles, and then even another with her and the district attorney, and I immediately realized that I had what appeared to be confirmation of George's suspicions.

"So what do you think of my power wall?" she asked jokingly.

"You know all of these people," I said, indicating the pictures on the wall, suddenly aware of the fact that I had not been able to suppress the amazement in my voice.

"Yes," she said in a manner that was very matter-of-fact. "I've met them at one time or another."

I pointed to a couple of the pictures. "So you know the governor and the mayor?"

"I have to confess that I've made generous contributions to many of their political campaigns, all perfectly legal, of course. Not that I'm particularly interested in politics, but when one is trying to do business in a strange country, one really needs to try and secure all the help she can get."

"I suppose you're right," I said, but my mind was racing with thoughts about this startling new aspect of Suzy's personality. I was having a hard time reconciling the girl that was in bed with me yesterday with this self-assured and successful businesswoman who stood facing me.

She raised her hand toward the wall with the diplomas and pictures. "Those things on that wall aren't hanging there for the sake of my ego," she explained. "They're up there simply because they look good for business. I'm just a woman, and I have to make men take me seriously enough to trust my abilities. They might look impressive to some, but to me, they're just a bunch of meaningless photographs."

I pointed to the book on the desk and asked, "And what about King Hussein?"

Suzy laughed. "He's actually a friend of a friend. I met him and his wife once when I was going to school in London. They are very unpretentious, down-to-earth people, easy to talk to, and both defi-nitely concerned about humanity, unlike most politicians. I'm just now finally getting around to reading his book." Her face suddenly became more serious.

"But you asked about the White Lotus Organization," she went on, "so I'll tell you about it."

She seated herself at her desk and motioned for me to take a seat in the chair directly across from her. "I've already told you about the significance of the lotus flower for me, so I won't go into that again. The White Lotus Organization is a company that I founded along with some partners in Hong Kong."

"Are your partners Triads?"

"Some might call them that. I prefer to call them businessmen."

I reached into my pocket for a cigarette before remembering that I had left the pack in my car. Suzy must have read my mind because she nodded toward a polished, dark wood cigarette box on her desk. I opened it to find that it contained imported Dunhill's. I lit one up and drew the smoke from the Virginia tobacco deeply into my lungs while savoring the sweet, unaccustomed taste.

"What exactly is it that your company does?"

"We do a lot of things, such as import and export, real estate in-vestment and development, funding and financing local businesses. Things like that. We have a restaurant in Monterey Park. Right now, we're in the process of building a large upscale shopping mall in San Gabriel."

"So you must be very wealthy."

She considered my statement thoughtfully before answering. "The company is very wealthy, Johnny. Fortunately, it has been al-lowed to prosper in this country. But don't forget that I have part-ners and investors. However, you are right. I am not poor by any stretch of the imagination."

"Why did you lead me to believe that you were a call girl?"

Suzy laughed. "You drew that conclusion all on your own, and I just played along with you for the fun of it. Actually, at one time, I did work at a massage parlor in Hong Kong to put myself through college."

"So I take it; now you've finally attained your dream, then."

She thought about that carefully before she answered. "You might say that in a way I have, just as you might say that in other, much more important ways that I haven't." She shifted in her chair and then looked straight at me. "Now why don't we get right down to the point of your visit? You're wondering if I had anything to do with Sheila's death, aren't you?"

That was pretty direct and to the point, so I thought I'd be direct and to the point. "Yes, I am."

"I see," she said quietly, looking down at her folded hands.

As if to explain myself, I added, "Your name and the name of your company did come up during the police investigation."

"I know it did, and I wish I could tell you why. But I am not at liberty to do so at this time. All I can tell you is that I did not kill her. Please don't ask me anything else about this."

"You know this makes it very difficult for me."

"I know it does, Johnny." She started to say something else but stopped. I could tell that she really wanted to confide in me, but something—and I don't know what—was somehow holding her back. Finally, she said, "All I can tell you to do, beg you to do, is trust me."

Almost as if on cue, her phone rang. I noticed that before she answered it, Suzy clicked on a cassette recorder hidden beneath some papers on her desk. An animated discussion in Mandarin ensued. It seemed as if something important had come up, and whatever it was seemed to be putting her on the spot. She seemed to be protesting about something, and her tone alternated between being angry and placating. I wished I could understand what was being said, but I couldn't, so that was that.

After the call ended, she clicked off the cassette recorder and said, "I'm sorry, Johnny, but something important has come up, and I'm very late for an important meeting. You'll have to go now."

I nodded at the cassette recorder. "You record all your phone conversations?"

She smiled. "I just record my end of it, so I can remember what I said in case I ever have to."

She reached over and took my hand and said, "Trust me, Johnny."

Chapter Eight

As I left Suzy's apartment, I reflected that even though I now had some answers, for whatever they were worth, I had come away with even more questions. Once again, it seemed as if I was getting nowhere fast. Suzy had asked me to trust her—and I really wanted to trust her, but I simply didn't know whether she was actually telling me the truth or whether she was playing me for a sucker all the way. There was no doubt in my mind that she was either a triad or was heavily involved with them, and I knew that the triads dealt in drugs and death. There was a link between her and Sheila, and I couldn't help but think that somehow there was a link between her and Sheila's death.

As I drove south on Fairfax, I wondered if George had gone back to the crime scene yet, so I headed back that way. When I got to Billie Rae's apartment building, I saw his car parked in front, so I parked behind it. I was about to get out of the car to look for him when I saw him leaving the apartment building, cautiously looking from side to side.

He spotted me, then walked over to my car, leaned in the window, and asked, "You had lunch yet?" I told him I hadn't, and he said, "Let's go to Farmer's Market. I feel like having a corned beef sandwich from Magee's."

"I'll meet you over there." George had, of course, uttered the magic words, triggering a whole barrage of memories of weekend childhood outings with the family that would inevitably end up at Farmer's Market with a corned beef sandwich from Magee's.

Over the years, the landmark Farmer's Market has grown from an empty lot at 3rd and Fairfax, where a few farmers sold their produce from the back of their trucks, to the bustling complex filled with the multitude of indoor stalls and shops that is there now.

Back in the early 1930's, an enterprising woman named Blanche Magee had noticed those farmers selling the produce from their trucks, and figuring that they might be hungry, she began bringing sandwiches in a picnic basket to sell to them, and soon she was selling her sandwiches to their customers as well. When the Farmer's Market officially opened in 1934, Magee's was the first restaurant there, and it's been there ever since.

George, who must have been really hungry, had ordered two corned beef sandwiches on rye with mustard and horseradish, and his eyes were carefully watching the server hand-carve the juicy, steaming meat.

I ordered mine French dipped on one of those freshly-baked Italian sub rolls, and then we both found a table on the upper deck and settled down to eat our lunch. "Did you get to see Suzy?" he asked with his mouth full.

Since I never learned to talk with my mouth full, I had to finish chewing and swallowing, before I was able to answer. "Yeah, but she really didn't tell me a whole lot. Something you might be interested in knowing, though, is that she's probably pretty tight with the mayor and the district attorney."

This managed to get George's attention. "Tight? What do you mean, tight?" His mouth was really full this time, and the juice from the sandwich was dripping from his mouth on down to his chin, and his eyes were beginning to water from the pungent horseradish, but he ignored all this and kept on eating while waiting for my answer.

"Apparently, she's been a big contributor to their political campaigns."

George's jaw dropped open. Then, after a brief moment of thought, he came up with yet another idea on the subject. "She probably has a judge or two in her pocket as well."

"I wouldn't be surprised." It has never ceased to amaze me what a whole lot of money is usually capable of buying.

"Interesting," George mused as he finished his first sandwich in one huge final bite and started in on the second one.

"I thought so too. She also insists that she had nothing to do with Sheila's death, although she as much as admitted that her business partners are Triads."

George was silent for a long moment while he finished eating his second sandwich. Then he wiped the grease off his mouth on his coat sleeve and asked, "So what do you think?"

"So what do I think about what?"

"Whether she's leveling with you about all this?"

I thought for a moment before answering him. "I really don't know what to think. She seems pretty forthcoming, but…" I searched for the words to describe what I felt but couldn't find them. "My gut instinct tells me that she's on the level, and I want to believe that she is. But there are some things that she's just not telling me. I just don't know, George."

George nodded and was silent once again. I couldn't tell if he was thinking about what I had just told him or whether he was contemplating getting another sandwich. At least his silence gave me a chance to finish mine. I never thought of myself as a slow eater, but compared to George, I guess that I'm a very slow eater. He watched me impatiently while I finished eating. There was a look on his face, as if he wanted to ask me a question. Finally, he looked into my eyes and asked, "Are you going to eat your pickle?"

"You can have it."

He picked up the kosher dill pickle slice and stuffed it into his mouth in a single swift movement. While he was chewing on it, he informed me, "When I got back to Billie Rae's place after the West Hollywood guys had left, I saw that the FBI boys were there in the apartment nosing around."

"Don't tell me—a tall Caucasian and a short Oriental?"

"That would be them. They were definitely looking for something." He pulled a well-used handkerchief out of his coat pocket and blew his nose, casually examining the result before putting it back in his pocket. "I laid low 'til they left, then I went in." He gave a dramatic pause, and then he smiled.

"So," I prodded him, "go on."

"I found something in Billie Rae's apartment that they all missed." He reached into his pocket again, and this time pulled out a small plastic evidence bag. "Take a look," he said. "I'm sure you know what that is."

Inside the transparent bag was something very familiar that I recognized from my army stint in Vietnam. It was a brass Zippo cigarette lighter like those you could buy back in Vietnam with your unit insignia and service date. This one boasted the crimson and yellow shield marked MAC/SOG bearing the white skull wearing a Green Beret cap.

The engraving on it read VIET NAM—HUE 65-66. The owner of that cigarette lighter had been in the Special Forces, in the Military Assistance Command Vietnam—Studies and Observation Group, or, in other words, someone who had been assigned to the Unconventional Warfare Task Force—someone like an experienced killer.

"You think this has something to do with her murder?"

"Turn it over."

I flipped the bag over and looked at the back of the lighter. There were a couple of drops of what appeared to be dried blood on it and a small bloody smudge near the bottom, and they didn't seem to be all that old. "Where did you find this?"

"You saw the way her arms were pointed toward the sofa?"

I recalled the crime scene in my mind, and then I nodded.

He went on, "I used to have a sofa just like that one when I lived in that old, furnished bachelor apartment on Ocean Boulevard. It has one of those fold-out beds, and because of that, it was really heavy, as I recalled. So it was just like the one Billie Rae had. I guess those guys were just too lazy to move it."

"You found it under the sofa bed?"

"It was almost near the wall, as if she'd deliberately pushed it under there during the struggle. So even if they gave a quick look in the space beneath the sofa, they wouldn't have seen it." He pulled a wooden toothpick out of his coat pocket and began picking his front teeth. George had a virtually endless supply of wooden toothpicks in his coat pocket.

"Well, I'll be damned," was all I could think of to say.

"There wasn't any dust on it, so it can't have been there for very long," he continued. "I have a feeling that somehow she managed to get it from her killer."

The implication of what he was saying had hit home. "So we could be looking for an ex-Green Beret who was in Nam sometime during the mid-sixties."

"We could be."

George followed this statement with a loud, massive belch, and the heads of those people sitting nearby turned and looked at us with surprise and awe. Noticing this, he said loud enough for everyone to hear, "Jeez, you got no manners at all, John. I can't take you anyplace."

I accepted the stares with a straight face and was glad that he had not decided to follow the burp with one of his super-loud farts as well, because that had usually been his modus operandi in the past. I could see in his eyes that the same thought had just been crossing his own mind. We were both thinking, at the same time, of our childhood and the old school days. For a brief moment there, it was almost like old times once again.

He gave off with a loud laugh before flipping away the used toothpick, retrieving the evidence bag from my hands, and putting it back into his coat pocket.

"I'm going to take this to the crime lab and have it checked out for prints and a possible match on the blood."

The shortest distance between two points is a straight line, but I had been following a maze that had so many different twists and turns that I was beginning to become confused and disoriented. And this was something that I was not used to and didn't like.

I've been a private investigator going on three years now, and never before had I experienced a case as thoroughly confusing as this one was turning out to be. No matter how many times I went over everything in my mind I just couldn't come up with any solid answers to the questions of who killed Sheila and why.

On one hand, we have the drug angle, which was probably the most likely angle to pursue. Sheila was supplying Billie Rae with cocaine. Billie Rae saw an Asian guy slip Sheila some heroin. Sheila also knew Suzie Huang. Suzie is in business with the triads, and the triads are usually involved in drug dealing. But they weren't really known for dealing in cocaine, which was pretty much controlled by the Mexican gangs and the South American drug cartels.

The triads dealt primarily in heroin and opium, but not as much in the United States as in Southeast Asia. Here, most of the heroin either came from Europe or Mexico. Sheila had been a recovered heroin addict, according to Suzy, but she had ingested opium not long before she was murdered. Suzie said she had nothing to do with Sheila's death, but could Suzy be trusted?

The FBI and the BNDD were also involved in this somehow, and George Lee had been ordered by his superiors not to continue with the murder investigation. His superiors had been intimidated by someone higher up in city government. Suzy donated money to the political campaigns of both the mayor and the district attorney.

At Billie Rae's murder scene, George uncovers a Special Forces cigarette lighter that may have belonged to a Green Beret stationed in Viet Nam sometime in the mid-1960s. That was about the time I had finished my own final tour there and was discharged and sent home. So what exactly was *really* going on here?

I decided that at least I had to set about and attempt to accomplish something. Since I was in the neighborhood, I stopped by the West Hollywood office of Hal, the agent, to see if he was familiar with the two names from the piece of paper that I'd found at Sheila's. It was a long shot, but it was worth a try. Unfortunately, I managed to draw a blank on both counts there.

Hal looked at the names on the piece of paper I had handed him carefully, then shook his head and said, "No, I've never heard of them," but he took down both their names anyway, said he'd check around, and promised to definitely give me a call if anything turned up.

Then I told him what had happened to Billie Rae, and he shook his head again at the very thought of another Hollywood tragedy brought about almost certainly as the result of the proliferation of so-called recreational drugs. Even though she worked on the fringes of the entertainment industry, she had still been a part of it, as obscure and unknown as she was, and she will always remain.

"Another young life wasted, another young life gone and forgotten forever," he mused, suddenly waxing poetic as he closed the large ring-bound model book he'd been working on. Hal was old-fashioned in many ways, but I had to admit that I shared his distaste for the rapidly developing drug culture in this country.

On the way home, I distracted myself by thinking of the gorgeous redhead who had been sitting in Hal's office shamelessly flirting with me. She was fresh talent, and she was hot—*really* hot. In fact, I was starting to get a boner just thinking about her. She smelled good, too. She gave off the sweet aroma of soap and shampoo, sugar and spice, and everything nice. The way she was coming on to me, I thought for sure that I was all set for a hotter than hot date this evening.

In fact, I was going over in my mind a way to lead into this when Hal noticed what was going on and, being the honest and straightforward guy that he is, told her that I wasn't a producer or a director, and that I wasn't a casting director either. Then it was as if, all of a sudden, someone turned off the gas on the stove. The flame went out, and she went back to filling out whatever form it was that she was filling out when I had first walked in. The momentary bubble had burst. Such is life in the big city.

When I got home and checked my phone messages, I was surprised to find a call from the sister of one of my old army buddies. Nuala Sullivan Doyle was a classic Irish-American beauty, a few years older than me, who had been widowed by the Vietnam War. Her brother, Sgt. Liam Sullivan, had been my squad leader and best buddy throughout the war.

We had both been discharged around the same time—me after I'd served my second tour of duty and Liam after his fourth—and when we returned to California, we both had been invited to live at Nuala's house in Huntington Beach until we were able to get our shit together and find places of our own.

I have always been grateful to her for that. Both of my parents had passed away, and I really had no place to go at the time. My mother died of cancer at the beginning of my second tour of duty in Vietnam, and my father followed her six months later after he suffered a fatal heart attack.

According to my sister, he really didn't want to go on living without my mother anyway. They had always been very close. In fact, I never even once heard them argue, much less fight, about anything, something truly unusual in a marriage, much less any kind of long-term relationship. So I guess I was very fortunate in that respect. Of course, the fact that they had a stable and enduring marriage never kept either of them from spanking me if the occasion called for it.

They were in their late thirties when I came along, somewhat unexpectedly, as I have been told. I have a sister ten years older than me who is married and lives in San Francisco, but we've never been particularly close—I suppose because of the age difference.

Nuala's late husband, Denny Doyle, had been an army helicopter pilot with the 1st Cavalry Brigade who was killed in action in Vietnam about three months before we got back. I'd never met him, but from what people had told me, I got the picture that he was a very nice guy.

I lived with Nuala and Liam at her home in Huntington Beach for about five months, and this was, for the most part, a happy, care-free period that may well have been one of the best times of my life. It ended when I finally got it together and managed to land a job with a company in Torrance that repossessed cars.

Repossessing cars wasn't a job that I particularly enjoyed, and I know for a fact that I wasn't very good at it, mainly because I simply hated taking people's cars away from them. And this was really not the way one should feel if one is going to be making a living by re-possessing cars.

But one thing I realized was that in a huge metropolitan area like Los Angeles, a car was very important to a person, and depriving that person of his or her car was, in a way, like taking away his or her freedom and livelihood. It just didn't sit well with me.

So one day the boss, who was definitely not impressed by my record as a re-possessor, gave me the assignment to follow his wife to see if she was cheating on him. He was a nice guy who had kept me on even though I was lousy at the job, so I agreed.

I stopped by a camera store not far from the Del Amo Shopping Center called Silvio's Photoworks and proceeded to invest a good deal of my hard-earned savings in an Olympus OM-1 35mm single lens reflex camera, a long telephoto zoom lens, and a few rolls of high-speed black-and-white film. Then I set about following the wife.

The wife was, of course, cheating on him, and when I provided my boss with the evidence in the form of the photographs I had taken, he paid me three thousand dollars and said, "Well, Wadd—I think we've found something that you're really good at, and you've saved me a fortune in alimony to boot. Why don't you become a private detective?" And I thought—you know, I think he's right.

I'd picked up some good investigative knowledge and contacts through running traces for the car repos, and aside from that, I had a lot of patience, and I particularly liked the fact that I could work my own hours and be answerable only to myself. I'd already invested in a camera—so I thought, what the hell, and took the three thousand and became a private investigator.

The message Nuala had left on my machine didn't say much. Only to please call her back and that it was important. She left both her work and her home number, and since it was only a little after three in the afternoon, I dialed her work. When she answered the phone, she immediately said, "It's about Liam, John."

"I thought as much. How is he?"

There was a momentary silence. And then she said, "He's dead."

This news hit me hard. I didn't know what to say for a long moment. All I could think of was a lame "Oh, Nuala," and then I finally got a grip on myself and asked, "How did it happen?"

Her voice broke as she replied, "He hanged himself."

This provided me with another great shock, even though the fact that he finally ended up committing suicide was not totally unexpected. "When did it happen?"

"Day before yesterday," she said. "I came home from work and found him there in the garage." She stopped talking for a moment.

I know it was hard for her to speak of this, and I wanted to tell her, "Stop; you don't have to say any more," but I didn't, and she continued, "I tried to get hold of you, but the number I had was no longer in service. Then there were so many things to do I forgot. I've only just been back to work this morning, and I got your new listing."

The realization dawned that I hadn't seen either her or Liam for over two years, and I'd not only moved during that time but had been so busy with working and then building up my PI business that I had not even managed to keep in touch.

"I'm so sorry, Nuala," I said. And then I hesitated before asking, "How are you holding up?"

"All right, I guess," she answered, but I could hear the tired sadness and bereavement in her voice.

"I'm coming down there."

"You don't have to, John. I know you're busy. You were his friend, so I wanted to make sure that you knew."

"I'm coming down there, Nuala. I'm leaving now."

She hesitated for a moment before she said, "If you want to come, Johnny, then it will be good to see you."

"I want to come."

"All right then. I'm at work now, but I'll be home at around five thirty. If you get there first, you know where to find the key."

Chapter Nine

The drive to Nuala's place in Huntington Beach generally took about an hour. Fortunately, I was able to hit the freeway before the start of rush hour traffic. The drive down gave time to reflect on the past. I thought about Liam Sullivan, who had always seemed so very much larger than life.

He had been a terrific leader, a real tough guy who put up with absolutely no shit from us but would never ask us to do something that he wouldn't do himself. He always looked out for the best interests of his squad and was consequently deeply respected by all of us.

Even after the war, he always addressed me as Private First Class Johnny Wadd to remind me that I did finally manage to earn a single stripe. We had experienced a lot of good times together and a lot of the bad as well.

I contemplated the things that had probably led up to his taking his own life. His suicide was something unexpected yet expected. To understand it, you have to go back in time and place to Vietnam and to the war that we had been forced to fight there.

The Sullivans were and are physically strong, big-boned people. Nuala is almost as tall as I am, and her only brother Liam was a few inches taller. Liam had been a genuine hero who had been awarded both the Silver Star and the Purple Heart for service to his country far above and beyond the call of duty.

But although his body was strong and his constitution courageous, his mind had been haunted by the horrors he had experienced and been a part of in the course of the four tours he had served over there.

Sgt. Liam Sullivan had returned home a hero, but he was not the same man who had left, and he would never again be that same man. He had done his part in the war—the part that had been assigned for him to do—but he had also become its victim. In his mind, he kept reliving the massacres he had been ordered to carry out—the wartime atrocities that he had been a part of.

His dreams were eternally populated by the faces of the men and women and the children he had killed. Much of this had happened even before I was myself assigned to join Liam's squad during my second and final tour of duty.

After I joined Liam's squad, I had been on one of those terrible raids with him, but unlike the other men, either through fear, incompetence, cowardice, or a combination of all three, I had just been unable to kill the family in the hut I had been ordered to clear.

I remember entering it and seeing an old Vietnamese man and a young woman huddled next to the cooking fire in the center of the hut, and a dark-eyed girl child cowering in fear in the corner.

None of them either moved or spoke a word. They just looked at me. I could hear the sounds of gunfire coming from the huts next to us, and a machine gun rattled on almost non-stop in the distance amidst the chaos and chorus of the shouts and screams.

Trying to do my duty, I aimed my rifle at the old man, and he looked up at me with an expressionless gaze and silently waited. The woman flinched, then closed her eyes and gripped the old man's soiled, sweat-stained shirt. The child stared wide-eyed. I pointed the rifle away from them and fired at the ground four times, then motioned for them to lie down on the dirt floor as if they were dead.

Right after they did this, Liam ran into the hut and said, "Are they all finished?" and when I nodded yes, he said, "Then let's get the hell out of here!"

Liam and I ran out of the hut, and while we retreated into the cover of the jungle, another squad came in with flamethrowers and set fire to all of the huts in the village. I don't know if that family ever made it out alive. Our orders had been to kill everyone in that village—men, women, and children—and then destroy it as if it had never existed.

After we had returned to California, Liam began telling me about his recurring nightmares. Then, one day, while we were in a bar drinking and getting pretty plastered, he asked me, "That family in the hut—you remember? You didn't kill them, did you?"

I replied truthfully, "No."

"I didn't think so," he said, nodding his head. "I saw no blood." He paused and looked at me for a long moment, then grabbed my shoulder. "Well, good for you," he said. "Good for you." And we never spoke of this matter again.

We did speak, however, of many things that he had been ordered to do and that he had done in the course of the war. His most startling confession came at another time when we were both very, very drunk, and he said to me, "You know what frightened me the most over there? It was not the enemy. No, I was not afraid of them. It was me that I feared the most, and it was because of the slaughter, John, the slaughter. Because God help me, but I got to the point where I was actually enjoying it; you hear what I'm saying—I actually liked what I was doing!"

He was silent for awhile, as if he was reliving something once again in his own mind. I didn't know what to say, so I said nothing.

He finished the drink he was holding and poured himself another, and then he continued: "While I was doing it, you know—the killing and all that, I mean. Well, I felt the power—I felt the power like God must feel when he holds in his hands the control of life and death. I'm telling you, in the middle of all that carnage and death, I felt so alive!" Tears were in his eyes, and he had begun slurring his words. I could feel the pain that was in his heart as he told me these things, and I wanted him to stop. Still, he went on, "And that's what scared me, John, that I could feel this way. That the beast in me had finally taken over. And now I know that I'm truly damned."

"Liam," I said, "you can't go on blaming yourself. You were only following orders. You were a good soldier, doing what a good soldier had to do. The guilt for the war is not yours to bear. The decisions, right or wrong, were made by others."

There was a long silence as he paused in deep reflection. "Before I went over there, I swear to God, I was a good person. I was a gentle person. I didn't even play football for Christ's sake because I was so big and strong that I was afraid I'd hurt somebody. But over there, well, we did do, I suppose, what we had to do."

I nodded my head in agreement, and he nodded his head, then drained his drink, but from the look in his eyes, I could tell that he knew deep inside that there was no way he would ever truly justify to himself not only his actions but also those terrible feelings of guilt that he had so remorsefully confessed to himself and which would haunt him to his dying day.

I watched as Liam slowly became a physical wreck because of that burden, which seemed to have consumed his entire being. He spent many of his days in brooding silence, and when night came, he was afraid to sleep. He began drinking more and more, much more than he should have, but the bottle offered him no real solace. He was not a lazy man, so he tried to work, but he couldn't seem to hold down a job longer than a week, or sometimes a month at the most. It bothered him that he was no longer the provider he once had been and that he had been reduced to being supported by his older sister.

His sister was good to him. She tried to comfort and care for him, allowing him to keep living in her house, and it is probably only because of her that he hung on for as long as he did. Even the last time I had seen him, well over two years ago, he had seemed to be at the end of his rope. Liam had been irrevocably damaged by what he had done in the war—not physically, even though he had been wounded twice—but mentally, and for that, they could find no cure.

He went to the VA Hospital and saw the doctors, and he talked to them, and they talked to him, but in the end, they could only give him sedatives to help him sleep, which only brought on the nightmare dreams, and they also gave him medicine that cured nothing, for it was not his body that was damaged but his soul.

I still have terrible dreams myself—dreams of things that I saw and experienced over there, horrifying nightmares of countless women and children dead and dying, men blown to bits both ours and the enemy. In these nightmares, I am still haunted by the stench of death, from the bloated corpses floating in the rice paddies of the Mekong Delta to the maggot-infested remains rotting in the sun, the all-pervading smell of fear, the repulsive odor of napalm, and burning flesh in the fires and the smoke of wanton destruction.

There are other things as well, far too horrifying and terrible to tell, that come and go in these dreams. And when I wake up, I'm drenched and shivering in the cold sweat of fear, heart thumping, and scared to death at the senseless horror of what one man is capable of doing to another.

I think that my salvation and the fact that I can still function as a rational human being lie in my cowardice and in my inability to kill those whom I find no need to kill. Still, I'm far from being a saint, and I am certainly not innocent. In the war, I did my share of killing, and I have my own guilt to live with. I killed not only men but also women who were trying to kill me—not many, but enough—and of course, this all still haunts me from time to time.

But I can live with it because, before I killed these people, I could see in their eyes that they wanted to kill me. When I looked into the eyes of the old man in the hut, the young woman beside him, and the child in the corner, I did not see this look. I saw only the questioning looks of innocents who wondered why this all was happening but had somehow resigned themselves to their fate.

There are things that we want to forget that we will never be able to forget. They come as flashbacks that always seem to insidiously return to haunt us when we are the most vulnerable—on those seemingly never-ending sleepless nights that we all dread.

Nuala's white Chevrolet Impala was already parked in the driveway beside her house when I arrived, and it occurred to me that she parked there because she could no longer go into the garage. She must have been watching from the window because she came to the door when I pulled up and parked out front.

She was wearing a simple, inexpensive white cotton dress, but even that looked good on her. Now in her late thirties, Nuala had put on a little weight, but on her it seemed appropriate, even sexy. Her long, strawberry blonde hair was tied up in a ponytail, which only emphasized the classic beauty of her facial features. She greeted me with a hug and a chaste kiss on the cheek.

"Well, John, it's been awhile." There was a slight smell of Scotch whiskey on her breath. "I decided to take off work early," she said, as if she needed to explain her presence.

"I'm sorry I've been so busy," I managed as a somewhat lame excuse. "I've been meaning to get down here and visit you and Liam but never seemed to get a chance." But still, I felt selfish and ashamed of the fact that I had ignored them for so long.

"Well, you're here now, so come in and have a drink," she said as she invited me into the house.

As I looked around the living room, I saw that it was pretty much the same as I remembered that it had always been. A large Christmas tree, a real one, stood prominently next to the fireplace, and I was reminded of the little artificial one in Wilma's small apartment. This one, however, had colorfully wrapped presents beneath it, and I wondered how many of them were for Liam. It was sad to think of the presents there that he would never receive or unwrap.

"Liam put up the tree before he…" The phone rang before Nuala could finish what she was going to say. "Excuse me," she said as she went off to the kitchen to answer it.

Left alone for the moment, I looked around the spacious room, which gave off the comfortable feeling of home—of a place that one could always go back to and find to be still there and unchanged. Like my parents home had once been to me until they passed on, and I myself had moved out and on to another life—a far less constant and stable life to be sure, but one that would be all mine.

I had come to learn that things do change and that most things in life are elusive and transitory. Still, I missed that sense of permanence, that sense of comfort and security that had once seemed to be eternal but was now no longer there.

On the wall was still the large photograph of her husband, Denny Doyle, framed in black along with his campaign ribbons and Purple Heart, and beside it, a similar photograph of Sgt. Liam Sullivan framed with his service ribbons, Silver Star, and Purple Heart.

I was overcome with the sad realization that what had originally been put up as nostalgic decorations had now become something of a double memorial shrine to the two men who were closest to her and whom she both loved.

On the table below these photographs were a number of other framed photographs, and some of these had not been there before. I remembered Nuala and Denny's wedding picture and the various pictures of all of them and their parents from childhood on. But what I was really surprised to see was the addition of a few framed wartime photos from Vietnam, and I was even more surprised to find that I was in several of them.

I tried to remember when and where those pictures had been taken. It hadn't been all that long ago, and yet now it all seemed as if it had been in another lifetime. The war was still raging in Vietnam, but my time to serve had come and gone. I only hoped that it would all end soon, for the sake of those still over there.

Nuala had come back into the room and noticed me looking at the pictures. "Even though he wanted so much to forget that time, there were some memories from it that he cherished." She seemed to be deeply engrossed in some kind of thought. Then she looked up and said, "The call was about the funeral, which is to be held this coming Sunday at the Veteran's Cemetery in West Los Angeles. He's to be buried with full military honors."

She was now on the verge of tears, and I went over to her and took her in my arms. She responded by holding me tight. "I don't know, John. This all has taken me by surprise. On that morning, that very morning, he seemed so cheerful and optimistic. He'd gotten up early and made us some breakfast, and he said he was going to see his friend Stuckey about a job at some construction site." She sobbed, and the tears began to freely flow.

"He was working construction, you know. It seemed as if everything was taking a turn for the better for him, and I was so glad, hoping that finally he'd found himself and managed to put the past behind. But then, when I got home…" Her voice trailed off, and I knew that she could say no more.

I could only imagine what it would have been like, her returning home to find that her only brother had taken his life in that horrible way. I struggled to find words to express my feelings because my heart went out to her, but I could find none that would not seem either trite or inappropriate. But I felt that I had to at least say something.

"He's at peace now, Nuala." I was trying to be reassuring but felt totally inadequate. "Finally, he's found the peace that he so wanted and needed."

"Yes, I know, I know," she said through her tears. "I realize that the real Liam died a long time ago. He died over there. He left himself over there, and the man who came home was no longer him. Still, he was my baby brother, and I loved him, and I will miss him. I will miss him terribly." I sensed the grief and ache of loneliness that she must be feeling as I held her tight and tried to comfort her.

She wiped the tears from her eyes. "Thank you so much for coming, John."

"Nuala…" I began, but I could not finish the sentence because as we looked into each other's eyes, we both simultaneously gave in to the feeling that overcame us, and our lips met in a long, deep, and soulful kiss, a kiss born of the urgent need to release feelings that had been hidden and long repressed.

I could taste the salt of her tears and feel the warmth of her breath. It was a kiss that seemed to last an eternity, and when our lips finally parted and I found that I could speak again, I confessed, "I've always wanted to do that, Nuala."

"I have always known," she said softly, "and I'm so grateful to you that you didn't do it at that time back then when I was still mourning for Denny and was still so very vulnerable." She lowered her head and continued, "I wasn't ready at that time, and you seemed to know it."

"It was hard for me to restrain myself," I admitted, "but yes, I knew it."

She smiled for the first time since I had been there and said, "You're a good man, John, and as Flannery O'Connor once wrote, a good man is hard to find."

"I read the story, and I only wish that I were a good man. And I'm not all that difficult to find."

Nuala laughed a high, joyful laugh like a little girl. "You are a good man, John, and don't worry. Denny Boyle was and still is the only man I will ever truly love. But sometimes I do get lonely, and a woman still has her needs, doesn't she, even though mine have gone unfilled for many years now."

She broke away from our embrace and walked over to where a bottle of twelve-year-old Glenlivet Scotch awaited on the sideboard. "So how about that drink now? Is Scotch okay? I hope it is because that's all I have."

"Scotch is fine," I answered, and she pulled the cork and poured us two stiff glasses.

"You take it neatly, as I recall."

"You recall correctly." I took the glass that she offered and downed a healthy swallow of the smooth brown liquid fire, which both warmed and relaxed at the same time.

She did the same, then, averting her eyes from mine. "I've put on some weight, you know. I'm ashamed for you to see me naked now."

"There's nothing to be ashamed of," I said as I took her in my arms and kissed her once again, this time longer and harder, just like I felt like I was getting down below.

We were both breathless when the kiss ended. She smiled and said, "Is that a gun in your pocket, or are you just…?"

"I'm just glad to see you," I admitted, both finishing her sentence and answering her question.

"You sure don't waste any time, do you?"

"I've been waiting for this for a long time."

"I have too, John. I've been waiting for a very long time."

I knew that Nuala rarely drank, and even when she did, she didn't drink much. Unlike her brother, she didn't have the taste for alcohol. I could tell that she was definitely feeling the effects of the Scotch and that it had already begun to lower her inhibitions.

We kissed again—another long, drawn-out kiss—and then I think that we both realized that the time had finally come.

"Come, John," she said breathlessly, taking me by the hand and leading me.

We went into the bedroom and undressed. When I turned to face her, she looked up at me and said, "My, but you do seem glad to see me, don't you?"

She had removed everything but her white cotton underwear, and the sight of her large, naked breasts for the first time stirred a powerfully erotic feeling in me. Her breasts had always remained hidden beneath a dress, blouse, or sweater before, and seeing them for the first time like this was akin to finally getting a taste of the forbidden fruit.

She noticed me looking at them and smiled shyly, then lowered her eyes. "I told you I've put on weight," she said.

"Oh, no, it's not that at all," I blurted out somewhat nervously. "It's just that I've always dreamed of seeing you like this."

Her eyes looked into mine and then down there again as she came over and squatted in front of me and took my cock in both her hands. "You're so much larger than I thought you were," she said before taking me without any hesitation into her mouth, which only ended up making me even larger, and even though she was not an expert in doing what she was doing, she did so with curious and sincere enthusiasm and, as I could tell from all of the pleasure that I was receiving, a good deal of enjoyment as well.

Eventually she took me out of her mouth, surveying what she had accomplished, and said, "Oh, my—look at that!" as she examined me curiously for a brief moment, then put me back into her mouth again and continued what she had been doing before, only this time using both of her hands as well as her mouth. She was learning quickly.

Finally, she stopped, got up, and kissed me on the lips. "I'm ready for you now, John," she said, and we moved over to the bed, where she pulled back the covers, then slipped off her underwear. She had a sexy bit of a belly, and the indentations from the elastic from her panties showed on it, but all this only served to turn me on even more. She was right when she said she was ready because I could feel with my gently exploring fingers that she was wet down there and wanting it.

She laid down on her back, and I took my place on top of her. I still couldn't believe this was happening. I felt her hands gently caressing my back, and I reached down and rubbed my cock along her moist slit, then slowly inserted myself. Then her hands gripped me, and she gasped, "It's been so long, for me."

In spite of her height and size, she was very tight and narrow, but because she was so wet, I could go in easily, and after a few long, slow strokes, she could take me up to the hilt. I could not believe that I was engulfed as I was inside of her, this wonderful woman who for so long had seemed so unattainable.

Some women moan either softly, loudly, or talk dirty talk or shout out their pleasure with screams or obscenities during sex. Nuala was not one of those. She is one of the quiet ones. But just because she internalized her experience didn't mean that she enjoyed it less.

I could tell by the rhythm and intensity of her breathing and the way her hands gripped the sheets that I was giving her pleasure, and I wanted to give her pleasure because she was certainly giving me immense pleasure.

I plunged deep inside her, trying to reach into the very core of her being, and she gasped and responded by meeting my thrusts with thrusts of her own. She had finally managed to unleash those long-suppressed desires, and I was totally enmeshed in the softness of her moist, burning heat. It was the kind of sexual experience that, up until now, I had only dreamed of, and I wanted it to last forever.

Nuala reached her climax quickly, and only then did she give out with a long breathy moan, indicating that she had come. When she finally opened them, I looked into those beautiful eyes of hers, and I kissed her, searching her mouth with my tongue, and she reciprocated with the thrusting of her own tongue. I could sense her still-growing need from the movements of her body and the feel of her flesh on mine. I could feel the passion stirring within her, the fires still unquenched after years of abstinence and self-denial.

My hands squeezed her large breasts, and my fingers rubbed and teased the hard nipples and large dark aureoles, forcing from her an uncontrolled sigh of wanton pleasure. I had not withdrawn from her, and I slowly began moving in and out again, gradually feeling her arousal growing stronger and stronger with each deep thrust and her desperate need engulfing me in the sheer heaven of its warmth as I continued working her step by step up to another shuddering, long-drawn-out climax before finally I could no longer control my own.

Afterward, as we both lay side by side exhausted on her bed, she put her hand on my chest and said, "Thank you, John."

Chapter Ten

By the time I got home, it was shortly after midnight. There was a strong winter breeze blowing in from the Pacific, and I could hardly wait to take shelter in the comforting warmth of my little house. I had not left the porch light on, and it was too dark to see enough to unlock the front door.

I had lit my cigarette lighter for illumination and was just beginning to insert the house key into the lock, when I noticed the tiny scratches and scrapes on the lock and a grave premonition came over me that something just was not right. Someone had obviously picked the lock to get into my house and made a very sloppy job of it.

I hesitated for a moment, wondering if anyone was inside waiting for me. Again, I felt foolish for not having thought to carry a gun. I carefully slipped my key in the lock, trying to be as quiet as possible as I unlocked the door.

I heard the click before flinging the door open, but instead of entering, I obeyed a sudden defensive instinct and quickly stepped backward and to the side, an action that probably saved my life as the concussion of a loud, explosive blast blew through the door, showering fire and shattered debris with an impact that propelled me backwards with such force that before I even realized it, I had landed on my side on the sidewalk, a good ten feet away.

I felt as if I had been shoved into a trash compactor, and been compacted and my ears were ringing, and it seemed as if I had gone deaf because I could hear nothing. All kinds of strange thoughts seemed to be running through my head, but I couldn't seem to concentrate on any of them long enough to know what I was thinking. I touched the right side of my head and felt the stickiness of blood, but I could feel no pain. I guess at that point, I must have been in shock.

The lights in the neighboring houses came on, and people clad in their nightclothes began appearing in front of them. When they saw the flames shooting out of my front door and me lying there, they rushed over to me, and only then did I smell the burning and saw that my coat was on fire, as they were carefully putting out the smoldering flames with their own bare hands.

And their mouths seemed to be asking what happened, but I only stared dumbly because I could not hear their voices. A surge of panic gripped me, and I shook my head and felt a popping in my eardrums. Then, almost miraculously, I realized that I must not be totally deaf because all of a sudden I heard the sound of sirens wailing in the distance but coming closer and closer.

Suddenly I had the strange feeling that I was being engulfed in the glow of a harsh light so bright that I was forced to close my eyes, but the brightness was still there, and a cold chill feeling came over me, and I wondered if I was dying or even possibly already dead. The last thing I heard was the murmuring of some unintelligible, echoing voices. And then I passed out.

When I came to, I tried to see through the haze that seemed to be trying to obscure my vision and first saw painfully bright lights and big shadows, and then I thought I could vaguely make out the figure of George Lee standing over me, but he was still sort of blurry, so I blinked my eyes a couple of times, and he finally came more or less into focus, first looking somewhat troubled, then looking suddenly relieved.

"Hey, Johnny," he greeted me, "welcome back to the world of the living."

I tried to say something, but I couldn't. What I wanted to say was, "What the hell happened?" My ears were still ringing, and I felt a sharp pain in my shoulder, and the right side of my head hurt. I reached up to feel a small bandage taped to it. The right side of my face felt like it had been badly sunburned.

Then I became aware of the strong antiseptic smell of Lysolled tiles, so I looked around and suddenly realized that I was lying on a very uncomfortable thing that tried to pass for some kind of a bed in what appeared to be a hospital emergency room.

"Where am I?" I finally managed to blurt out, but my mouth felt full of cotton and my vision was still a little hazy.

"Good, you can talk." And then George answered.

"Just barely," I struggled to say.

"Well, you're at St. John's in Santa Monica. So what happened, John?"

"That's exactly what I was going to ask you."

"What do you remember?"

I tried to think, to remember what had happened, but my head seemed to be full of cobwebs. I began wondering if I had amnesia or something like it—some kind of loss of memory. I closed my eyes and tried even harder. Think, I told myself, straining my concentration to the very limit.

It seemed that no matter how hard I tried, I just couldn't remember. I was starting to feel even weaker, and my head was throbbing with pain. I was on the verge of giving up when something seemed to suddenly click, and things slowly started coming back to me. Images—dark, fuzzy images—but images nonetheless.

"I'm beginning to remember something," I said hopefully.

First, I saw myself driving in the night and pulling up in front of my house. I hadn't turned the porch light on before I left, so it was very dark. I got out of the car and felt the chill blast of the cold winter wind. I walked up to the door and reached into my pocket for my cigarette lighter so I could illuminate the lock, so I could put the key in it.

"I got home and opened the door, and then—a bomb?"

"That's what it looks like," George confirmed. "Your front door is history, and your living room is a total mess."

"Great," I muttered sarcastically. I remembered the explosion now, my front door being blasted to bits, and the sudden shock of feeling like I was hit by a sledgehammer before momentarily flying through the air.

It had sort of been like some kind of bizarre out-of-body experience, the kind that people said they had when they momentarily hovered on the brink of death.

Reality intruded once again with the sound of George's voice. "Hey, look at it this way. You're lucky to still be alive."

"Yeah," and I thought that was one way to look at it all right, but I sure didn't feel anything close to lucky, even though I did realize that I was indeed lucky to be alive.

"I woulda really missed you, you know. If you had kicked the bucket," George said.

"I didn't know you cared, George."

George reached into his pocket and pulled out his pack of Viceroys. He had already taken one out and put it between his lips by the time I got around to saying, "I don't think you can smoke in here," even though the thing that I really wanted the most right now was to light up a cigarette myself.

"Oh yeah, I guess you're right." He seemed somewhat distracted as he put the cigarette back in the pack, as if he was contemplating something either very important or very profound.

"What's on your mind?" I asked.

"I was just trying to put a couple things together in my head," he said.

"Did they come together?"

He shook his head and said, "No."

His next question to me was more like a statement of obvious fact, and he said it in a very serious and not a casually joking manner. "You get the feeling that somebody doesn't like you?"

"I'm definitely getting that feeling," and I was also getting an even worse headache, and I didn't really know how much longer I would feel like talking.

"Any idea who it might be?"

Unfortunately, I didn't have a clue. "I wish I knew."

"This is getting serious, John," and all of a sudden he was very serious, perhaps even somewhat concerned. "Maybe you should think of backing off."

"And let you have all the fun, fat chance of that."

"Well, don't say I didn't warn you. You're getting awfully close to that meat grinder, you know."

He stepped aside when the doctor came by to briefly examine me. Then the doctor told me that he had put a couple of stitches in the side of my head, but despite the fact that I had some minor burns and was pretty bruised and battered and dinged up a little from the flying debris, I would probably live.

He wanted me to stay in the hospital overnight so they could observe me in case there was anything that they might have missed. With head injuries, he told me, sometimes something unexpected showed up later. Better to be safe than sorry.

Of course he wasn't paying the hospital bill, I thought, but I didn't say anything. With that settled, he gave me a shot for the pain, which he said would relax me and probably eventually put me to sleep.

The doctor left, and George moved back into position beside my bed to inform me, "We're treating your house as a crime scene, and we have the bomb squad going over it to see what kind of evidence they can find."

"Think they can figure out who did it?"

"You never can tell. They just might find something that points the way. There was a small fire from the blast in your living room, but a couple of your neighbors managed to put it out before the fire department arrived. We'll seal the hole that used to be the front door with crime scene tape, but you better see about getting a new one as soon as you can."

I said "Thanks," even though the knowledge that a hole had been blasted in the front of my house, which pretty much now made it open to the world, was sort of disconcerting. Fortunately, I didn't have a whole lot of stuff in it that anybody might want to steal.

The shot that the doctor had given me had begun to make me feel a little better. The pain in my head was starting to go away, and a relaxed, comfortable feeling was beginning to glow throughout my body. I was even beginning to feel a little sociable, so I turned to George and asked, "You manage to come up with anything this afternoon?"

"Actually, yes, I did. We found out that the real estate guy, Alex Eastman, also has another name. His real name, or at least the one on his birth certificate, is Alex Eliott, and under this name, he not only had some priors for possession with the intent to sell but also a hell of a lot of unpaid parking tickets as well."

"That's interesting."

"Yeah, we thought so. Anyway, we hauled his ass into the station and leaned on him a little bit." The expression on George's face indicated that this move had probably proved to be successful.

A sudden inspirational thought occurred to me. "Tell me he was a Green Beret who was stationed in Vietnam."

"Nah, no such luck; he was 4F. Never even went over there."

"Shit," I muttered, trying hard to hide my disappointment.

"In fact, the guy turned out to be such a wuss that he fell apart in no time and began spilling his guts like a hog in the slaughterhouse. He admitted that Sheila had been supplying him with coke but had stopped a couple of months ago. He also confessed to having gone through her place looking for drugs, but he swears that he didn't find any."

"You believe him?"

George considered this for a moment. "About as much as I believe anybody."

"She must have stopped supplying him around the time she got clean."

George thought about that one, too. "That probably makes sense. That is, if this girl Suzy is really on the up and up about whatever she's been telling you." He took a stick of gum out of his pocket and unwrapped it, then plopped it in his mouth and began chewing noisily.

Almost as an afterthought, he reached back into his pocket, pulled out the pack of Spearmint, and offered me one, but I graciously declined. I didn't know if my jaw still worked, and I didn't feel like I was quite ready to find out.

He shrugged his shoulders, chewed on his gum for a moment, then looked up at me. "Anyway, chew on this, pal. Somebody thinks you're enough of a threat to want to kill you."

"Not a very comforting thought," and it wasn't, so I decided to change the subject. "So what else is new and exciting?"

"Billie Rae's autopsy is scheduled for sometime the day after tomorrow. They're real backed up at the coroner's just now. But then again, I guess we already know what killed her."

"Yeah," I agreed, and then another thought entered my mind. "They manage to get any prints off that lighter you found?"

"Aside from Billie Rae's thumbprint they found a partial that belongs to somebody else. It's not much to work with, but they're working on it, so let's just keep our fingers crossed."

"I think that lighter might turn out to be the best lead we have so far."

"You're probably right about that," George said thoughtfully. "I've already turned it in as evidence. Needless to say, the West Hollywood boys weren't exactly thrilled that I looked around their crime scene and found something that they missed."

"But their case is linked directly with yours."

"That's what I told them." He sighed and said, "But then again, I don't really have a case, now, do I, since I've been warned off on investigating Sheila's murder."

"But you can keep looking into Billie Rae's murder while I keep looking into Sheila's."

He thought about that for a moment before saying, "You know, you really don't have to be risking your ass just to be helping me out with this case."

"I thought it was you that was helping me out."

"You're a funny guy, John."

"Yeah, I'm just a barrel of laughs." I tried to smile, but my face hurt too much. I was beginning to feel lethargic and tired. It had really been a rough day.

George must have felt that way too, because he yawned. "Well, I'm gonna go home and see if I can get a couple hours of sleep." He got up and started to leave, then turned around to face me. "Do me a big favor and at least try and stay out of trouble for the rest of the night, will you?"

"I'll try."

George left, and I closed my eyes and almost immediately nodded quietly off to sleep.

Chapter Eleven

Thursday, December 21, 1972

The next morning was somewhat cloudy and overcast when George picked me up in front of the hospital and dropped me off in front of what was left of my house. He would have come in with me for a while, but on the way, a call came over on the car radio that he had to respond to.

"I don't have time to watch your back right now, so turn around once in awhile and keep an eye out for yourself," were the comforting words he left me with.

The first thing I noticed was that there had been quite a bit of damage to the front door area, but it wasn't as bad as I had expected. I made my way through the crime scene tape to find that inside the house was another story altogether.

The first thing that greeted me was the water-logged, burned-out remains of what had once been a great leather-covered sofa. And all that remained of a wooden coffee table was a bunch of charred splinters.

The blast had done considerable damage to the front entryway, and the walls would have to be repainted. The carpet in the living room area was water and flame damaged and would also have to be replaced.

The bar area and kitchen had miraculously escaped destruction, and I was relieved to find that the phone as well as the television set was still in good working order. I played back the messages on my answering machine. There had been a call from Suzy, which I immediately answered.

"Well, you're up bright and early," she greeted me.

"I just got home after spending the night in the hospital," I told her. She seemed unusually alarmed about this, so I told her what had happened.

There was a long silence after I had finished. When she spoke again, I could hear the concern in her voice. "I'm worried about you, Johnny. I believe you to be in great danger, perhaps even more so than you realize." When she phrased things this way, it reminded me that English was not her first language. There was a long pause, and her silence told me that she was seriously considering something.

"I've got a feeling that you know more than you're telling me, Suzy."

"I wish that I could tell you what I suspect, but I can't."

"Somebody's out to kill me, and whoever it was came very close to succeeding. I've got to know what's going on."

Finally, she said, "You're just going to have to trust me, Johnny, and I'm going to ask that you do me a favor. There is a man that I want you to see. His name is Frankie Funai, and you will find him at the Sun Kwong Restaurant on North Spring Street in Old Chinatown. He's there every afternoon between twelve and one, but please go see him today."

"Tell me, why should I go see this person?"

"I believe he has answers to some questions you might have. Promise me that you'll go see him."

"All right, I'll go see him."

"Thank you. It's really all that I can do for you right now." She hesitated a moment, as if she wanted to say something else. Then she added, "And Johnny, please be careful."

I would definitely heed her advice, I thought as I hung up the phone. Things were beginning to happen that I had no control over, and this was beginning to scare me. I don't like being scared. I had to get out there and find out what was going on.

At least now I had some kind of idea about what to anticipate. I was somewhat used to the thought of danger lurking around every corner, but I had never expected it to enter my own home. A man's home is supposed to be his castle, but this man's castle had been violently breached.

With this discomforting thought in mind, I called my landlord and told him what had happened. Needless to say, he wasn't all that happy about it, but he said that he'd be over to replace the door and take a look at the rest of the damage.

I told him I'd pay for everything, and he said, "Damn right, you will, and see that this doesn't happen again." I assured him that it wouldn't. He's a good landlord, and I really didn't want to lose the place, which was conveniently located for work and just about right on the beach for relaxation.

Before I left the house this time, I went to the bedroom closet and retrieved my Walther PPK/S from where I had hidden it. I checked to see if the barrel was unobstructed and that it was clean, then loaded it with seven .380 ACP hollow point rounds. It wasn't a particularly powerful handgun because it didn't have a whole lot of stopping power, but it was still capable of wounding or, if necessary, killing.

The main reason I was taking it was because it was small, light, dependable, unobtrusive, and easy to carry. In a situation where I really needed a gun, I would much rather have my Colt Python 357 Magnum with me, but I really didn't feel like walking around carrying a bulky and heavy weapon like that today.

At any rate, the little Walther autoloader would be much better than nothing, I thought as I slipped it into the small leather hideaway holster and clipped it to my belt.

Almost as an afterthought, I reached up to the closet shelf and took down the old, dusty cardboard box that contained the old photographs and memorabilia from my past that I had stored away. I was grateful to my sister for saving this stuff for me, even though I rarely ever looked at it.

I rummaged through the box until I finally found what I was looking for. The wallet-sized graduation photo of Sheila brought back some memories that now were best left forgotten and buried in the past. I put it in my billfold and replaced the box back on the closet shelf.

The area in downtown Los Angeles that is known locally as Old Chinatown stretches east from Sunset Boulevard to College Street, encompassing the area south of Hill Street and north of Alameda Street. When you drive past the multitude of ethnic shops and businesses on North Broadway and North Spring Streets, you almost get the sense that you are actually somewhere in East Asia.

There are large garish signs in Chinese, Vietnamese, Cambodian, and occasionally English. The people you see on the streets are nearly all Asians. Caucasians tend to frequent the more tourist-oriented area known as New Chinatown, which is a few blocks away.

Sun Kwong Restaurant turned out to be one of those little hole-in-the-wall family-type places that was frequented primarily by the local Chinese population. When I entered, I was greeted by the appetizing aroma of steamed, stewed, and stir-fried food that seemed to float out of the open door of the kitchen.

It made me realize that I hadn't even thought of eating since leaving the hospital, and since I hadn't eaten all day, I was now ravenously hungry. The large crowd inside the restaurant indicated that the food was either very cheap or very good, or perhaps a fortunate combination of the two.

It was the height of the lunch hour, and the clatter of dishes mixed with the periodic shouts from the kitchen and loud conversations in sing-song Cantonese at the tables. The menu posted on the wall near the entryway was in Chinese without any attempt at an English translation, and I couldn't help but notice that I was the only Caucasian in the place.

The next thing I noticed was a kid who couldn't have been older than eighteen, sitting on a chair next to the door, who was following me with his eyes. I looked around the place, and my eyes came to rest on the person, who was obviously Frankie Funai.

For some reason, I had expected him to be an older man. This guy appeared to be in his early thirties, which is around my own age, although with Asians it's sometimes really hard to tell. I can usually differentiate the facial characteristics between Chinese, Japanese, and Koreans though. He was Chinese.

Frankie was seated at a small table toward the back near the kitchen, a table that gave him an unobstructed view of both the front and back entrances to the restaurant. It was a position that allowed him to see whoever came into the place, make a hasty exit, and quickly disappear at the first hint of trouble heading his way.

He was quietly sitting there, eating a large bowl of noodles, but his eyes had not left me from the time I had walked in. I made my way past the crowded tables, dodging a harried, fast-moving waiter, until I stood next to him at the table. "Frankie Funai?"

He looked up at my face and studied it carefully. I must have looked like shit because of the bomb blast, and I could tell he was somewhat curious about my battered appearance, but he didn't ask anything, and I didn't tell anything. He didn't offer to shake hands but made a motion for me to sit across from him.

"And you must be Johnny Wadd." He didn't wait for an answer and continued, "I hear that you're a private investigator, Mr. Wadd." He spoke English without the slightest trace of an accent of any kind, which indicated that he had probably been both born and raised here.

"Yes, I'm a private investigator."

"Well, I don't like talking to cops, and I don't like talking to private investigators. I'm only speaking to you this one time as a favor to Suzy Huang, so ask your questions and make them good ones."

He was concise and to the point, so I decided to be concise and to the point. "What do you know about Suzy Huang?"

"She's a very powerful and influential person in the community. But you must know this already. You're wasting my time."

Frankie went on eating his noodles. Like George, he was capable of carrying on a conversation while eating, but unlike George, he thankfully didn't talk while his mouth was full of food.

I decided to clarify my question. "I want to know about her involvement with the triads."

"She has their backing for certain business ventures."

I contemplated this and asked my next question. "Like drugs?"

He smiled before he answered, "If you mean Chinese medicine and medicinal herbs, then yes, I do believe that one of her companies imports these things, the same one that imports foodstuffs and supplies for markets and restaurants."

"No, I mean drugs like heroin and opium."

"Mr. Wadd, the triads on the East Coast may deal in heroin and opium, but on the West Coast they are generally involved in other businesses. Far more profitable businesses with much less risk and competition, I might add."

"Care to elaborate?"

"No, but I'll tell you this with certainty. Suzy Huang would never get involved in dealing with the product that killed her mother."

"But what about the triad organization that Suzy is involved with?"

"That organization is primarily in the import-export and insurance business."

I knew Frankie wasn't going to tell me what they imported and exported, so I didn't even bother to ask. I did know for a fact that the 'insurance business' meant extorting the local Chinese-owned merchants for protection money, and I wasn't at all surprised that Suzy's triad was somehow involved in that racket.

I knew from a previous case that many of the merchants and businessmen willingly paid the triads for protection because, most of the time, the police showed little or no interest in helping them or solving their problems.

The particular case I happened to remember involved a Chinese liquor store owner in South Central Los Angeles who had been robbed three times by the same teen-aged gang banger. The police took down the information each time but were either too busy or too lazy to follow up, so nothing was actually done about it. In disgust, the owner went to his local triad, who signed him up for their insurance policy.

They caught the young gang banger on his fourth robbery attempt and forced him to work in the store until everything he had stolen was repaid. The gang banger apparently liked the job because he decided to go straight and stay on, and from what I understand, he's still working there to this very day.

Frankie looked up for a moment as the waiter approached the table and plopped down a small white teacup and dirty grease-stained menu in front of me. I looked at it and saw that it was written in hand, entirely in Chinese. Since I was unable to read Chinese, I pushed it away. The waiter shrugged and left, and Frankie looked back at me.

"Now I have a question for you, Mr. Wadd."

"Go ahead and ask."

"What do you know about the triads?"

"I know that they're gangsters—sort of like the Mafia."

"In a way, that is true, and in a way, it is not. The Triads are descended from secret societies in China originally formed to fight against government oppression. Over the years, to maintain their power, they began to engage in illegal activities, and this became so profitable for them that they became wealthy and powerful, and in turn, they became the oppressors. Do you know who Chiang Kai-shek is?"

"Of course I do. He's the leader of Free China."

"Free China—now that's an interesting expression. Well, he is the leader of the so-called Republic of China in Taiwan, the China that, as you know, our country recognizes and backs. But did you know that he was put in power with the backing of the Triads and still maintains his hold on power with their support?"

"I didn't know that," I said, but I wasn't at all surprised. If I had learned anything at all from the Vietnam War, it was that our country had a penchant for supporting and backing perhaps the worst, most corrupt dictators the world has ever known.

In Vietnam, we were supposed to have been fighting that war to save the people there from the Communists, but it didn't take long to realize that most of the people preferred the Communists to the repressive and corrupt regime that we had forced on them under the guise of democracy and kept in place with our military power.

Still, it was all in the best interests of our country, and whoever suffered didn't seem to matter much in the scheme of things as long as our political and economic status quo was assured. And so it all still continued.

Frankie had finished his lunch and had lit a cigarette. He smoked unfiltered Lucky Strikes, and he apparently smoked a lot of them because the thumb and index finger of his right hand were stained yellow by the nicotine. His fingers were impatiently tapping on the table, and he looked as if he wanted to get the hell out of the place. "Any more questions, Mr. Wadd?"

"Did you know Sheila Ross?"

He was quiet for a moment. He picked up my teacup and wiped it out with a clean paper napkin before filling it with tea. Then he surprised me by answering, "Yes, I met her once." He thought carefully about what he was going to say next, and then he said it. "If you must know, I supplied her with a small quantity of opium at her request."

His frank admission also surprised me. I took a sip of tea and decided to go for broke. "Did you also supply her with heroin and cocaine?"

"No, I did not."

I can usually tell when someone is lying, and Frankie didn't seem to be lying about this. Still, I could not help but say, "And why should I believe you?"

"Two reasons," he replied without hesitation. "First, because I have no reason to lie to you, and anyway, I do not tell lies, and second, because I promised Suzy to answer whatever questions you asked truthfully."

Then he looked up at me and said, "Look, I know that this Sheila Ross was your friend, and you are investigating her murder, so I'll tell you this, and I'll only tell you once."

He snuffed out his cigarette in his teacup, looked me directly in the eyes, and continued, "If you really want to find out who killed her, you have to look not in Chinatown but closer to home." He stood up and retrieved his coat from the back of his chair. "And now, Mr. Wadd, it's been nice and all that, but I believe that our pleasant conversation is finally over."

"Please, just one more question."

Frankie heaved a heavy sigh and sat back down. "Ok, ask."

"What do you recommend that's good to eat in this place?"

"Have the House Special Wonton Noodles. It's what I have every day for lunch." He got up to leave. "And Mr. Wadd…"

"Call me Johnny."

"Johnny, I was just going to say—if you ever happen to see me again, I would appreciate it if you would just please pretend that you didn't."

I watched him leave, and as he approached the door, the young guy who had been sitting by the entryway watching me quickly got up and opened the door for him, then followed him out.

After lunch, I realized that I wasn't in any particular hurry to get home. In all honesty, I just wasn't anxious to run into my landlord and have to answer any questions he might have about the events leading up to the current state of his property, so since I happened to be in the area, I decided to set about on a leisurely stroll through Chinatown.

The overcast sky still hinted at the possibility of rain as I walked the few blocks over to New Chinatown, a development that was the realization of a dream by the Chinese-American community leader Peter Soo Hoo. With the help and support of the local merchants and residents, he had managed to transform the area into a stylized version of the old streets of Shanghai, which ultimately made New Chinatown one of Los Angeles' major tourist attractions.

I continued my stroll through the spacious Central Plaza, which was designed back in the 1930s by now long-forgotten Hollywood art directors and set designers, and noticed that not much seemed to have changed from the time I'd been there last, which must have been at least a good couple of years ago.

I also remembered that Sheila and I had come here a couple of times during our first year of college to explore the shops and then eat dinner at General Lee's Man Jen Low Restaurant.

As I walked on, I wasn't surprised to find that the same old shops still displayed their tourist-oriented wares, and the large, fancy restaurants still promised the same old familiar Cantonese food for the faithful as well as much more exotic and elaborate fare for the palates of the more adventurous.

The old buildings housing the multitude of curio shops and restaurants still displayed the interesting fusion of Chinese and Western architecture that made the place unique. Some of the old stores and markets had been there for years, but I knew for a fact that many had changed hands since the beginning of the current decade after the influx of the new ethnic Chinese, Vietnamese, and displaced Cambodian and Laotian immigrants had begun arriving at our shores in growing numbers from Southeast Asia.

Like everywhere else in Los Angeles and in the world, things in Chinatown were in a period of transition. Most of the original immigrants who had founded Chinatown were hard-working people from the Toisan district of China.

Many of them had first come to this country to work on the railroad gangs in the previous century, and it was their descendants who had formed the majority of the Chinese-American population in the United States.

It had also been their dialect of the Cantonese language that one had usually heard spoken here. And it was their particular style of Cantonese food that has traditionally been found in most of the Chinese restaurants in Los Angeles as well as most of the Chinese restaurants across the country. But that, too, was rapidly beginning to change.

As a direct result of the Vietnam War, a good many ethnic Chinese from Vietnam and Cambodia had begun immigrating to the United States. Naturally, and as a matter of course, lots of them had ended up right here in Chinatown, where they felt more comfortable being among their own kind.

This new group of emigrants and refugees brought with them their Teochow and Fukinese dialects of speech as well as their own specific styles of regional cuisine. One suddenly became aware that there was much more to Chinese food than those old familiar dishes that we'd originally grown up with.

They arrived at a time when many of the first and second generations of original immigrants were ready to retire, and since most of their children and grandchildren had entered into professional careers and moved to the more affluent areas of the city, they sold their Chinatown businesses to the new immigrants.

It was the continuation of a cycle that had begun in the last century, and now, in this one, had resulted in a new diversity that made life all that much more interesting.

There were some colorful holiday decorations up in a few of the stores on North Hill Street, in spite of the fact that many of the Chinese living in the area didn't celebrate Christmas. Thankfully, there were no loudspeakers blaring out those obnoxious Christmas songs that supposedly put you in the buying mood for the holiday season. I went into one of the larger grocery stores and soon found what I was looking for.

The last time I had been in that particular market, I'd seen several different beautifully hand-painted porcelain tea sets from China, consisting of the traditional teapot along with six traditional cups that came in the traditional, luxuriously padded wicker storage and carrying case. I had thought at the time that they would make a nice gift.

I had decided to get one of those fancy tea sets as a Christmas present for Wilma, even though it cost a little more than I really wanted to spend. Fortunately, I managed to talk the pretty young salesgirl into gift-wrapping it for me with some appropriate paper that I managed to score from the curio store next door. Fortunately, because one thing I was really terrible at was wrapping presents, which was probably why I seldom gave any. It was the first time I'd done any Christmas shopping in years.

Before I left the market, I stopped at the deli section, where they sold a variety of barbecued, roasted, and cooked delicacies, and picked up one of those whole roasted ducks that I'd seen hanging there to give to George.

Chapter Twelve

The rush hour traffic had just begun, and it took me a good forty-five minutes to get to where I was headed, even though I had wisely chosen to take the streets after realizing that the Santa Monica Freeway would be more like a parking lot than an express roadway. It was a negligible choice because traffic, even on the surface streets, was terrible.

When I finally managed to make it to the Westside, I stopped at Wilma's and dropped off her present. She was both surprised and grateful that somebody had thought to remember her, and just seeing that happy look in her eyes made me feel good. Sometimes it takes so very little to bring a bit of joy to the lonely and forgotten.

Then I headed on over to the Santa Monica Police Station to see if George was still there in his office. He was. I found him seated at his desk, trying to look busy with some paperwork. He looked up when I walked in, and I presented him with the somewhat greasy parcel containing the roasted duck.

"Merry Christmas," I told him.

"What in the hell is this?" he asked, then curiosity overcame him, and as he sniffed the package, a sort of smile came across his face. He carefully unwrapped the waxed brown butcher paper, and his face positively beamed when he saw what it was that I had brought him. I guess I had made him happy too. Score two for me and all in one day, no less.

"John," he said. "You remembered how much I love these things!"

"How could I forget?" We had spent many happy days of our youth exploring not only just about all the Chinese restaurants in the area, which, being of Chinese descent, George was familiar with, but experiencing the wide variety of other ethnic cuisines that the cosmopolitan city of Los Angeles had to offer as well. It was one of the very few interests that we shared in common.

The cop in him kicked in. "So you were in Chinatown," he deduced. "You must've had lunch with Suzy Huang," he smiled.

"No, as a matter of fact, I had lunch with a guy named Frankie Funai."

George's expression suddenly soured. "If I were you I'd stay away from that guy. He's bad news with a capital B."

"You know him?"

"Hell, I know all about him. So does just about every other cop in LA. If there's anything illegal going on in Chinatown or Little Tokyo you can bet your sweet ass that he has his slimy little hand in it." He shook his head in barely contained annoyance before continuing.

"The frustrating thing is that we've never been able to pin anything on him. He's got a record a mile long, a lot of arrests, but not a single conviction. The guy is as slippery as an eel in a Chinese rice paddy. But believe me, eventually he'll slip up. And when he does, we'll be right there to take him down."

This was all very interesting. I wondered what Suzy's relationship with Frankie actually was. There was also something else very interesting that had been nagging at me, so I brought it up. "This guy is obviously Chinese, but he has a Japanese name. What's the story on that?"

"It's a long story."

"I got the time."

George looked at his watch as if he didn't before finally deciding to settle back in his chair to tell the story. "When your friend Frankie was just a baby, he was abandoned in the doorway of a small grocery store on First Street in Little Tokyo."

"A Chinese baby was abandoned in Little Tokyo?"

"It was a highly unusual thing in itself—a Chinese woman leaving her baby in Japantown. Just wasn't something that was done back then because, as you well know, there's no love lost between the Chinese and Japanese, and especially so when you take into consideration what was happening in China at the time."

"The Japanese had invaded China and were committing all kinds of atrocities against the Chinese people," I said, recalling my knowledge of history.

"You going to keep fucking interrupting, or are you going to let me tell the story?"

"Sorry."

Having properly admonished me, George continued. "So the old Japanese couple that owned the store was named Funai, and they had no children of their own, so they took him in and raised him. Sort of unofficially adopted him, if you know what I mean."

I nodded that I did, and he continued. "Well, a few years pass, Pearl Harbor is bombed, World War II rolls around, and all of the Japanese here on the coast have to be sent inland to those concentration camps, or whatever the hell it was that they called them."

"They were called relocation camps."

"Yeah, that's what they were called; relocation camps, internment camps—same fucking thing. But Frankie wasn't allowed to go with them because the Funais, you see, never legally adopted him, and he was Chinese anyway, and the Chinese weren't considered to be any kind of threat to the nation."

"Of course, because they were our allies at the time," I reflected, before I realized that I was interrupting George again. But then there was something I had always wondered about, so I took the opportunity to ask him. "Tell me, during World War II, did you have to wear one of those buttons that said 'I am Chinese'?"

"I was just a baby, shithead; how would I remember?"

I guess that question answered my question, so I asked another. "So they broke up the family?"

"Yeah," he went on. "At that time, Frankie was about five years old; he was only a small child, so they sent him to an orphanage—that old place that used to be on Adams Boulevard, I think it was. Well, anyway, the kid didn't like it there, though, and after a year or so, he ran away and grew up on the streets of Chinatown instead." He paused at this point of the narrative and lit up one of his Viceroys.

Then he continued. "He was just a kid, and there he was living from hand to mouth in alleys like some kind of homeless person. The story has it that some of the shopkeepers and restaurant people there took pity on him, and they clothed and fed him, so the kid managed to survive. He swept out the shops, took out the trash, did odd jobs, you know, stuff like that in return."

I nodded that I understood what George was saying. "Eventually he was running bets for the bookies and gamblers. You know how much those Chinese like to gamble. When he became a teenager, one of the local gangsters took him under his wing, and the rest is history."

"That's an interesting story."

"It is if you like melodrama."

By the time I got home, the landlord was gone, and I had a new door. It was a good, strong, solid, unfinished wood door. He'd left the keys for me in my mailbox, which was very thoughtful of him, along with a bill for the door and an estimate on what it was going to cost to do the repairs on the inside of the house.

I looked at the estimate and groaned inwardly as I realized that it was going to eat up a healthy chunk of my savings. I realized that I was going to have to come up with a paying case very soon in order to keep on living in the style to which I had become accustomed.

Not in the mood for any more major surprises, I examined the new door very carefully before inserting the new key and cautiously opening it. This time, I was not greeted by an explosion. I noticed that there was a strong smell of fresh paint about the place as I walked in. I was also taken aback by the barren look of the place.

Apparently my landlord had hauled off the damaged furniture because the living room was totally empty except for the things that had been hanging on the wall and a small pile of my personal stuff that he'd thoughtfully placed on the bar.

Whatever had been left undamaged stood stacked up against the wall in the small dining area next to the kitchen. The carpet had been pulled up from the living room floor, exposing the bare, unfinished wooden flooring, and two of the walls had been newly painted a clean-looking white.

The other two still showed signs of the explosion and fire, but the cans of paint and other painting materials were still there where the painters had left them, and I supposed that the job would probably be finished tomorrow. I could tell that the place was going to look like new in no time.

There were four calls waiting for me on the answering machine. Two were from Hal, but it was too late to call him back at his office, and I didn't have his home number, so I left getting back to him for tomorrow. The other two were from people I didn't know who were trying to sell me things.

One of them wanted to sell me magazine subscriptions, which

I didn't need or want. The other wanted to sell me life insurance. Great timing for that, I thought, and for a brief moment, I actually thought about calling that guy back. But I didn't, and I erased all the messages instead.

The kitchen was pretty much the same as it had been before the bomb blast, and I looked around for something to eat before realizing that I was really more tired than hungry, so I looked around for something to drink instead.

To my utter dismay, I found that I was all out of the hard stuff, and the only thing I managed to come up with was half a bottle of red wine in the refrigerator. I couldn't remember how long it had been since I'd opened it, but it still smelled and tasted okay, so I polished it off while contemplating what I had to do next. The thing is, at this point, I really didn't know what it was that I had to do next.

Aside from the brief history lesson, the meeting with Frankie hadn't been all that productive. Again, I wondered what his connection with Suzy Huang was and if I could trust what he had said about her. I really couldn't figure this guy Frankie out. He was obviously some sort of shady underworld character, but the question that bothered me was—is he a killer?

He had freely admitted that he'd sold Sheila some opium. I wondered if he was the Asian guy that Billie Rae had seen with Sheila, the one she thought had brought her the heroin. What did he mean by telling me that to find Sheila's killer, I'd have to look not in Chinatown but closer to home? It was another meeting that had ended up producing more questions than answers. And still at the center of everything, of course, was Suzy Huang.

At that point in my reverie, the phone rang. It was Suzy. "I was just thinking about you," I admitted.

"And I was thinking about you," she said. And then she got right to the point. "How did the meeting with Frankie go?"

"He's an interesting guy. But I still have more questions than I have answers for."

"I know. Just be patient. Everything will eventually fall into place."

"I'm beginning to wonder about that."

She was quiet for a moment, and I thought we had been disconnected. And then she said, "Believe me, Johnny. I'm not lying to you."

Well, for the time being, I thought, I'm just going to have to believe her. "When am I going to see you again?" I asked hopefully.

There was another short silence, and then she said, "I've got a big business deal to wrap up, and then I'll have some time."

I didn't know whether she was stalling or not, and all I could think of saying was, "Business deal, huh?" and after saying it, I hoped that it didn't sound as if I were too disappointed or suspicious.

"Yes, Johnny. It's a very important one that I've been working on for a long time now." She hesitated, as if she were thinking of what to say next. "Give me a couple of days to settle everything, and after that, perhaps you'd like to come over for dinner?"

"I'd love to," I replied, and my outlook suddenly brightened at the prospect.

"Until then, take care of yourself, Johnny."

"It's always my first priority."

After she hung up, I wished that I had asked her some questions about Frankie. I also realized how much I missed seeing her. For better or for worse, I was starting to become somewhat emotionally attached to this gorgeous but enigmatic female. In other words, I cared about her more than I wanted to admit.

Which was probably not smart at all, but then again, I had never been very smart when it came to women. Still, my gut instinct told me she was sincere, and I usually trusted my gut instinct, even though it occasionally proved to be wrong. I just hoped that it wasn't wrong this time.

The wine had stimulated my appetite, so I overcame the feeling of inertia that had been gripping me and opened the can of imported Italian tuna in olive oil that had been sitting in the cupboard for at least the past two years. I searched through the cupboard again but could find nothing else that appealed to me.

I looked in the fridge and found a small jar of marinated mushrooms, a chunk of Monterey Jack cheese, and half a head of iceberg lettuce that would be somewhat edible after I cut off the rust-colored parts, so I made a sort of antipasto salad, which I devoured along with the two remaining slices of stale bread from which I carefully picked off the largest spots of mold. I made a mental note to do some grocery shopping soon.

Having finished my hastily improvised meal, I was washing the dishes while watching the sun set outside my kitchen window and had just begun contemplating making up a shopping list for the groceries I needed when the doorbell rang. I thought about ignoring it, but it rang again and again, and then it was followed by some loud and overly persistent knocking.

"All right," I shouted, "I'm coming," then I muttered a sincere but very audible curse as I dried my hands with my clean but ragged dishtowel and made my way to the front door, hoping against hope that it wasn't George again. It wasn't. Instead, I stood face-to-face-with two of the most unwelcome guests I could possibly have imagined.

"New door?" Ferret Face, the FBI agent, greeted me as he rubbed two fingers of his right hand along the unfinished wood of the new front door that I had just opened. He looked from the door over to me, and our eyes met.

"Yeah, I haven't had time to paint it yet."

His pie-faced Oriental friend stood beside and slightly behind him. He was dressed in the same navy blue blazer I had seen him in before. The FBI agent had changed from his black suit to a dark blue one, but it still showed off his abundant dandruff. Both were chewing gum and looking at me as if they expected me to say something else. When I didn't, Ferret Face sighed deeply and said, "Well, aren't you going to invite us in?"

"I'm really not in the mood for company this evening."

"Tough," he said as he pushed the door open, almost knocking me over as he sauntered on in, followed by his smiling but dangerous Asian-American sidekick. He looked around the living room and gave out with a low whistle. "Well, what in the hell happened here?"

"I'm redecorating."

"So I see." He nodded his head and looked around some more, as if he were taking in all the details of my domain and what was left of my early Pier 1 furniture and décor. His Oriental buddy looked around too, only not quite as curiously. He simply stood around by the door as if he were blocking it, and if he saw something of interest on the floor nearby, he kicked at it. I remembered from bitter experience how much this guy liked to kick. He was probably some kind of frustrated soccer player.

"Nice place you have here," Ferret Face commented while nodding appreciatively, "close to the beach and all. You probably really enjoy yourself, what with all those scantily clad babes hanging around out there on the sand during the summertime."

He chuckled and went over to the window to check out whatever view it was that he could see before he turned back to me and said, "But I guess you've figured out that this isn't exactly a social call."

"I hope not. I'm very picky about my friends."

"Now that was sort of uncalled for, wasn't it, Conrad?" Conrad nodded in agreement. "Oh, and you know something, it just sort of occurred to me that I don't think we've ever been properly introduced, now, have we?"

He paused for a brief moment, and I had the somewhat uneasy feeling that he was about to rectify that situation. And I wasn't wrong, because before I could even begin to say anything, he continued.

"Well, this here's Special Agent Conrad Yama with the BNDD." Conrad gave me his moon-faced smile, which revealed a gold-capped front tooth, but didn't bother to extend his hand. I wouldn't have shaken it anyway. Ferret Face went on with his patter. "You might say that Conrad and you share something in common."

Needless to say, I couldn't wait to hear what that was. Ferret Face ignored my obvious disinterest and proceeded to ramble on: "You see, when his grandfather came over from Japan, well, the immigration official that was processing him shortened his last name from Yamanaka to Yama, just like your grandfather's was shortened from Wadja to Wadd."

After saying this, he gave off a strange laugh that sounded like he was sort of both coughing and hiccupping at the same time. Conrad just scowled and attempted to look menacing.

Ferret Face eventually recovered from his bizarre fit of laughter. "And by the way," he continued, still in his falsely friendly tone, "I'm Mark Ulrich, FBI."

Now that the formal introductions were out of the way, I was actually somewhat surprised to learn that Ferret Face really had a proper name. He also had a hand, which he extended and which I ignored.

He shrugged his shoulders and retracted his hand. "Still some hard feelings, huh, Mr. Wadd," he said, shaking his head as if he regarded me as an irredeemably sad case. "Or should I call you Johnny?"

"I think I'd prefer if you called me Mr. Wadd."

It was getting late, and I was beginning to grow very impatient with this highly unwarranted intrusion. When I spoke, I realized that the tone of my voice must have made this pretty plain. At any rate, I figured that the time had come to get down to brass tacks.

"Just what is it that you want?" I asked in as civil a manner as I could come up with under the circumstances.

Ferret Face—I much preferred to refer to him as that—cracked his knuckles and managed a hideous grin. "We just thought maybe you needed a little reminder to keep your nose out of our business."

My mind flashed back to a very painful memory from not so very long ago, and I began to feel a dull ache in my ribs. I followed a subconscious urge to cross my arms to protect them. I didn't know what these two had in mind, but I definitely wasn't looking forward to a replay of what happened in Sheila's garage.

"I said that I heard you loud and clear the first time you told me that."

"Ah, that's what you said," he said, "but I don't think you were really paying full attention, Mr. Wadd." He shook his head as if this act added some kind of emphasis. Then he shook his finger at me, which was something that had the tendency to annoy me even more than I was already annoyed. "You've been a bad boy, you know. You just keep right on interfering."

"What do you mean?"

"Didn't you pay a visit to a woman named Suzy Huang?"

"I don't see that it's any of your business if I did."

"Oh, but it is our business, isn't that right, Conrad?" Conrad nodded in agreement with Ferret Face and smiled. Ferret Face smiled back at him and went on. "You see, she's what we call a person of interest in the investigation that we're conducting. In fact, she's what we might call a person of extreme interest, if you catch my drift."

"I'm trying to."

"Well, try a little harder."

"So what exactly is it that you're getting at?"

Ferret Face moved closer to me, as if he had something confidential to confide. I drew back a little in an awkward attempt to evade his horrible halitosis. This only had the effect of making him move even closer, so I gave up and simply resigned myself to my fate. He came in close to my ear and said in an almost whisper, "Well, this woman we're speaking of might just be involved in some things that you don't really want to get involved in."

"Shouldn't I be the judge of that?"

"No, we'll be the judge of that." He made this pronouncement with a finality that indicated that it was carved in stone.

I figured at this point that I'd had all the pleasure of their company that I could take. In an effort to be as courteous and charming as possible, I told them, "Well, if that's all you have to say, don't let the door hit you in the ass on your way out."

"I hope you realize that we're dead serious, Mr. Wadd," he said, and in an effort to underline a significant point after a dramatic pause, he repeated the words "dead serious," and this time with even more emphasis. To that, he added, "And believe me, this is our final warning." He had placed a big emphasis on the word "is" and he also put in another one of his dramatic pauses to allow a little time for those words to sink in.

"Alright, I've been warned."

"Just make sure you keep out of this. It's none of your business, and you're not to see, talk to, or call this woman again. You hear?" When he got overly serious or excited, his Alabama accent seemed to flare up in full force.

The realization finally sank in that George was right on the money when he thought my line was being tapped, and now I suppose I knew more or less for sure that my phone was bugged. Otherwise, how else would they have known that I made a telephone call to Suzy?

So they must be listening in to all of the other calls I made as well. I wondered if it was legal for the government to do that without some kind of court order or something. And what kind of country is it that we are living in if it was, I thought, and suddenly, being just the average citizen that I was, a strong sense of outrage overcame me, accompanied by a helpless feeling of paranoia.

Ferret Face must have somehow sensed how I was feeling because he appeared as if he was very pleased with himself when he moved in on me once again and said, "Have I made myself absolutely clear?"

"I said I heard what you're saying."

"Then I'll take it that you also fully understand my meaning this time." He turned to his little buddy and asked him, "You think he fully understands my meaning, Conrad?"

Conrad shrugged as if he either didn't know or he didn't particularly care and didn't have any opinion on the matter, one way or the other. And then Ferret Face suddenly wheeled around and threw a left-handed punch right in the direction of my breadbasket.

My body tensed, and a look of sheer panic came across my face as I raised my arms in an attempt to ward off the blow, but he pulled the punch just in time, and after tapping me playfully on my belly, gave out with a loud guffaw, followed by his trademark cough and hiccup laugh.

When he finally managed to fully recover his equilibrium, he said, "What are you, Wadd, some kind of pussy or something? Why don't you at least try to fight back?"

"I don't like the odds."

He shook his head as I was some kind of really sad case before turning to his buddy and saying, "I think we can take our leave now, Conrad. I'm sure Mr. Wadd would like to spend some time to contemplate his future."

The more the man said, the more I found that I disliked him. But then again, there was really not a whole lot to like about either of them. I struggled to keep my anger under control as I ushered my two most unwelcome guests out the door.

As they were leaving, Ferret Face turned back to me and said, "Don't forget, Mr. Wadd. You've now been warned more than once." His face contorted into a kind of grimace that seemed to be seriously trying to turn into a smile. "The next time it's most definitely not going to be a warning."

I almost expected him to give off with another one of his strange cough-hiccup laughs, but much to my relief, he didn't, and instead he and his silent partner just turned around and walked on off into the cold, chill darkness of the winter night.

After closing the door, I hastily lit a cigarette and quietly decided that I would have given my left nut for a stiff drink. For one reckless moment, I seriously contemplated heading over to the Marina to the bar at Charlie Brown's Steakhouse to get that drink, but an overpoweringly strong feeling of ennui prevented me, which was probably all for the best.

I could visualize myself sitting at the bar there, drinking way too much and spending way too much money, only to wake up tomorrow morning feeling like death warmed over. I shuddered at the thought.

Instead, I walked over to my bar and carefully examined my

telephone. I unscrewed the caps from the listening and talking ends but found nothing unusual inside. I checked out the answering machine and also found nothing. Then I checked around the whole surrounding area for some kind of miniature microphone or transmitter and still came up empty.

Then it occurred to me that there could possibly be some kind of outside line tap, but I really didn't have the faintest idea about what to check for there.

Even though it was still early, it suddenly occurred to me that I had just been through a long, hard day. I tried to think back on all I had done to have accomplished so little, but my thoughts were becoming a little fuzzy, and I decided that it wasn't worth the effort.

I just felt like I was dead tired, and I suddenly realized that I was still suffering the aftereffects of having barely survived the explosive blast of the night before. No wonder I was feeling so totally fucked up.

With this in mind, I thought that it would be better for me to get some rest so I could recharge my batteries for the ordeal that I knew lay ahead. I was sure that there was going to be a final showdown in the very near future, and this time I really wanted to be ready for whatever was going to come down the pike.

I was tired of being beaten up, stomped on, blown up, and threatened. The next time things got rough, I was determined that I was the one who was going to have the upper hand. So I headed for the bedroom and decided to make an early night of it.

Chapter Thirteen

Friday, December 22, 1972

The next morning I was up bright and early, and as I left my house and walked over to my car, I noticed the surfer who lived in the house directly opposite mine loading his sky blue Greg Noll surfboard onto the top of his battered and weathered late 1950s era wood-sided station wagon, no doubt in preparation for another day to be spent enjoying life out on the shimmering winter waves of the beautiful blue Pacific.

In spite of the fact that it was definitely wet-suit weather, he was dressed only in knee-length Hawaiian-patterned swim trunks and a well-worn, unbuttoned faded red aloha shirt over an even more well-worn and faded blue Primo Beer t-shirt.

He was starting out a little late for the Dawn Patrol, but that group of hardy early morning diehards consisted mostly of the younger surfers who went out way before the crack of dawn, hoping to catch some wave action before they had to put away their boards and head for either school or work. The fact that the weather had been unusually cold lately didn't seem to bother most of the surfers because this type of weather usually results in the bigger and better waves.

Compared to the youngsters of the Dawn Patrol, my neighbor was a slightly older guy—not all that old, but older—meaning, like he was in his middle or late twenties. So I suspected that he would be heading out to surf during what was known as the Gentleman's Hour, which usually started around 9:00 AM, at a time after most of the youngsters had already cleared out and left the beach.

He was one of the neighbors who had been among the first to come to my aid after the explosion the night before last, so I walked on over to thank him.

He had just finished tying down his board, and he looked over at me as I approached him. "Hey, how you feeling, man?" he asked as a manner of greeting.

"I'm still alive," I replied. "Thanks for helping me the other night."

"No problem. I'm sure you'd do the same for me." He scooped up his long, sun-bleached blonde hair with both his hands and, with a quick and experienced movement, fastened it into a ponytail on the back of his head with a thick rubber band.

Then he rubbed the unruly stubble of his sun-bleached blonde beard and looked curiously at my battered and scarred face and asked, "So you're all right, now?"

"Yeah, I'm as all right as can be expected, I suppose."

He hesitated for a moment, then spoke up. "At first we thought it was some kind of a gas leak, you know, that caused the explosion." He scratched his head and continued. "But when we went into your place to put out the fire, we could smell the gasoline, and it looked more like someone had planted some kind of bomb."

"You're right there."

"Wow, you must have really pissed off some heavy dudes, man."

I simply nodded my head and didn't say anything. He looked at me for a moment, then nodded back, and I could tell he was thinking about it, but fortunately he was polite enough to respect my privacy by not questioning me further about the matter. I decided then and there that I really liked this guy, in spite of the fact that I was truly envious of the great tan that his skin sported.

Even though we lived across the street from each other and knew each other by sight, we had never been formally introduced, and it occurred to me that I didn't know his name, and I'm sure that he didn't know mine. Deciding to remedy that situation, I extended my hand and formally introduced myself.

"My name is Johnny Wadd."

He accepted my hand and shook it. "Chuck Carter."

"Glad to meet you, Chuck," I said.

"The feeling's mutual."

It was just a long shot, but I thought I'd ask anyway. "Chuck, do you remember if you happened to see anyone nosing around my place that day?"

He gave my question some serious thought before shaking his head. "No, not really," he said, "but then I wasn't around most of the day. There were some really serious six and seven-foot swells out at Malibu, and I was sort of hanging out over there from early in the morning until really late in the afternoon."

He told me that he would keep his eyes on my place whenever he got the chance and promised to let me know if he saw any suspicious characters loitering about or anything out of the ordinary going on.

After saying goodbye and taking my leave of Chuck Carter, I drove downtown to the Original Pantry on Figueroa, where I sat at the counter and read the Los Angeles Times while enjoying a leisurely breakfast of bacon and eggs washed down by three hot cups of black coffee. I had a little time to kill before Hal opened up his little agency office in West Hollywood, which would be my next stop.

Since my phone at home was probably bugged, tapped, or whatever the Feds had decided to do with it, I had decided to go over to his office and talk to him in person rather than advertise my every move to whoever might be listening and monitoring whatever I was doing or planned to do.

At ten on the dot, I pulled my Porsche up in front of the Santa Monica Boulevard storefront office just as Hal was in the process of unlocking the door. He looked over and noticed me, waved at me, and then opened the door and motioned for me to come on in. By the time I walked through the door, he had already removed his coat and was just seating himself at his desk.

"Early bird gets the worm," he said.

"You got a worm for me?"

"I sure do. One of those names you gave me the other day," he said as he put on his reading glasses, pulled open his desk drawer, and removed a small sheet of yellow notebook paper. He looked up and motioned for me to take a seat. I sat down in the chair across from him. He looked closely at what he had written on the sheet of paper.

"This girl named Kathy Heller," he continued. "It turns out she works crew on a lot of independent films as a production sound mixer."

"I knew you'd come through for me, Hal."

"Don't I always?"

"Yes, I would have to admit that you do." I was particularly grateful that he had followed up on this lead because things were beginning to look pretty sparse on this investigation so far.

"You have any contact information on her?"

"She's not one of my clients, but one of my sources told me that he thought she's currently working on a Bill Margold film that's shooting over in Pasadena. I checked it out and found out that she is, so I talked to Bill, and he said you're welcome to come on the set today around lunch time if you want."

I looked at my watch. "What time would that be?"

"Lunch time on his set usually starts around one o'clock, give or take, which was why I was trying so hard to get hold of you yesterday. I called you twice and left messages. Where in the hell were you, by the way?"

"Don't even ask."

"It's that bad, huh?" He looked closer at me, and a frown came across his face. "It looks like somebody's been using your face for a punching bag."

"Not only my face, but the rest of me too," I informed him. I didn't think it would be wise at this point to tell him about the explosion.

He shook his head and said, "Here's the address of the house where they'll be filming," as he handed me the small sheet of note-book paper. I noticed the name of the street, which was in one of the older neighborhoods of Pasadena. A neighborhood where there were a lot of the old-money mansions and big old houses, usually inhabited by descendents of the old-time California families and the very well-heeled nouveau riche.

"You know where it is?"

"I'll find it."

"I'm sure you will. The phone number written down there will reach the production manager just in case you get lost."

"Thanks, Hal. I owe you one."

"By my count, it's more like you owe me two."

Hal was always good at keeping count when it came to favors owed. "And if I know you, you'll be sure to collect."

"You can just bet your sweet ass I will."

The tattered street map of Los Angeles and Vicinity that I usually used to find places I was totally unfamiliar with in this vast metropolis was literally coming apart at the folds. Unfortunately, one of those folds was in the section of Pasadena that I was looking for, and the tear had completely obliterated the street I was trying to find. I stopped at the nearest gas station and picked up a new map.

The maps were free, but I wished that they were printed on more durable paper. It seemed that all you had to do was unfold and re-fold them just a few times before they began tearing at the folds and falling apart. The new map, fortunately, showed me exactly where I had to go.

The old house in Pasadena that was being used for the soft-core skin flick shoot was up a long, heavily wooded driveway, a discreet distance from the quiet, tree-lined neighborhood street. It wasn't one of the old mansions that the area was famous for, but it was a very large two-story house that probably had at least five bedrooms and a huge den, as well as a big old white tiled kitchen.

This is where the catering service had set up and was serving lunch. There was also a pretty good sized dining room, which was conspicuously devoid of diners because it was currently being used as a set. I wandered around, asking for the production manager, and finally ran into somebody who pointed me in the right direction.

The production manager led me through the house, past the large dining room, which was being used as the set, and out the back door. There was no pool in the back yard, but there was a huge patio, a well-tended, healthy green lawn ringed with rose bushes and beds of other various types of flowers, and a good-sized guest house. The warming sun had begun to filter down from behind the scattered dark clouds that still threatened rain.

Kathy Heller was an attractive girl in her early twenties with short, curly black hair and a boyish figure. She was dressed in a clean and pressed white t-shirt and baggy khaki cargo pants with lots of pockets and was seated on an aluminum equipment box on the patio wearing reflective sunglasses.

She was slowly eating what was left of her catered lunch, which was on a plastic plate that was perched precariously on another aluminum equipment box placed directly in front of her. At the same time, she was reading a hardbound copy of the Anna Kavan novel Julia and the Bazooka. Her expensive Nagra tape recorder was on the metal sound equipment cart, which was securely parked right beside her, as if she didn't want to let it out of her sight.

I walked over to her and said, "Hi there."

She looked up at me, smiled, and said, "Hi there, yourself."

I studied my double reflection in the chrome-colored lenses of her sunglasses and decided I didn't look all that bad, considering all I'd been through in the past few days. I couldn't see her eyes, but I knew that she was studying me.

"How do you like the book?" I asked in an awkward attempt at making conversation.

"It's all right," she replied. Then she took a sip from her can of Pepsi Cola.

"I just finished reading Ice," I lied. Actually, I'd read it something like two years ago, when it first came out. "Great book," I added.

She took off her dark glasses and looked at me a little closer. Without her dark glasses, she looked a little like Jacqueline Bisset. She also had beautiful green eyes to go along with that friendly smile, and something inside me seemed to melt as I felt an immediate and positive physical attraction. I had the almost certain feeling that she also felt somewhat of a similar attraction, and I sincerely hoped that I wasn't wrong.

"Do I know you?" she asked.

"Johnny," I said, extending my hand, trying to exude a sense of bravado and feeling of confidence that somehow, in her presence, I really didn't seem to actually feel.

She took my hand and held it in hers for a moment before saying, "I'm Kathy." A slightly puzzled look came across her face. "Are you talent? I haven't seen you with the crew."

"I'm neither," I admitted. "I'm a private investigator."

"Really?" she said, in a tone that somehow indicated that she didn't quite believe me.

"Really," I answered, in as positive a tone as I could muster. "Approved and licensed by the State of California," I said as I showed her my badge. She looked at it carefully and nodded. I put it back into my pocket.

She positioned a folded piece of notebook paper in the book to save her place and closed it. "So are you like a technical advisor for this film or something?" she asked, expressing some interest.

Puzzled, I replied to her question with a question of my own. "A technical advisor?"

"Yeah, the hero of the thing we're filming is a private detective."

"No, I'm not a technical advisor," I said, now realizing why she had asked that question. "Actually, I came here to see you."

She put her sunglasses back on. "Yeah, sure," she said, and this time I could tell that she really believed I was bullshitting her.

"Honestly," I said with as much honesty as I could muster.

She laughed, showing a nice set of beautifully white and even teeth. "Well, it's the first time I've ever heard that being used as a pickup line."

"I definitely would like to figure out some way to persuade you to go on a date with me. But I really do have a few questions I would like to ask you about a case I'm currently working on."

She appeared genuinely puzzled this time. "What could I possibly know about any case that you may be working on?"

I was about to answer her when the assistant director called out loud enough for all to hear, "We're back! Let's go, people—everyone back on set!" I looked at my watch. It was barely after 1:45. It had been a very short lunch.

Kathy shrugged and stood up. "I have to get back to work," she said as she unlocked the wheels on her sound cart and started pushing it toward the set.

"How about joining me for dinner tonight at Musso and Frank?" I blurted out on the spur of the moment, hoping against hope for a positive response.

She stopped and considered my proposition for what seemed like a long moment. Then she took off her sunglasses again, looked me up and down, and then smiled that meltingly beautiful smile of hers.

"All right," she said.

"Great!" I exclaimed, and I have to admit that I truly meant it.

She pondered something for a brief moment and looked at her watch. It was a large man's military-style chronograph watch with a gold-colored expandable watchband, and it looked out of place on her tiny wrist. "The shoot's been going pretty good so far today, and Bill always works fast, so we should wrap here about five or six. I could meet you there, say at eight?"

"I'll be waiting for you at the bar."

Chapter Fourteen

I had a good six hours to kill before my dinner date with Kathy, so I headed toward home, stopping at the cleaners along the way to drop off the bag of laundry I'd been carrying around in the trunk of my car for the past week.

Then I stopped at a discount furniture store on Pico Boulevard and bought a comfortable off-white sectional sofa and love seat combination, which they said would be delivered on Tuesday morning to replace my old, burned-out one.

I'd probably regret buying white, but it was the only way it came in the style of sofa that appealed to me. While I was at it, I also bought a sturdy wooden coffee table and a couple of matching end tables. I was now all set in the furniture department.

After that, I made a quick stop at Johnny's near the corner of Sepulveda and Washington Place to refuel on a pastrami dip sandwich and a large root beer, and since I seemed to be on a roll with regard to getting some chores done, I made a longer stop at the Food Giant Market and went on a grocery shopping spree to restock my larder and bar.

Since I didn't want to get caught short again, I probably ended up buying much more than I needed, and I realized that I had when I was trying to find a place to fit everything in my little sports car. But then again, I simply figured that my stocking up would end up being a good thing when push came to shove. I was now pretty confident that I was set to weather out the remainder of winter with sufficient food and drink.

When I got home and carted all the stuff I had bought into the house, I found that there was one message waiting on my answering machine, and it was from a woman I had never heard of before named Sophie Steinman. I quickly put away the groceries and the booze and returned the call.

Sophie Steinman sounded older and Jewish, and she said she saw my ad in the yellow pages, and then she asked me if I found people. I told her that I did, and she told me that she had someone she wanted found.

We then arranged to meet at her house in Beverly Hills in about an hour. I was getting excited. A house in Beverly Hills usually spelled big money, and at this stage of the game, I could really use some big money. If this panned out, it would be my first paying case in over two months. Business was finally starting to look up, I thought, with great expectations.

My expectations took a sharp and sudden nose dive when I saw Sophie's house. She lived in Beverly Hills, all right, but at the very edge of it on a quiet middle-class residential street between Olympic and Pico Boulevards. The street was quiet because, so far, the area seemed to have resisted the current trend toward the construction of apartment buildings.

Her house was a small single-story two-bedroom tract house that looked like it had been built sometime back in the early 1940s. The lawn was brown and neglected, and overall, the house had definitely seen better days. I mentally adjusted my rate down to the bottom of the scale.

The plump little woman who answered the door introduced herself as Sophie Steinman before she cheerfully invited me in. She appeared to be in her middle sixties, wore wire-rimmed granny glasses, and was dressed dowdily in a somewhat conservative fashion that seemed to be a little behind the times.

The furnishings in her living room were also a little behind the times—spare and tasteful, but not particularly elegant. However, everything in the house seemed to be well ordered and neatly arranged. In fact, the place was immaculately clean, as if cleanliness was somewhat of an obsession with her.

She invited me to sit on a large, plum-colored velour sofa that may have been fashionable two or three decades ago and politely asked if I wanted some coffee or tea. I declined her offer of refreshments, opting instead to get right down to business. She sat down on the matching love seat opposite me.

"You mentioned on the phone that you wanted me to find someone."

When she spoke, I heard the light inflection of the Yiddish accent that I had heard on the telephone. "Yes, Mr. Wadd, but first I have to know how much you charge for such a service."

I told her that my fee was a hundred dollars a day plus expenses.

She hesitated for a long moment before finally asking, "And how much would they be, these expenses?"

I explained to her that the expenses entailed the cost of gasoline or plane tickets for whatever travel was required or whatever cash outlay for various incidentals that I would have to make in the course of the investigation. She considered this silently for awhile. To break the silence, I assured her that I did not pad the account or bill for any frivolous or unnecessary expenses.

She looked up at me and said, "I can see that you're an honest person, and so I will be honest with you. I'm a widow, and I'm not a wealthy woman by any means, but I have more than enough to get by. I don't need much. My husband passed away last year. He left me a small business, which I sold, and some insurance, and of course we had some savings, so I have more than enough to get along on. We also own an old apartment building in the Mar Vista area of West Los Angeles, from which I collect rents. Of course, nowadays, with such high property taxes and the costs of repair and maintenance and all that, being a landlord is more of a cross to bear than a blessing. But anyway, I wanted you to know that I can afford to hire you. That is, I can afford to do so for a while, at least."

Sophie told me that her husband had been killed in an automobile accident when his car had been struck head-on by the car of a drunk driver. He died instantly. He had been on his way home from his small shop in Culver City, where he sold stamps for collectors.

She herself had always been just a simple housewife, and she freely admitted that she had absolutely no head at all for business. Since they had no children, she had ended up selling his shop along with all of its stock to an old friend of his. This was all very interesting, but I was wondering where she was going with all of this. She still hadn't said anything about who she wanted me to find or what exactly it was that she wanted me to do for her.

At this point, I felt obligated to tell her that I was currently working on a case and would be unable to devote full time to hers, but assured her that I would only bill her for the time spent working on her case—if she wanted me to take the job. She shrugged this off. "What I want you to do for me is not so very urgent. So there's really no big hurry, young man."

Sophie then explained that the other day she was going through her husband's documents and papers to put everything in order for tax time, which would be coming right around the corner, when she came across something that puzzled her.

At this point, she got up and went over to an old oak roll-top desk and opened it. She reached in and took out a postcard-sized photograph, looked at it for a brief moment, and then brought the photograph over and handed it to me.

It was one of those souvenir gag-type photographs in which three people stuck their heads through the holes of a painted wooden set so that they seemed attached to the cartoon bodies, which in this case happened to be the representation of a family on a small, compact ocean liner. The picture appeared to have darkened with age, but the image was still clearly discernible.

It had been taken at the photo shop on the Santa Monica Pier, according to the legend that was printed on it. The first of the smiling heads stuck through the hole was that of a balding middle-aged man. The second smiling head belonged to a pretty young black woman who appeared to be in her early twenties.

They were depicted standing on the deck of the cartoon ship. The third head, which stuck out of one of the port holes below them and looked smilingly up at the other two, was that of a male child of about four or five years of age who bore a distinct resemblance to both the man and the woman.

"That man in the picture is my husband, Solly," Sophie explained. "From the way he looks, I can tell that it's not a very recent picture."

"Who are the other two?"

"I have absolutely no idea," she said, looking steadily at me. "They are the people who I want you to find."

The words '& Coin' on the sign, which read Steinman Stamp & Coin Center, looked like they had been added at a much later date and almost as an afterthought. The tiny one-man shop not far from the San Diego Freeway on Washington Place was wedged between a locksmith's shop on one side and a small used book store on the other in a nondescript building that had seen better days. All three stores looked as if they had probably been partitioned off at one time long ago from a single large one.

Across the street was a Polynesian-themed take-out food place with a window full of colorful signs offering the promise of a wide variety of delicious and inexpensive Hawaiian and Chinese take-out dishes. Both sides of the street comprised a small commercial area that seemed like an island in a neighborhood that was surrounded by a sea of apartment buildings that appeared to have been built in the 1940's and 1950's.

Inside the shop, several shelves housing what appeared to be hundreds of ring binders lined the wall behind a long glass display case containing a bewildering array of collectable stamps and coins that ran the length of the narrow store, ending at a desk where a thin, fragile-looking grey-haired man who had the appearance of an absent-minded professor now in his late sixties sat carefully examining a colorful set of postage stamps mounted in a large old green Morocco leather collector's album. The old man raised his eyes and looked up over his spectacles as I walked up to him.

"Can I help you with something?" he asked in a voice that echoed an accent somewhat similar to that of Sophie.

"Samuel Rubin?"

"That's me."

I introduced myself and explained that I had just come from seeing Sophie Steinman.

"Wonderful woman, that Sophie," he said. "This used to be her husband's shop, but I suppose she already told you that." He studied my face for a moment until he seemed satisfied with what he saw. "So what can I do for you, Mr. Wadd?"

I explained the purpose of my visit and how Sophie had hired me to find the two people who were in the photograph that I handed to him. Samuel Rubin looked at the picture carefully before shaking his head. "I don't have a clue as to who those people are," he said, "but from the look of it, my friend Sol must have had some kind of secret life on the side." He shook his head in amazement. "So secret even I didn't know about it, and believe me, over the years Sol confided in me a lot."

He looked at the picture again before handing it back to me. "The child sure looks like he might be Sol's son, doesn't he?"

"I think that could be very possible," I replied.

"Then it doesn't surprise me that Sophie would want to know where he is. They always wanted children, you know, but Sophie was incapable of conceiving."

This threw an interesting light on Sophie's motives. I had wondered why she wanted so much to locate two people who were complete strangers to her.

Samuel told me that he had known Solomon Steinman for over ten years. He had come to know him first as a customer and later as a friend. Sol, he said, had emigrated here in the mid-1930's, when the Nazis were beginning to come to power in Germany. Sol's father, also named Solomon, was a moderately wealthy publisher and professional philatelist who eventually had been exterminated along with the rest of his family that had remained in Germany at Dachau.

Solomon Senior had sent his only son, who was twenty-six years old at the time, to America along with most of the family jewels, which had been carefully sewn into the lining of his coat, and a large steamer trunk containing a modest fortune in collectable postage stamps.

After arriving here, young Sol had used the money he brought with him to open a stamp shop in downtown Los Angeles. The business had flourished almost from the beginning, since stamp collecting at that time was a very popular pastime. It had been a far simpler time then, long before other things in an ever-changing world began to occupy everyone's spare time.

Sol was a clever and capable businessman, and his shop continued to prosper not only during the war years but on through to the late 1950's, when the interest in sedentary hobbies like collecting postage stamps finally began to wane and such things as television became far more popular as a means of leisure home entertainment. At the same time, the rent for the prime real estate of the downtown shops continued to rise.

Sol then saw the light and relocated his business to the present location at the edge of Culver City, where the rent was much more reasonable and there was also a lot of convenient street parking available for the customers. There were a lot of apartment complexes in the area, as well as a vast new residential area, which would bring him even more customers than he had before.

"So he opened this shop here in 1960?" I asked.

"No, he opened it back in the early days of 1961. It was February 3rd, to be exact," he said with proud certainty.

"I must confess that I'm amazed by such a precise memory."

He shrugged my comment off. "I can remember this very well because it was on my birthday, and I came here to this new stamp shop that had just opened to celebrate it. In fact, I was his first customer," he informed me proudly. "That ten-dollar bill you see on the wall there," he said, pointing to the framed 'first customer' memento taped to the wall behind him, "was mine." He shrugged his shoulders and let out a chuckle. "Of course now it's mine again, so to speak."

"Everything eventually comes full circle, I suppose."

Samuel laughed in agreement and continued. "You see, I lived right down the street, a block away. Still do. Stamps and coins have always been a passion for me. Some people go to work and then spend all their hard-earned money in bars drinking, in restaurants eating expensive meals, or in department stores buying fancy clothes. Me, I spent my money buying stamps and coins. They provided me with entertainment and relaxation. They were my own personal drug of choice."

He took off his glasses, rubbed his tired eyes, and ran his fingers through his thin gray hair. "But now I'm an old man, and I have no wife, no children. And over the years, I have had so much pleasure from my hobby that I wanted to share it with others. That's the reason why, when Sophie said she was selling the business, I told her that I'd buy it."

"So, how is business?" I asked to keep the conversation going. I couldn't help but notice the conspicuous absence of customers in the shop.

"I have to confess that business isn't all that great, but it does pick up from time to time, and I don't have much to do anyway since I retired from Douglas Aircraft a couple of years ago. This gives me a reason to get up every morning, and when you get to be my age, believe me, you really need one. And to be perfectly honest, the rent here is very affordable."

"Still, with business being so slow, you must have had second thoughts."

"No, I don't at all regret taking over this place because not only do I enjoy so much what I'm doing, but now I finally have a chance to dispose of my coin collection, which is actually what is keeping not only the store going but is keeping me in groceries as well. Sol never sold coins so his business gradually went downhill. Now stamps are out and coins are in, so go figure."

"So Sol's business wasn't doing all that well?"

Samuel made a dismissive gesture with his hand. "It didn't matter all that much to him. He had already invested his money when the times were good in real estate. Sol even thought about buying this building, too, but the landlord would never sell. Still, he owned his house, and he owned an apartment building, so he had some income from the rentals. They didn't need much. They lived very simply, he and Sophie."

"How well do you know Sophie?"

"Not all that well to begin with, but well enough to have gone to their house a few times for dinner before Sol passed away. She cooks a mean brisket that Sophie does." He thought for a moment. "Both Sophie's family and mine originally came from Russia, from the Ukraine. Not the same village, of course, so we didn't know each other back then. We were both just small kids when our families came over. Her folks originally settled in Canada, in Alberta, and mine settled here."

"So, how did she end up in Los Angeles?"

"From what I understood, she had an aunt who lived down here. One year Sophie came down to spend the summer with her, and she then met Sol, who had only recently arrived in Los Angeles himself. I guess that must have been back in the middle 1930's."

He paused a moment, calculating something in his head, and finally seemed satisfied with his conclusion. "Anyway, they both fell in love with each other and were married. And not only that, but they stayed happily married for over thirty-some odd years. So there you have it—life and love in Los Angeles."

He picked up a box of Russian Sobranie cigarettes from his desk and offered me one. Those cigarettes, which are three quarters filter and one quarter dark Balkan Yenidje tobacco, are a little too strong for my taste, so I politely declined but lit up one of my own while he proceeded to light up one of his.

He drew the smoke from the pungent, dark tobacco deep into his lungs and expelled it. A look of extreme pleasure came across his face, and he said, as if in explanation, "I know smoking is not good for you, so I allow myself only two of these a day."

"I'm trying to cut down myself," I lied.

He took another long puff, obviously savoring the experience before he continued, "You know, Sophie's basically just a quiet sort of person who keeps pretty much to herself. She's a simple house-frau, if you know what I mean. Doesn't even know how to drive a car, you know. The shop is closed on Sunday, so I take her to the market once a week, now that Sol is gone."

"Do you know if Sol had any other close friends with whom he might have confided?" I asked hopefully.

Samuel thought seriously for a moment before replying. "I can't really say that I do, although he did mention that every morning before he came to the shop, he had breakfast and kibitzed with the other guys that hung out at Shep's Deli over there on Pico."

I had passed by Shep's Deli many times on my travels down Pico Boulevard, so I knew where it was. I could visualize the gathering of old men sitting there in one of those large red vinyl booths, telling each other stories of escapades past and present over endless cups of coffee. I decided that it might indeed be a good idea to pay a visit there to see if any of Leo's old cronies might be able to shed some light on the situation.

Outside, the sky had begun to darken, and I looked at my watch and had decided that it was time to leave when something in the nearby glass showcase caught my attention. I took a couple steps over for a better look.

What I had noticed was an old paper bundle tied with brown twine and sealed with red sealing wax in the middle of the package, where the twine intersected. The bundle had been torn open at the side, and hundreds of colorful little square and rectangular pieces of paper the size of small banknotes had escaped and were surrounding it. I looked closer at the pieces of paper and noticed the fantastic expressionistic artwork and German wording on them.

Most of the designs were truly unique and amazing, as well as extremely colorful and varied. Some depicted representations of the Madonna and Child, while others showed a leering bright red devil with his pitchfork or a grim-visaged Golem.

Still others showed medieval town scenes, pastoral scenes, sailing ships and seaside scenes, elephants and other animals, dancers in provincial costumes, workers and soldiers, as well as beautifully engraved portraits. My curiosity was aroused.

"What are those?" I asked, pointing at them.

"Those, young man, are notgeld."

"Notgeld?"

"It means 'not gold' in German, or, if you like, paper money," he explained. "It was emergency currency that was issued in Germany and Austria in the period between 1914 and 1923. You see, World War I had devastated the economy there, and a terrible inflation followed, making the country's existing currency virtually worthless."

He took a deep breath before continuing. "Since the Reichsbank couldn't print new currency and get it into circulation fast enough to keep up with the spiraling inflation, the various local provinces or even city governments and businesses began printing their own money to keep the economy going, resulting in these colorful pieces of paper. Sol brought that bundle of notgeld over from Germany with him when he came here."

"That's very interesting. I'd never heard about it before."

"If you look closely at them, you can see reflected the chaotic post-war history of Germany—from the grim ashes of defeat to the irreversible economic collapse that led to the chaos and confusion that resulted in the inevitable but terrible emergence to power of the National Socialist Party, the Nazis."

Samuel opened the case and picked up one of the notes. It was beautiful, even though it depicted a somewhat horrifying expressionistic rendering of the Grim Reaper. "You see here what the denomination is on this one. It is One Hundred Trillion Marks."

He was right. That's what the banknote said. "Is it valuable?"

"Value, young man, is in the eye and mind of the beholder." He replaced the note in the showcase and continued. "At the time it was issued, it might have bought a couple of eggs."

"One hundred trillion marks for just a couple of eggs?"

He shrugged his shoulders. "You see, young man, so bad was the inflation by that time that a few days later it was probably worthless. As a piece of history, yes, it has some value. As a collectable piece, yes, it has some value. Otherwise, as currency, it's no longer worth the paper it was printed on."

All of this information about something I'd never known about before was proving to be very enlightening, but it was starting to get late, and I remembered that I had what had a good chance to turn out to be a hot dinner date as well as another case to work on.

I thanked Samuel Rubin for his time and valuable information, gave him my business card in case he happened to remember anything else, and headed on over to Hollywood in great anticipation of my date with Kathy Heller.

Chapter Fifteen

The Musso & Frank Grill on Hollywood Boulevard has been around since 1919 and prides itself as being the oldest restaurant in Hollywood. It is pretty much the same place as it was back in the old days, when all the great legends of the motion picture and the literary world dined and drank there.

The bar serves excellent martinis, and the likes of John Barrymore, W.C. Fields, Errol Flynn, Ernest Hemingway, Nathaniel West, William Faulkner, F. Scott Fitzgerald, Thomas Wolfe, and Raymond Chandler used to hang out and drink there. Needless to say, the atmosphere of the place is marvelous.

Among the notables from the Golden Era of Hollywood that the dining room has served are Greta Garbo, Bette Davis, Orson Welles, Boris Karloff, and Edward G. Robinson. Gary Cooper and Joel McCrea usually ordered their mouth-watering steaks, which were cooked for them on the same old, well-seasoned wood-burning grill still in use to this very day.

Even as far back as the era of silent motion pictures Rudolph Valentino came there for their spaghetti, and Charlie Chaplin was a regular who usually had boiled lamb with caper sauce for lunch. Most of the current breed of show business legends and industry movers and shakers still patronize this restaurant, which has become a veritable institution. Many deals have been made and contracts signed within the confines of those old wooden booths.

I've always enjoyed eating at Musso's, and I've done so often enough that I've gotten to know the manager, a sweet little old man named Jesse, fairly well. One day, while I happened to be shopping at the nearby Hollywood Ranch Market, I caught sight of Jesse there and noticed that he was struggling to carry all his bags of purchases, so I went over and helped him get them to his car. Ever since then, he's always looked after me whenever I would go to Musso's.

Jesse greeted me when I walked through the door and asked if I wanted a table. I told him that I did, but that I was meeting someone at the bar for drinks first. Since I had arrived a few minutes early, I found a place at the crowded bar and ordered one of their glorious Tanqueray Martinis, which always ended up being almost two martinis because along with the martini came a little glass carafe that contained the rest of what had been generously poured into the cocktail shaker—a wonderful Musso & Frank tradition.

It was Friday night, and the place was becoming very packed. I sat contemplatively at the old wooden bar and enjoyed the drink while soaking up the unique atmosphere, wondering if all the ghosts of all those great men who used to drink here were still hovering around. Somehow, it felt as if they were.

Eight o'clock came and went, and then eight thirty. I was on my third martini and feeling absolutely no pain when nine o'clock rolled around, and I was beginning to get the uneasy feeling that I had been stood up.

Then she walked into the room and looked around, and, seeing me, strolled up to the bar and sat down on the bar stool that I had been saving for her. She ordered a Bombay Martini with extra olives, then turned to me and apologized for being late.

She was still dressed in the same clothes she had been wearing on the film shoot, with the exception of the addition of a brown World War II-era wool Royal Air Force surplus aviator's jacket. She carried one of those soft leather patchwork handbags that closed with a drawstring, the kind that came from Morocco.

"The shoot sort of went to shit after you left, and we ended up going overtime. We didn't wrap until almost eight thirty," she explained. "Sorry, I didn't get a chance to change. I just came straight on over here because it was so late."

The bartender brought her martini, and she tossed it down with a couple of serious swallows, emptied the carafe of additional martini in her glass, downed it, and immediately ordered another. "I needed that," she said as she started in on her olives. I didn't doubt her. She must have had a long, hard day. "So what was it you wanted to talk to me about?"

I decided to come directly to the point. "Do you know someone named Sheila Ross?"

Kathy furrowed her brow in thought and replied, "No, I don't believe I'm familiar with that name."

A sudden thought occurred to me, and I reached for my wallet and pulled out Sheila's photo. I handed it to Kathy. She looked at it, and recognition dawned on her face. "Oh, so her name's Sheila Ross. She looks real young here. What is this, some kind of high school picture?"

"Yeah, when was the last time that you saw her?"

She thought for a moment and said, "Must've been around three weeks ago—it was actually the first and only time I ever saw her. Like, I didn't even know her name. So what's this all about?"

"She was murdered. I'm investigating her death."

She looked at me incredulously. "What? Are you serious?"

"I'm dead serious."

Kathy appeared thoughtful for a moment. "What happened to her? I mean, why was she killed?"

"That's what I'm trying to find out. You say you only saw her that one time, about three weeks ago?"

"Yeah, a friend of mine—Grace London at Rapid Sound Services—set up a meeting with her. She called me and told me that she had someone who was interested in buying something that I had. So we got together, and I sold it to her. She paid me in cash, and that was that."

Grace London was the other name on the piece of paper that I had found beneath the magnet on Sheila's refrigerator. Now that more pieces of the puzzle were coming into play, my curiosity was really aroused.

"What was it that you sold to Sheila?"

"It was a small wireless microphone and transmitter set that I had built into a pendant. You know, like the kind you wear as a necklace around your neck. This one was a thick, round gold-plated pendant with a lion's face in relief, a really pretty design."

"Sounds like it might be a pretty expensive item."

"Yeah, well, it is. I make these things for film work. Sometimes there's no place to hide a mike or boom in a scene, so I have to get pretty creative with the sound recording equipment."

I nodded that I understood what she was saying, and she went on, "I also sold her a miniature tape recorder receiver that activated itself with voice control, which I'd modified to work specifically with the pendant. You see, the transmitter in this case is so small that it's only effective for about twenty feet, so the recorder would have to be either somewhere on her person, in a purse, or in something close by. But apparently that was just what she wanted."

"I see," I said. "Did she tell you what she was going to use it for?"

"No, she didn't, and I didn't ask."

I thought about this and wondered if Sheila might have intended to blackmail somebody—but then again, blackmail really didn't seem like something that the Sheila I once knew would do. What could she have possibly been doing with a hidden recording device?

I finished my martini and caught Jesse's eye. He came over and led us to my favorite corner booth, which I noticed he had been saving for me for the past half hour. I casually slipped a folded twenty into his palm, and he simply smiled and said nothing as he walked away.

"You eat here often?" Kathy asked.

"Once in a while," I replied. "When I feel like I can afford it," I added, because Kathy was a girl who seemed like she appreciated honesty.

"I noticed that Jesse likes you. He doesn't seem to like all that many people, so you should feel honored. You've heard the story about Charlton Heston, haven't you?"

"Yeah, I have." The story goes that one evening Charlton Heston happened to show up at Musso's with some family and friends at the peak dinner hour and was told by Jesse that there would be quite a long wait for a table because they were so busy. Heston asked Jesse if he knew who he was, and Jesse replied, "Yes, I know who you are, Mr. Heston. And there's still going to be a long wait." Heston and his party left, and from what I understand, he's never been back since then.

"Apparently even Moses has a problem getting a table here during the peak dinner hour," I said.

She looked up at me and smiled. "But I have a feeling that you probably wouldn't."

I shrugged my shoulders, and we looked through the menu. Musso's has a daily menu printed for each and every day of the year that they are open. It doesn't seem like something that was absolutely necessary, but it was, after all, a tradition. And a traditional place like Musso's takes such things very seriously.

We decided to share a Crab Louie with imported Roquefort, and for the main entrée, she ordered the Fillet of Sandabs Saute Meuniere and I ordered the Porterhouse Steak medium rare.

"Do you want to have wine with dinner?" I asked.

"No," Kathy said, picking up her martini and finishing it. "But I'll have another one of these."

"Make it two." I said to the waiter, who acknowledged my request by nodding before taking his leave.

While we were waiting for the food, we discussed our mutual interests in books and music. Aside from having read a couple of novels by Anna Kavan, we both enjoyed reading Paul Bowles, Nevil Shute, B. Traven, and Georges Simenon and thought that except for *Pnin* and *Lolita*, that Nabokov was probably somewhat overrated. She didn't share my taste for the guilty pleasure of Warren Murphy and Richard Sapir's *The Destroyer* novels, but then again, I suppose you can't kill 'em all.

We both also had fairly eclectic taste in music and enjoyed listening to all kinds of classical music, including but not limited to Schubert and Dvorak. The jury was still out on opera, which neither of us listened to very much, but we did like to listen to recordings of the early blues singers such as Bessie Smith, Robert Johnson, Blind Lemon, and Memphis Minnie.

Both of us were also into The Rolling Stones, The Doors, Jimi Hendrix, Santana, Fats Domino, and Linda Ronstadt, as well as some folk singers, early Carter Family recordings, and Hank Williams Senior.

"I heard on the news that Joan Baez is going to Hanoi to deliver Christmas presents to the American POW's," she said. "I think that's so cool."

"That's a dangerous place to be right now, especially with President Nixon's Linebacker II bombing raids," I speculated.

She shook her head. "I doubt that even a totally psychotic asshole like Nixon would think of continuing the bombing over Christmas," she said.

I wasn't so sure about that, but I sort of agreed with her opinion about our president being somewhat of a psychotic asshole. Nixon had his good points, but unfortunately, these were being rapidly overshadowed by his bad points. Even though he claimed to be trying to negotiate an end to the war over there in Southeast Asia, the manner in which he and his generals were doing it seemed to be pretty ineffective and heavy-handed and the situation appeared to continue to be going from bad to worse.

But anyway, I thought, with a feeling of relief that must have been similar to that of someone who's finally finished all their formal schooling, I'd already done my duty and played my own reluctant part in that hopeless fiasco. Sadly, I also realized that whatever I had managed to accomplish over there while risking life and limb hadn't really amounted to a hill of beans in the final scheme of things.

Bringing myself back to the present and the here and now, I could see that during my long silence, Kathy had been intently studying my face, and there was a quizzical expression on hers. I felt the question coming, and there was no way I could stop it.

"Were you over there?"

"Yeah," I answered somewhat uncomfortably. The way things were going nowadays, it was hard to get away from the subject of the war, no matter how much I wanted to.

"What was it like?"

"It was far worse than you could ever imagine."

"You don't like talking about it, do you?"

"No, I suppose I don't."

Fortunately, the arrival of two fresh martinis and the Crab Louie managed to put an end to that particular conversation. Our waiter split the salad up for us into perfectly equal portions, and we added the dressing ourselves. Kathy dug into the salad with undisguised gusto. "I'm starving," she apologized needlessly. "I haven't eaten a thing since lunch."

"And I interrupted that. Sorry."

She shook her head as if telling me to dismiss the thought, and we both continued to eat quietly.

Kathy quickly finished her salad, and to break the silence, she asked, "How do you like it? Being a private investigator, I mean."

"I like it fine. I can pretty much set my own hours, and it's something that I'm good at doing."

"Do you find missing people and stuff like that?"

"I've done a few missing persons cases," I replied. I decided not to tell her about Sophie and the new case I had just taken on. Instead, I told her, "Once, I even found a dog that was stolen."

She laughed. "Must have been a pretty valuable dog," she

commented as she took a sip of her fresh martini.

"It was," I said, finishing my salad and pushing the plate away from me. "Mostly, I'm just hired to gather evidence for divorce cases. It gets pretty boring sometimes, just sitting in my car, waiting and watching for something to happen. It can be pretty dull work."

"But right now you're working on a murder case. That sounds pretty exciting."

I hesitated for a moment before saying, "The victim in this particular case was someone from my past."

She nodded her head to convey mute understanding and thoughtfully didn't pursue the matter any further. The waiter returned bearing our entrees on a large oval aluminum serving tray, which he set down on a folding serving caddy.

He skillfully boned the Sautéed Sandabs for Kathy before serving them to her, and then, with a practiced flourish, he placed the plate containing my thick Porterhouse, which was perfectly grilled to medium-rare perfection and swimming in its own juices, garnished only with a couple of tasty sprigs of watercress in front of me. At this point, conversation pretty much ceased until we finished our dinner.

"The fish was delicious," she said.

"So was the steak."

She pulled a pack of Marlboros out of her handbag and offered me one. I accepted it, and as I put it between my lips, our waiter came over with two small glass ashtrays, which he placed in front of each of us with one hand while he wordlessly lit our cigarettes with the other. Then he proceeded to clear away our dinner dishes from the table.

"Thank you for inviting me to dinner," she said as she exhaled a long stream of smoke that slowly dissipated into little curls that gradually dissolved their way toward the ceiling.

"It was most definitely my pleasure." At this point, I seemed to have exhausted my conversational repertoire and was trying to figure out what to say next that might hopefully lead to something interesting for the rest of the night. But all I could think of saying was, "Would you like an after-dinner drink?"

She smiled a most inviting smile and replied with an invitation that I was not about to refuse. "Why don't you come to my place for one? I don't live very far from here."

Chapter Sixteen

Kathy had an apartment that occupied the entire second floor on top of an old four-car garage behind a main residence on a quiet middle-class residential street a couple of blocks west of Highland and a few blocks below Beverly Boulevard in the area of Los Angeles, just south of Hollywood.

The houses in the neighborhood there looked like they had been built in the 1920s and 1930s. The apartment Kathy lived in was split into three rooms: a pretty, good-sized combination living room and dining room area with a small kitchenette, a separate bedroom in the back, and a small bathroom with a tub and shower.

The first thing I noticed when I walked in was a wall piled high with books, mostly paperbacks but also a good number of hard-bound books and mostly fiction, all neatly shelved on improvised bookcases made of pine boards laid on top of concrete building blocks.

There was also a fairly large collection of LPs of all varieties, from classical to rock, economically housed in several wooden Scotch crates that had been stood up on end. On top of the Scotch crates was a turntable and what appeared to be a state-of-the-art amplifier and receiver. A pair of stereo speakers cased in dark wood flanked each side.

In the center of the room reposed a comfortable-looking dark brown faux leather sofa that was partially covered by a colorful Mexican blanket. In front of the sofa was a glass-topped coffee table with a small pile of *American Cinematographer* and *Time* magazines, a large book of Hieronymus Bosch paintings, a hand-painted wooden box from India, and a white ceramic ashtray that advertised Cinzano vermouth and contained a little green book of matches from Yee Mee Loo Restaurant in Old Chinatown.

Against the wall opposite the sofa beneath the colorful Che Guevara poster, which provided the sole wall decoration, was a Sony color television set that had been placed on top of four sturdy wooden milk crates. On top of the television set was an empty, straw-covered Chianti bottle that had been converted into a makeshift candle holder.

Everything was orderly and neat, and the apartment appeared to be lived in but very clean. A multicolored glass-beaded curtain separated the living room from the bedroom and bathroom. There was a slight hint of sandalwood incense in the air, along with another vague but slightly overpowering smell, perhaps patchouli.

"Nice place," I said.

"I like it. I have enough room in here, and the rent's reasonable. The landlord and his wife live in the house out front, and they take good care of the place."

The dining area was dominated by a large rectangular piece of plywood laid flat on top of two saw horses, which appeared to serve more as a work table than a dining table because it was covered with sound equipment parts and pieces, a soldering iron, assorted little screwdrivers, pliers, and other tools. This girl was mechanically inclined, something I definitely was not.

"So is this where you make your customized microphones?" I asked.

"That's my little workshop," Kathy affirmed as she opened one of the kitchen cabinets and took out two brandy snifters and a three-quarters-full bottle of Drambuie. "This is all I have," she said somewhat apologetically.

"It will do fine," I said, taking one of the snifters. She uncorked the bottle and poured me a healthy dram before doing the same for herself. She raised her glass, and we made a silent toast. A sip of the sweet but potent liqueur burned nicely going down.

Kathy took my hand and led me over to the sofa, where she set the bottle down next to the little wooden box on the glass-topped coffee table. I excused myself to go to the bathroom, and when I returned, she had made herself comfortable on the sofa and was smoking a cigarette.

"Would you like some coffee?" she asked. I simply shook my head in reply. I rarely drank coffee at night. We each took a healthy sip of the liqueur, and she finished her cigarette and stubbed it out in the ashtray. Then her eyes suddenly lit up as another thought occurred to her. "Do you want to do a doobie?"

I contemplated that offer. Sure, I'd smoked a lot of grass over in Nam, just like everybody else. But those have been extenuating circumstances, and nowadays I don't usually smoke marijuana because, as a rule, I prefer to always be in total control of my thoughts and actions, and grass has a tendency to make me feel a little too laid back and my thoughts somewhat erratic and uncontrollable.

I could see that she was reading my hesitation, and I didn't want to appear to be too uptight, so I replied, "Sure, why not," and this motivated another one of her beautiful smiles. She reached for the little wooden box on the coffee table, opened it, and removed a pack of cigarette papers and a plastic baggie half-full of what appeared to be some pretty high-grade cannabis.

"Panama Red," she said as if no further explanation was necessary. She proceeded to roll a joint while I went over and examined her extensive and eclectic record collection. She had a good many records that I was familiar with and even more that I wasn't. In the mood for something in the latter category, I pulled out Pink Floyd's *The Piper at the Gates of Dawn* and put it on the turntable.

As the music came out of the speakers, Kathy lit the joint she had just rolled, looked up, and said, "Good choice." I listened to the music and thought that it was strange but somehow appropriate, and I was surprised to find that I really liked it.

I sat back down next to her and took another deep sip of the Drambuie, feeling its warming glow rush down to the depths of my stomach. Kathy handed me the joint. I took a deep draw and held the smoke in my lungs as long as I could before I erupted in an uncontrolled fit of coughing. Kathy laughed as I grimaced and handed the joint back to her.

"I guess this is something you don't do on a regular basis," she said as she expertly took another toke.

"You guess right," I replied.

The Panama Red proved to be some really stony stuff, indeed. It wasn't long before we were both giggling like a couple of certified idiots while we tried to articulate to each other the seemingly profound insights that had managed to enter our pot-buzzed brains.

My mind and awareness seemed to be expanding into areas into which they had never expanded before, and I pushed away a sudden fleeting feeling of paranoia as I did the best I could to try and go with the flow.

The flow was alternately warm and exciting, and my initial uneasiness gradually gave way to a more relaxed sense of being when I realized that, in spite of the fact that I didn't feel like I was in full control of myself, by the same token, neither was she.

And then we got the munchies. We raided her fridge and found some left-over Thai takeout which, in my condition, turned out to be some of the most delicious stuff I had ever tasted, in spite of the fact that we were sitting there on the floor of her living room eating it cold.

We feasted on delicious pork spareribs, the remains of a Thai barbeque-style chicken, and some kind of spicy red curry dish with beef. With each bite, it was as if I suddenly became aware of the intensity of each individual spice that went into the making of those tasty delicacies in the white cardboard containers. When we eventually moved on to munching on the contents of a bag of Fritos, the amazing taste sensations continued.

We smoked another joint, and eventually we somehow ended up in each other's arms. Once we were in each other's arms, I really couldn't remember how we got there, and it puzzled me for a brief moment, but then I decided that it probably really didn't matter.

Kathy looked at me and smiled, and then our faces slowly moved together and our lips met in a kiss. It was a long, warm kiss, just the lips at first, and then she opened her mouth, and our tongues met and slowly began to get to know each other more intimately.

By this time, I was totally aroused, and I could feel myself getting rock hard. At least I thought I was getting rock-hard. I was so stoned that I really wasn't sure, so I had to look down there to see that I was. In fact, my erection was even straining uncomfortably against the tightness of my trousers, and it threatened to rip the distended material of my pants and burst out at any minute.

Her hand went down and brushed against my erection, and I could feel her hesitate for a brief moment before it proceeded to continue, curiously feeling the length of it. "My God, what is this?" she said.

"It's what you think it is."

She felt it again. "You're very big, aren't you?"

I shrugged and replied, "Size doesn't really matter."

She smiled again—that sweet, heartwarming smile of hers. "You want to screw me, don't you?"

"How could you tell?"

"I have to be honest with you and tell you that it's not something I would ever do on the first date," she said softly but firmly.

I didn't even try to hide my disappointment. "I had a strange feeling you were that kind of girl."

"I'm really not a prick teaser, if that's what you mean."

"That's not what I meant at all."

"Then you're very perceptive," she said, "and it's very important to me." She kissed me again before slowly pulling back. "It's not that I don't want to, because I do, you know. Just not tonight, because first of all, it's so very late, and I haven't had a chance to shower tonight, and I'm really so stoned and so tired."

"Don't worry about it."

Her hand reached over and gently caressed my face. "If we did it tonight, it wouldn't end up being as good as it should be, and I want it to be. And to be quite honest, I do have the pressure of having to get up to go to work super early tomorrow."

"I understand."

"Do you, really?"

"Yes, I do."

"You'll take a rain check, then?"

"I'll take a rain check."

She smiled once more and cuddled against me. I could smell the faint odor of shampoo in her hair, and the soft warmth of her body sure wasn't helping my painfully neglected erection to go down.

"The film I'm working on wraps on Monday," she whispered in my ear. "Call me any time after."

That sounded like a plan, so I told her, "I will."

She stood and reached out her arms to help me to my feet. As I stood before her, she looked down at the still-prominent bulge in the area of my crotch. Then she looked back up and smiled at me.

"No hard feelings?"

"No hard feelings."

At the door, we had a final kiss, and this was the longest, most passionate one as she ground herself against my erection, which would not seem to go down. "Go now, quickly, please, before I change my mind."

I thought that changing her mind might not be a bad thing for me, and for a brief second, I thought about pressing the matter. I could be pretty persuasive if I wanted to be. But then I realized that it might probably be a bad thing for her, and in all honesty, for some reason, I really didn't want to get started off on the wrong foot with her. So I decided to respect her wishes to leave, and as I was leaving, she said, "Next time, dinner will be on me."

"I'm going to take you up on that," I said before walking somewhat unsteadily off into the night.

I headed toward the street, where I thought that I remembered parking my car. I was still a little stoned, but not too stoned, I hoped, to drive. The last time I was stoned and drove a car, I had felt as if I were actually floating above the road.

It had been a sort of unsettling experience, but I had somehow managed to survive it, but just barely so, and I hoped that I would not be floating home once again tonight.

In a way, I was kind of relieved that things with Kathy had ended the way that they did this evening. I hated to admit it, but for some unexplainable reason I had been feeling a little guilty about being unfaithful to Suzie, and that was an unusual feeling indeed for someone who is a dedicated rounder like me.

I don't know why I felt that way. It wasn't as if she and I had made any kind of commitment to each other. In fact, I really didn't even know how Suzie really felt about me. And in all honesty, I really wasn't quite sure how I really felt about her.

"I suppose," I said aloud to myself and the unhearing darkness of the night, "that it's just one of those strange, unexplainable mysteries of life."

I finally found my car, still unmoved from where I had parked it. I got in, started it up, and as I began driving down the dark residential street, I realized that I was still pretty high.

By high, I mean that I felt as if I were ten feet high above the quiet road, and I realized that I would have to drive slowly and extremely carefully and just hope that no one noticed me. I cautiously headed my car toward the quiet tree-lined residential area of Highland Avenue, where I hung a hard right and drove south toward Venice Boulevard.

To my surprise, I noticed that the car behind me did the exact same thing. It appeared to be following me, and even though I was driving slowly it also seemed to be driving slowly, in a deliberate effort to keep its distance. I wondered who could be following me or if, in reality, anyone was actually following me, and then I shrugged it off as a feeling of paranoia from being so buzzed by the grass.

But when I turned right on Venice Boulevard to head toward the beach and home, the car behind me also turned right.

Of course, this could all still be just a coincidence, but at this point, I was seriously beginning to doubt that assumption. I slowed down even more to see if the car would pass me, but instead it deliberately slowed down to maintain the same distance behind me. I was starting to get really spooked.

The car was still far enough away that I couldn't make out the specific make and model, but what I could tell was that it was a mid-sized car of American manufacture, and the color appeared to be black. I was suddenly feeling cold sober, and my heightened senses were on immediate alert.

The black car kept tailing me in the distance, and I was beginning to feel more than a little uneasy about it, so when I got to the Sepulveda Boulevard intersection, I gunned my Audi through the end of a yellow light, just managing to get past the beginning of the red as, out of the corner of my eye, I saw a police car parked and patiently waiting on the right. Fortunately, the cop didn't come after me.

The black car that was following me saw the police car too and stopped at the light. Breathing a sigh of relief and carefully keeping to the posted speed limit, I managed to put some distance between myself and the black car. I made certain that it was completely out of sight before hanging a left off of Venice and quickly making my way home down the darkened side streets.

Chapter Seventeen

Saturday, December 23, 1972

The next morning I was awakened by the annoyingly persistent sound of the doorbell ringing, and when I answered it, George Lee stepped in carrying a box of a dozen donuts from Mrs. Carlson's Donuts and two extra-large takeout cups of coffee. I could tell from the way he was holding the box that the donuts were still hot, and the odor that assailed my nostrils told me that they had probably just recently been made. The coffee smelled like it was pretty fresh as well.

"Are you going to make a habit of waking me up?" I asked grouchily, still somewhat groggy from the previous night's dissipation.

He handed me one of the oversized cups of coffee, which I accepted with grateful appreciation. The aroma was wonderful, and I could tell right away that it was black and strong, which was just the way I liked it. I was already beginning to forgive George in my mind.

"What, you gonna sleep all day?" he asked as he walked into the kitchen, where he deposited the box of donuts on the kitchen table and opened it.

I followed him into the kitchen while looking at my watch and murmured defensively, "It's only eight o'clock, man." I tried hard to stifle a yawn, but I couldn't. "But thanks for the coffee."

"You're welcome," he said, more magnanimously than he should have under the circumstances. "Since you were thoughtful enough to bring me that roasted duck the other day, I thought I'd bring you breakfast this morning. You get first choice."

I peered into the box to check out his selection and helped myself to one of the still greasy glazed ones.

George picked up and expertly shoved a chocolate donut in his mouth and swallowed it almost whole after chewing three or four times. He reached in for another and proceeded to polish it off in the same way while I was still nibbling at mine.

"I got the report on Billie Rae's autopsy," he said between chews. "Guess what they found lodged in her esophagus?"

I almost choked on a piece of donut in mid-swallow, but my interest immediately perked up. "What?"

"A brass button," he said before he popped a third donut into his mouth. "They said it looks like it came from a coat or something. It was a fairly big one."

Now this was an interesting development. "Think it belonged to the killer?"

"I think it probably did," he replied. "That is, unless she just got off on swallowing buttons, you think?"

"I seriously doubt that," I said, although, in all honesty, I had to admit that Billie Rae was more than a little kinky.

He took a big, slurping sip of coffee. I took a small sip and not only burned the hell out of my mouth but also ended up sending a painful lava-like flow down into my chest because the coffee was scalding hot. George must have a mouth made out of asbestos.

But thankfully, the coffee was starting to wake me up. My mind was clearing, and my head was spinning with all kinds of thoughts. "Billie Rae must have torn off the button during her struggle with the killer. This girl was no fool. She knew that she was going to go down, so she swallowed it to leave us some evidence to follow."

"Yeah," George nodded in agreement. "She left us that and the cigarette lighter." I could tell that he was somewhat amazed at this girl's resourcefulness in leaving behind clues. He confirmed it for me by saying, "If only more victims could think like her, it would end up making my job a whole lot easier."

"You get a look at the button?"

He shook his head. "I'm going over to the morgue now to have a look at it. Want to come with me?"

There are a lot of places where I don't mind going, but the City Morgue was definitely not one of them. "I think I'll pass. Did the autopsy report tell you anything else?"

A serious look came over his face. "Unfortunately, yes." He put down his coffee, pulled a cigarette out and tapped it on his hand, and looked at me. "It confirmed that she was beaten up real bad and that she was tortured before her throat was slit." He put the cigarette in his mouth, lit it, and blew out a long stream of smoke. "All of the fingers on her right hand were broken."

What he had said had conjured up an unpleasant picture, and like it or not, that picture was forming in my mind, and I sure didn't like the way it looked. It was making me think about something I really didn't want to think about. "Like, whoever it was that killed her wanted some information."

"You hit the nail on the head."

"It might explain all that screaming the neighbors heard." I paused for a moment, deep in a thought that was leading me to an unsettling conclusion. "It also might have been the same thing as what happened to Sheila."

"It's exactly like what happened to Sheila," he said as he snuffed out the cigarette. He picked through the box of donuts and chose one with sprinkles. "The medical examiner even thinks that the same knife was used on both victims," he continued while chewing on the donut. "Both bodies showed the same left-to-right cutting action done as a single stroke." He finished the donut and slurped a sip of his coffee.

"It was real professional, like the guy's an expert at what he does," he continued. "The wounds indicate that he uses a really sharp knife with probably a seven-inch blade, and he must be pretty strong too, from what the depths of the cuts seem to indicate."

I thought about the cigarette lighter that George had found. "You think that the killer might have been a Special Forces assassin at one time—like a Green Beret or someone like that?"

"It's a distinct possibility. They're trained to kill like that, aren't they?"

I nodded affirmatively and briefly pictured in my mind someone sneaking behind their victim, commando style, and ending their life with a quick, single motion by slitting their throat. I cautiously took another sip of coffee while I tried to digest all this new information.

"So a left-to-right cut," I said thoughtfully. "The killer must be right-handed."

"Shit, most people in the world are right handed, John," he said. "So what the hell does that tell us?" He shook his head. "Absolutely nothing."

"You're right, I was just thinking out loud," I said defensively.

Billie Rae had left us some significant clues that could possibly identify her killer and help solve the mystery of her death, but first we needed to come up with some solid suspects so we could use those clues to nail him.

I could see the wheels turning in George's head. "You know something," he finally said, "those West Hollywood detectives questioned the neighbors but weren't able to come up with anything." He shook his head. "I don't buy that. With all the screaming that was going on, somebody must have looked out their window and seen something."

"Stands to reason," I concurred. "I think you might be right."

That decided him. "I think I'm going to do some checking around myself."

"Well, it sure can't hurt anything. By the way," I said as the thought occurred to me. "I've come up with a lead that may mean something." I then proceeded to tell him about my meeting with Kathy Heller and went into detail about the recording equipment Sheila had purchased from her.

There was a puzzled look on George's face. "Sounds like Sheila was going to try and blackmail someone," he mused.

"It sure seems like it," I reluctantly agreed.

"I wonder what would make her want to do something like that?" I could tell that he was fishing to see if I had any more information.

I shook my head. "I only wish I knew."

There was a long silence, as if he were debating with himself whether to believe me or not. "Who do you think it could have been?" he finally asked, even though by now I'm sure he suspected that I didn't have the answer to that one.

I shrugged my shoulders and could only say, "Beats me."

George continued, "This other girl, the one who put together the deal you mentioned—what's her name?"

"Grace London. She works at Rapid Sound Services over in Hollywood."

George picked a glazed donut out of the box and looked at it before taking a bite. "I take it you're going to follow up on her."

"I'm going over there this morning."

"Good," George said before wiping the sugar from his mouth with a quick, practiced swipe of his right hand. "Let me know if she tells you anything."

"I will," I said as I took another sip of coffee. By now, it had cooled off enough to be somewhat safe to drink, so I took a healthy swig.

"Another thing," I added. "I've taken on a case, a paying one."

"About time you realized that you have to work for a living."

I shot him the bird with my left hand and walked over to the bar where I had left my coat the night before and pulled the photograph Sophie had given me out of the pocket. I walked back and handed it to George.

"I'm trying to track down this woman and the child."

George took a quick look at it. "It looks like it was taken a few years ago."

"I believe it was."

"Have any idea how long ago?"

"Not really."

"No names, of course."

"No names."

George's brow furrowed, and he looked at the photograph again. "Something about the woman looks familiar," he said. He looked at the photograph again carefully, trying hard to recall what looked familiar about her. He finally gave up. "I just can't seem to place her right now, but I know I've seen her." He shook his head and handed the photo back to me.

"Maybe it'll come back to you," I said hopefully. George was terrible with names, but he was pretty good with faces. If that one looked familiar, I would bet good money that he had run across her somewhere sometime in the past. I just hoped that eventually he would remember where.

"Maybe," he said. "By the way, who's the guy in the picture, the old guy?"

"His name is Sol Steinman. He used to own a stamp store in Culver City."

"You mean the kind of store that the stamp collectors go to?

I nodded, and George thought hard for a moment, then said, "Well, it doesn't ring any bells right now, but I'll let you know if and when it does."

"I'd really appreciate it."

I hesitated and then told George about the black car that had followed me last night after I left Kathy's place. I could tell that he was a little disturbed by this. I have to confess that I was a little disturbed by it myself.

"So you didn't get a real good look at the car or the driver?"

"No, it was too far away. And after I ran the light, I was just trying to put some distance between myself and the tail."

"Be careful, John. I definitely don't think we're dealing with amateurs here."

"I don't think we are either."

"So pay attention to me. If you see that car again, try and get a good look at the license plate if you can, and give me a call immediately. I'll run the number through DMV so we can find out who owns the car. Don't confront the guy or do anything stupid, now, you hear."

I nodded my head and said, "Loud and clear."

"Good, maybe we can keep you alive after all."

Before George left, I told him about my unexpected visit from the Feds the night before last and asked him what kind of trouble I would be in if I decided to fight back.

He thought for a moment before replying, "I don't know, John, but I'll be glad to join you to even out the odds if you want to find out. Whatever you decide, give me a call."

"I couldn't ask for anything more." I patted my pocket. "I've got your card and your pager number."

He started to leave, but turned around and said, "Why don't we get together for dinner this evening and compare notes?"

I didn't have anything planned, so I answered, "That sounds good to me."

"How about Pancho's place then—say around seven?"

"I'll be there."

George headed out the front door, and I headed for the shower.

Chapter Eighteen

The sun was peeking out from behind the clouds as I pulled my car into the beach parking lot, got out, and followed a couple of morning fishermen as they walked purposefully down the Santa Monica Pier. I stopped when I reached the building that housed the carousel and saw that the little photographer's shop beside it was closed.

The sign on the door informed me that the shop opened at 10:00 AM. I looked at my watch and saw that I still had fifteen minutes left to kill, so I descended the well-worn wooden stairs to the beach and sat down on the sand to silently contemplate the ocean.

The air was fresh and brisk, with only a light breeze blowing from the northwest, and the relative quiet was disturbed only by the sound of the crashing waves, followed by the sound of bubbling froth as the waves washed on shore and then slowly receded in their never-ending cycle.

These sounds were occasionally punctuated by the screeching of the various flocks of sea birds as they flew around doing their thing in the sky above. I lit a cigarette and quietly pondered the manifold wakings of mankind.

A little after ten, a tall, bearded middle-aged Caucasian man, probably in his fifties, showed up. He was dressed in threadbare, dark brown corduroy pants and a tan turtleneck sweater. His closely cropped brown hair was sprinkled with a lot of gray, and he was carrying a large, battered, and scarred brown leather briefcase. I couldn't see what color his socks were, but from all that I could see, this guy was totally color coordinated in earth tones.

I couldn't help but wonder if he made a conscious effort to do this. I watched him as he fumbled with a large ring of keys before finding the right one. He unlocked the photo shop, and I walked over and followed him in.

When he turned around to look at me, I introduced myself and handed him the photograph that Sophie had given to me. He had a questioning look on his face, but he accepted it. Before he looked at it, he reached into his coat pocket and pulled out a pair of tortoiseshell-rimmed reading glasses, which he put on.

He turned on the lights so he could see better, and then he took a cursory look at the front of the photograph before turning it over and carefully examining the back of it. He looked up at me with a neutral expression and handed the picture back.

"Yeah, that was taken here." His eyes scanned the room, and he pointed at the far wall. "There's the ship set over there." Sure enough, there was the painted wooden cartoon ship flat leaning against the opposite wall. It was stacked up against two other flats. I could plainly see that it was the same as the one depicted in the picture, somewhat the worse for wear with the passage of years, but still, it was obviously the same one.

"Was it you who took the picture?"

"Yeah, I took that picture," he stated with confidence.

"Would you happen to know who the people in it are?"

He shot me an incredulous look. "You've got to be kidding," he answered with a deliberate snicker. "You know how many of these things I take in the course of a single day and for how many years I've been taking them?"

"Just thought I'd ask," I said. "I had a feeling it would be a long shot."

"Well, you're right about that." He thought for a moment. "I can tell you one thing, though. The picture was taken around ten years ago."

That was a surprising but important bit of information. "How can you tell?"

"By the photo paper," he replied, moving closer to me. I noticed that his sweater had holes in it and smelled of mothballs. He pointed to the picture that was still in my hand. "Turn it over, and you'll see."

I did as he told me to, and he pointed to a barely discernible watermark logo on the back of the picture. "See how age has darkened it. It's that cheap paper made by an East German company named Orwo." I looked closer and saw the words in the logo. He was right.

"I remember this paper because one time I managed to get a batch of it at a really good price and then wished I hadn't. It was terrible stuff. I only used that particular print paper for a few months, and boy, was I glad when I finally ran out of it. That was around ten years ago."

"So this photograph was taken around 1962."

The photographer thought for a moment, making a rapid calculation in his mind before he confirmed my calculation: "Yeah, 1962 was when I took that picture. It was sometime between the summer and fall of 1962. I remember now. That's when I was using that paper. It would definitely be no earlier or later than that."

It wasn't a whole lot, but at least it was something, and I was beginning to feel good about it. The information I gathered from the photographer told me that the child in the picture must be around fourteen or fifteen years old by now. That meant if he was four or five when that picture was taken, Sol must have had a relationship with the woman in the picture during the period when he had his store downtown, since he didn't move his business to Culver City until February 3rd, 1961.

This also meant that the woman in the picture would be ten years older by now, which would probably put her age-wise in her early thirties. Well, the case was starting to develop, and I felt as if I had made a good start. Now if I could only find out just exactly who the woman in the picture was.

As I drove along Pico Boulevard, keeping a wary eye out for anyone who might be tailing me, I thought about stopping at Shep's Deli on my way to Hollywood to see if I could possibly learn anything more. Then I decided that it was probably a little too late in the day to catch any of the early morning breakfast kibitzers who might have known Sol.

I knew from previous experience that those guys usually hung around shooting the shit for a few hours after they had their breakfast, but they usually cleared out with the approach of the early lunch crowd. Although I seriously doubted that talking to them would serve to shed any more light on the situation, you could never really tell.

There was always that off chance that an old acquaintance might drop some obscure remembered detail that could ultimately lead to a break in the case. Stranger things have happened, so I knew that I'd eventually have to go there and give it a try. But not right now. I was too anxious to find out what Grace London could tell me about Sheila.

Rapid Sound Services was on Seward Street, in an area where a lot of different businesses provided various goods and services to the motion picture industry. It was located in a small white Spanish-type building that recalled the once popular Southern California architectural style of the 1930s.

The company sold and rented sound equipment to the entertainment business, which not only included movies and television but the music recording business as well. It also housed a post-production sound mixing facility and editing rooms, which were available for rental by the day, week, or month.

Grace London, I learned, was one of the people who handled the equipment sales and rentals. When I got there, the showroom was a hive of activity, and I had a much longer opportunity than I needed to study the merchandise and look around the place while I patiently waited for her. I was amazed at the variety of equipment and accessories that were needed and available to record sound for movies and music for records.

In the meantime, whenever I got the chance, I looked over at Grace, appraisingly trying, of course, to be as discreet as possible. She had a light complexion, and her long, thin face was not at all unattractive. She also had reddish blonde hair that fell to her shoulders.

She appeared to be in her early thirties and was dressed neatly in a conservative dark blue suit. She wore a frilly white silk blouse, and she gestured a lot with her hands when she talked.

Eventually she wrapped up her sound equipment sale, finished with her customer, and walked over to me. Close up, she didn't look quite as good as she did from the distance. There was a certain hardness about her face, even though she did have some appealing girlish freckles that spread across the top of her nose and over to her cheeks.

"Sorry that took so long," she said. "You were waiting to see me?"

I introduced myself, but when I told her what I wanted to talk to her about, she suddenly became very uneasy, and she looked around furtively before she finally said, "I don't think we should discuss that here."

"Why don't you let me buy you some lunch?" I asked hopefully.

She hesitated again before looking at her wristwatch. "All right," she said. "Do you know where Huston's is?"

"You mean the barbeque place?"

"That's the one."

"I'll meet you there in thirty minutes."

Huston's Texas Style Pit Barbeque is a semi-grubby little eatery of the walk-up to the counter and order variety that has been at its location across the street from the main branch of the Hollywood Post Office on Wilcox Avenue since World War II. I'd eaten there a couple of times and recalled that while the atmosphere was not much to speak of, the food was good enough to make you want to go back.

Inside the place the walls were graced with colorful but indifferently framed movie posters and lobby cards from various independent Hollywood B-pictures of the 1940s and 1950s, mostly obscure and semi-obscure Westerns with stars that most people had never heard of.

The mouth-watering smell of smoked meat permeated the place, and I was uncomfortably hoping that Grace, who was standing in line next to me, didn't hear my stomach making the gurgling sounds that it was making.

When it came our turn, we each ordered one of their delicious wood-smoked slow-roasted pork sandwiches, along with a side of coleslaw and a large plastic cup filled with iced tea. I paid the tab and watched while the meat was being expertly chopped up and heaped in a generous pile onto the waiting buns.

We were quickly handed our orders, and we took our trays of food and sat across from each other at one of the small but clean, formica-topped tables situated next to the wall.

"I've only had this job for a few months, and I don't want to lose it," she said as she squeezed the juice from her wedge of lemon into her iced tea. "Sheila came to me at work, and we didn't have what she wanted to buy."

She took a small bite of her sandwich, and I took a large bite of mine, and then I asked, "She wanted to buy a small, easily hidden wireless microphone, right?"

Grace picked a strand of pork from between her front teeth

with her fingernail. "Yeah, she told me that she needed a miniature microphone and transmitter unit and a small receiver and recorder combination. I asked her what she needed it for, and she told me that she needed it for something very important."

"Did she tell you what it was that was so important?"

"Not really. Anyway, I knew that Kathy made that kind of equipment, so I thought I do them both a favor and arrange the meeting so she could buy it from her. If my boss found out about that, he'd fire me for sure."

She took a long drink of the iced tea and looked up at me as if she were seeking some kind of assurance.

"I can promise you that he won't find out about it from me," I assured her, hoping that this would do the job. I watched her nibble at her coleslaw for a moment before I asked, "How long have you known Sheila?"

She seemed nervous about answering that question at first. Then she shrugged her shoulders, sighed, and admitted, "I suppose you'd find out eventually. We met at rehab."

She hesitated for a moment before she continued, "For awhile there, I had a major problem with cocaine. It's not a problem now." She looked around for some wood to knock on and settled for the cheap artificial wood veneer paneling on the wall.

She took another bite of her sandwich, but I could tell that at this point she wasn't really hungry. She looked up at me and asked, as if she needed further confirmation, "You say that Sheila was killed?"

I nodded. I didn't want to spook her, but I also knew that it usually was better to be honest. "That's what it looks like."

She shuddered, then pushed away her sandwich and said, "I had a strange feeling that it would end up like this. Because I knew it was dangerous—what she wanted to do."

My interest instantly perked up. "What was it she wanted to do?"

She picked up her napkin and chewed on it nervously for a moment, searching for the words to convey what she wanted to say. Then she continued, "After she finished rehab, she hooked up with someone—I don't know who it was, and Sheila would never say—but she started going on this crazy crusade-like thing, you know, against drugs."

"You don't have any idea who this other person was?"

"No, like I said, Sheila wouldn't say. Anyway, from the way she was acting, I got the idea that they were both going to try and do something very stupid, you know, like bringing down some of the big guys."

I thought carefully about everything she had just said. Some pieces were finally beginning to come together, and this was all starting to become more and more interesting—and more and more complicated as well.

"You mean they wanted to go up against the dealers?" I asked.

"I got the feeling that they were after a much bigger game than that. I think they were after the really big guys—the guys that were actually bringing the stuff into the country."

"It's simply foolish to get involved with people like that. Most of those guys are so ruthless they would kill their own mothers if they saw a profit in it," I muttered, more to myself than to her.

"No shit, Sherlock," she said in a sarcastic tone that indicated she was well aware of that pretty obvious fact. Then she looked cautiously around to see if anyone was within hearing range before she quietly revealed, "I think she'd found out something about a big shipment that was supposed to be coming in or something, but she didn't actually tell me what it was. Maybe that's why she wanted to buy the recorder."

"You think she wanted to use it to get some evidence?"

"Yeah, that's what I think."

"She told you that?"

Grace hesitated, and then she said, "Not directly, no, but well, it's kinda obvious, isn't it?" She moved in closer toward me and lowered her voice, as if she wanted to tell me something in confidence. "Actually, she wanted me to go in with them, to help them and all, but I told her that I really didn't want to have anything to do with what they were into. I like living too much."

Chapter Nineteen

My talk with Grace London had confirmed my suspicion that Sheila's death was directly related to the drug trade. She had also given me something very important to follow up on with her revelation that Sheila had been involved with someone else in her ill-fated undercover operation.

Now I only had to find out who this person was. I wondered if it was Billie Rae because she was close to Sheila and because she, too, had been murdered in the same violent manner as Sheila had been. Had she held something back from me out of fear or for some other reason?

And then there was Suzy. She told me that she had met Sheila at a clinic where she donated her time when Sheila was recovering from her addiction to heroin. Now more than ever, I was curious about what exactly their relationship had been since I remembered that Suzy had been so very tight-lipped about it.

Frankie Funai, who was obviously a friend of Suzy's, had, by his own admission, supplied Sheila with some opium. I had the distinct feeling that Suzy was somehow more involved in all of this than she let on. In what way, I didn't know, but I was sure going to find out.

I went to the nearest phone booth and dialed Suzy's number, but all I ended up getting was an answering machine. Checking my watch for the time, I realized that it was too late to try and corner Frankie at his lunchtime hangout in Chinatown, so instead I decided to call Grace London at Rapid Sound Services, but was told that she had gone home for the day.

I cursed myself for not getting her home number and not getting the name of the rehab clinic where she and Sheila had met. Next, I tried to call George Lee on his direct line at the station. This got me to another answering machine, so I left him a message on it, then dialed his pager and left the number of the phone in the phone booth.

The sun was high in the sky now, and I was feeling its warming heat as I patiently waited for George to call me back. Five minutes later, the phone in the booth rang. George had returned my page. He was still in the field, canvassing the neighborhood in the vicinity of Billie Rae's apartment, trying to track down anyone who might have seen anything on the day that she was murdered.

"I think I'm onto something, George," I told him. Then I asked him if he, by any chance, remembered the place where Sheila had been sent to rehab. I hit pay dirt there. Not only did George remember the name of the place, but he also gave me the address, which he happened to know very well because another cop—his former partner and mentor—had gone there once as a patient to dry out. George had been a regular visitor there, so he knew where the place was. My day brightened even more when he gave me the name of one of the nurses there.

Mary Alvarez had been one of our classmates throughout grade school and Junior High. I didn't remember ever seeing her in high school, but by then, I suppose, her family had moved into another school district. We hadn't really been close friends, as I recalled, but I did remember that in grade school she'd had a brief infatuation with George.

It took me about twenty minutes to drive from Hollywood to the affluent community known as San Marino, where the clinic was located.

The Carl F. Weiderman Clinic was named after the son and heir of a wealthy Los Angeles oil tycoon. Young Carl had succumbed at an early age to the substance abuse that had plagued his short and uneventful life, and his father had built and funded the rehabilitation clinic bearing his son's name in this quiet, upscale neighborhood in San Marino in his memory.

Of course, I had learned all this by reading a brochure while waiting for Mary Alvarez. After reading the brochure, I took a quick look around the place and could see that what had probably initially begun as a sincere humanitarian gesture was now probably operating as a profitable enterprise. According to the brochure, the cost of a stay at this clinic was not particularly cheap. Sheila had obviously gone first-class all the way.

It was easy to recognize Mary as soon as she stepped into the lobby, even though she was no longer the thin young girl that I could still picture in my mind's eye. Over the years, Mary had put on a little weight. Her round, somewhat plain, but friendly face was somewhat fuller, but it was still the same familiar face. The most attractive thing about her was those mischievous eyes, which still twinkled knowingly, and her short, black hair, which was still short and black.

I stood up, and the stout-figured woman who looked so familiar turned toward me, and a smile of recognition dawned on her face as she walked over to where I was standing.

"Johnny," she greeted me. "It's been such a long time!" She gestured for me to sit back down and she sat down next to me.

We spent a few minutes catching up with what we both had done since we'd seen each other last. After we had finished compressing about seventeen years into four or five minutes, she asked me if I'd seen George lately, and I told her that we were currently working together on a case. And then I told her about the case we were working on.

Mary didn't show the surprise that most people had shown upon learning of Sheila's death. She'd already read about it in the small single-column article that had appeared four days ago on the third page of the *Los Angeles Times*. It was pretty much standard coverage for the suspicious death of a non-celebrity in a city that had more than its share of suspicious deaths.

"She was a patient here for awhile, you know."

"That's what I wanted to talk to you about, Mary."

Mary debated with herself for a moment about whether she should talk about someone who had been a patient there. And then she apparently made a decision about it and said, "I suppose there's no harm in telling you that it was quite a surprise to see her after all those years—especially the way she was when she first came here. She was in really bad shape." She shook her head as if to emphasize that fact. "You wouldn't believe what bad shape she was in. I think she was glad to see me, someone that she once knew."

"I'm sure she was. I can imagine how hard it would have been to face something like this under the care of a complete stranger."

She nodded and continued. "You know, when we were kids,

Sheila and I weren't all that close, but when she came here, we started to get to know each other a little better. She told me that she had a little son that died and that she had been stuck in a marriage that wasn't a very happy one."

"Her marriage with Scott McGinnis, you mean."

"Yes, can you believe that she married him? Anyway, she admitted that he didn't beat her or anything like that, but she also said that as time passed, he had become increasingly cold toward her."

She thought briefly about what she was going to reveal next. "I got the feeling from what she told me that she really didn't love him to begin with, and when he became aware of that fact, I guess he just began to shut her out."

She stopped for a moment as if something suddenly occurred to her, and then she looked up at me and said, "Hey, you used to go out with Sheila, didn't you?"

"Yes, but that was a long time ago."

Mary nodded her head as if she understood and continued. "Well, anyway, after their son died, it only got worse. She said that it was as if he blamed her for their son's death, but what was even worse was that she blamed herself. She carried a tremendous burden of guilt.

"That's what her drug addiction was all about. She had been trying to dull all of the guilt, hurt, and the pain with prescription drugs. Of course, it didn't work, and she eventually ended up just becoming addicted to them. It's the same old, familiar story.

"When she eventually resorted to heroin, things finally began to get out of control. Her heroin addiction ended up totally destroying her marriage, which made her even more depressed and determined to escape from reality. As you probably know, she was eventually arrested and only released on the condition that she would come here to receive treatment for her addiction."

"But when she left here, she was cured, right?"

"We treated her successfully, yes, but nobody is ever really cured of alcohol or heroin addiction, Johnny. We can get the drugs out of their system and try to help and counsel them, but the craving is still always there, and it's a day-to-day situation to keep the need under control and to keep from relapsing."

She looked up at me. "You're familiar with the craving for a cigarette from nicotine addiction, aren't you?"

"Boy am I," I replied honestly.

"Well, multiply that times a hundred, and you'll get some sort of idea what she was up against."

Mary had made her point. I thought of another question to ask her. "Did you have a patient here named Grace London around the same time?"

She didn't need to even think about that one. "Yes, actually, she was Sheila's roommate during her stay here."

"Did they become friends?"

"I suppose so. At least they appeared to get along well with each other."

So far, everything that Mary told me seemed to pretty much confirm what I had already learned. I decided to ask the question that I had been waiting to ask.

"Do you know someone named Suzy Huang?"

"Of course I do. Miss Huang has donated quite a bit of money to the clinic, and she also spends time here working with the patients to try and help them recover and get back to leading a normal life."

"Why do you think she does this?"

Mary shrugged her shoulders. "Because she likes to do it, I suppose. I never asked her."

"Do you know her very well?"

"Not particularly. She's here from time to time, and sometimes we talk. But she never says very much about herself."

"What do you talk about, then?"

"Mostly about the patients and how they're doing. What can be done to help some of them along, you know, stuff like that."

I pondered what she had said for a long moment before asking, "What else can you tell me about her?"

"I don't know a whole lot about Miss Huang other than that she seems to be very wealthy as the result of some kind of business that she owns. I know that she's given jobs to several former patients who had lost their previous ones because of their substance abuse."

"From what I keep hearing about this Suzy Huang, she almost sounds as if she were too good to be true."

Mary thought about this for a moment. "Well, she seems like a really nice person. But then again, I'm sure she has her own agenda. Doesn't everyone?"

After leaving the clinic, I tried calling Suzy again but still only got her answering machine. This was starting to become frustrating. I had to talk to her because I now had the feeling that only she could clear up some of the nagging questions that had been raised in my mind.

I desperately needed her help because I was still putting two and two together and getting three. There was a big locked door that had to be opened, and somehow I had the distinct feeling that Suzy had the key.

I still had some time on my hands before I was due to meet George at Pancho's, so I stopped downtown to check out the two remaining stamp and coin shops that were still in the area. I drew a complete blank at the first one, the larger of the two, which seemed to devote most of its space to the more speculative and profitable coin side of the business.

Most of the people there were younger types, and all of them had either never heard of or didn't know or remember Sol Steinman at all. But when I visited the second shop, a much smaller one-man store that was devoted more to stamps than coins, I hit pay dirt.

"Of course I remember Sol," the thin, wrinkled gray-haired man who introduced himself as Emmanuel Berkelouw replied.

He looked like he was a hundred years old, but from the way he moved around, I deduced that he probably wasn't older than seventy. He took off his reading glasses and looked me up and down before continuing. "I haven't seen him for a long, long time now. How is he?"

I told him that Sol was dead and then showed him the photograph and explained that I had been hired by his widow Sophie, to locate the woman and child in it. He scrutinized the picture carefully before looking up at me and saying, "Sure, I know who that girl is. That's Angie."

He was as surprised as Samuel Rubin had been at the resemblance between Sol and the child. He had no idea at all that Sol had been having a relationship with that girl.

Angie, it turns out, had been a waitress at the small lunch counter on the upper level at Grand Central Market on Hill Street, which was only a couple of blocks away from where Sol's old shop had been. Unfortunately, she no longer worked there, and since the place had changed ownership two times in the last decade, no one had either remembered or heard of her. I'd come up against another stone wall, but at least now I had a name for the mysterious woman in the picture.

Chapter Twenty

George was already waiting for me, sitting at the counter with beer in hand, when I arrived at Pancho's Family Restaurant at seven on the dot. Pancho looked up from the large T-Bone steak he was cooking on the grill and greeted me with a "Hola, Johnny!" as I slipped onto the seat next to George.

Since it was Saturday night, the jukebox was going full blast, and the place was packed. I was lucky that George had saved me a seat.

"I thought you said seven o'clock," I said, looking at my watch.

"I did. I came early. You've got to drink two to catch up."

He made a hand signal to Alicia, the waitress, and pointed to me, and she dug into the large beer cooler and pulled out two cold Negro Modelos, which she expertly opened and placed in front of me. George was snacking on a small plate of fried pork bits called chicharones.

Pancho didn't give you anything like chips to snack on unless you ordered and paid for them, and if you did, he would make them up fresh by cutting up a stack of fresh corn tortillas into the familiar triangles and then deep-frying them.

The chicharones, however, were always free if you happened to be lucky enough to be there when he made a batch of them.

Pancho is the Mexican name for Frank, but Pancho's real name is Rosario, and he was originally from the state of Zacatecas in Mexico. His rural roots had influenced his cooking, which resulted in pure and simple, unadulterated home-style Mexican food at its finest.

He had also done his apprenticeship for many years as a fry cook at various restaurants before opening his own place, so the American side of his menu offered steaks and chops as well as an unforgettable fried chicken. These could be had with either beans and rice or freshly made French fries hand-cut from a king-sized Russet potato. It was always difficult to decide what to eat at Pancho's because anything and everything was first-rate.

In spite of the excellence of the cuisine, you might say that the restaurant was only a slight step up from a dive. Housed in a unique round building probably built sometime in the 1920's, the restaurant contained about eight pedestal-based dining tables of assorted sizes, surrounded by a variety of matched and mismatched chairs, a jukebox that constantly blared new and old Mexican rancheras, corridos, and canciones, and an L-shaped counter that also served as the bar and seated about ten people. The ten people that sat on those stools were usually the regulars.

Set against the wall behind the counter was the kitchen, which consisted of an industrial-sized refrigerator and an industrial-sized stove that had a grill and four burners on which large pots of menudo, Chili Verde and Chile Colorado were always simmering, a steam table, a deep fryer, a large refrigerated case where the beer was kept cold, and a large kitchen sink. Pancho prepared the food in full view of anyone and everyone.

"Boy, that steak looks good," I said as Pancho pulled it off the grill and plopped it onto a huge platter. The tantalizing aroma of garlic and grilled beef juices floated up to my nostrils as it passed me on the way to its destination. "You decide what you're going to eat yet?"

"Not yet. I'm still contemplating it," George replied as he took another deep pull on his Budweiser long neck.

Suddenly, two more beers were set down in front of us. I looked up at Alicia, who craned her neck toward the end of the bar, where a weathered Mexican man wearing a soiled and well-worn straw cowboy hat sat. "Chris buy," she said.

This was pretty much the extent of Alicia's spoken English. Even though she could understand most of what you said to her in English, she rarely spoke the language.

Alicia was a little on the hefty side, but her pretty face and out-standing physical attributes far outweighed this slight disadvantage. Her subtle but expressive gaze hinted at the forbidden sensual pleasures her voluptuous body was capable of. Everyone at the bar counter would love nothing more than to crawl into her pants, but unfortunately, she made herself very unattainable. She had a husband back in Mexico, where she also owned a ranch.

George and I both raised our beers to Chris and said in unison, "Thanks, Cristobal!" He touched the tip of his hat in return. Cristobal was a regular fixture at Pancho's. Any given weekday from four o'clock on or Saturday beginning at noon, you'd usually find him sitting on the same stool at the end of the bar counter, and he'd remain there drinking long-neck bottles of Coors beer until closing time.

"What does Chris do?" I asked George.

George looked over at Chris, and then he looked back at me. "He's a tree trimmer," he replied. George pretty much knows what everybody does for a living. I don't know how he comes by this knowledge, but he seems to always have it. "He owns his own business, and I think he has a contract with the city to keep the trees looking good."

"I was wondering why he always has those chainsaws in his truck." Tree trimming could be hard and dangerous work. I could see why he always came here to chill out at the end of the day. He looked over and saw me looking at him, and he raised his beer in a silent toast. I picked up one of mine, returned the toast, and took a deep swallow. The cold amber liquid felt good going down. I hadn't realized how dry my throat was.

I looked at the counter in front of me and saw that I now had three beers to finish. The way things usually went around here, there would soon be more. One thing these Mexican guys truly enjoyed doing was buying the house a round, so I didn't waste any time getting started.

Thinking back on it, I realized that George and I had known Pancho for a long time. Before he had this place, he operated what he called Pancho's Lucky U Café, which was little more than a long counter that seated eight people in front of the cooking area and the one and a half booths which could seat an additional six at the back of the narrow rectangular room that adjoined the notorious West Los Angeles bar on Santa Monica Boulevard known as the Lucky U.

This was back in the early 1960s, and even then Pancho had a dedicated and loyal following. Aside from the drunks that staggered in from the open door of the Lucky U Bar and his steady Mexican clientele, the place was frequented by students from UCLA, and these included Jim Morrison and Ray Manzarek, who were soon to become famous members of the rock group The Doors.

Morrison died last year, but Manzarek still comes to Pancho's new location once in awhile. So does the new California Secretary of State, Jerry Brown, who, from time to time, shows up with Linda Ronstadt when he's in town. In spite of the fact that some cool people enjoy eating here, the place hasn't really been discovered by the trendy set, which is probably a good thing.

Aside from Alicia and the other waitress who worked for him, Pancho's is basically a one-man operation, and as such, he can not only pretty much control the quality of the food he serves but also the way it is cooked. I've seen too many places go downhill once they become too well known and the crowds start to show up.

"I think I'll have the T-Bone Steak, medium rare," George said, "with papas fritas and a salad, beans and rice on the side, tortillas de maiz."

"You think or you know for sure?" Pancho asked as he wiped the sweat from his forehead with a napkin.

"I know for sure," George said decisively. Pancho grunted his approval of the choice he had made.

George had made the decision for me. Even though the Chili Verde stew here was the sublime dish that I usually always ordered, tonight the steak just looked to be too good to pass up. "Make it two," I said, and Pancho simply nodded silently, obviously pleased at the choice I had made as well. Of course, the steak is the most expensive item on the menu.

"So what was this something you were onto?" George asked.

I told him about my meeting with Grace London in Hollywood and then about my visit to the rehab clinic in San Marino and what Mary Alvarez had said. As I explained what I had learned, I could see that he was carefully pondering the implications of everything.

"What did you think of Mary Alvarez?" he asked.

"What's that got to do with anything?"

"Humor me."

I realized that George might have some personal feelings in that direction, so I tried to be both honest and tactful. "Overweight, but not unattractive," I replied.

"Would you do her?"

I thought about that one for a moment. "Yeah, I suppose," I said, shrugging my shoulders.

He stared at me for a long moment. I could tell that he was

contemplating something profound, and I probably didn't want to know what it was. So I kept quiet too. "I wish I could figure out this Suzy Huang," he finally said.

"I wish I could too. For some reason, everything seems to revolve around her."

"It sure does," George agreed. "Have you tried pumping her some more?"

I caught George's corny double entendre but just replied, "I tried to get a hold of her all day today, but she's not answering her phone." And then a thought occurred to me. "The last time I talked to her, she told me that she was going to be tied up with some kind of big business deal. Maybe she's out of town. I'll try and corner Frankie in Chinatown tomorrow and see what I can find out."

George grimaced at the mention of Frankie's name, but he didn't bother to say anything because he realized that, whether he approved of it or not, I simply had to talk with the guy. The sooner we could resolve the issue of Suzy Huang's involvement, the sooner the case was going to be solved.

"Did you find out anything from Billie Rae's neighbors?"

He gave me a look that revealed his disgust before answering, "Not much, unfortunately, even after spending the better part of the day there." George was obviously troubled by something. He finished his bottle of beer and immediately started in on the one that Chris had bought.

"There was one thing, though," he continued. "An Ethiopian college student who heard the screams looked out of his window and thought he saw an Asian guy in the vicinity, but he was too far away to be able to describe him. He did say that the guy was wearing a white shirt."

"Well, that's something, but you know what? I haven't seen a single Ethiopian in that neighborhood."

"There's lots of 'em there. They just keep to themselves."

I shook my head. I don't know whether George was putting me on or not, but I could tell that he was depressed by the lack of progress he had made for all the effort he had put out in the course of the day.

"So you think this Asian guy might have something to do with Billie Rae's murder?"

"It's a possibility. Or maybe he was just a delivery guy for some

Chinese take-out food place. Who the fuck knows?"

"Could even have been you that he saw." I interjected.

George looked up at me and thought for a moment. Sometimes he forgets that he looks like an Asian. Hell, he's so American, sometimes even I forget that his ancestry is Chinese.

"Nah," he said, shaking his head. "I wasn't wearing a white shirt that day."

Suddenly two more cold beers were set down in front of us, and I looked up at Alicia, who craned her neck to the left of me and said, "Mundo buy." The beers were starting to pile up in front of me faster than I could drink them.

We both looked over at Mundo, nodded our thanks, and raised our beers to him in a toast. Edmundo was a gardener, or as they are called in California, a landscape artist, who had a number of clients in the affluent nearby areas of Bel-Air, Brentwood, and Pacific Palisades.

I quickly downed the beer I was drinking, only to see that I still had three full ones in front of me. I had to start getting serious about my beer drinking or my macho reputation would take a deep loss.

"You're falling behind," George said, but he didn't really have to remind me. I was feeling thirsty and suddenly very hungry as I watched our steaks sizzling on the grill.

Pancho had finished peeling two large potatoes and was cutting them into thick slices to throw into the deep fryer. I polished off the beer I was drinking and started in on the next one. I was beginning to get a warm and pleasant buzz.

The food arrived, and I was pleased to see that Pancho had thoughtfully included a small dish of his fabulous Chili Verde pork stew along with it. At Pancho's, you can have your cake and eat it too. He also put a small dish of pickled whole jalapenos and a little platter of fresh yellow chilis—the kind we called yellow hots—between us, just in case we wanted to kick the heat up a notch or two.

George doused his steak with Pancho's tongue-blistering hot sauce made of crushed dried red chili pequin steeped in water and seasoned with a little crushed oregano and garlic powder.

I did the same, but not quite as liberally. The addition of the hot sauce is what made Pancho's steaks truly unique, but most people could only tolerate a small amount of it.

I watched George as he cut a healthy slice of the hot sauce-slathered steak, wrapped it in a corn tortilla, and proceeded to polish it off, chasing each bite with a jalapeno and a yellow hot. Remember I said that George has a mouth that must be made of asbestos? Well, I'm also relatively certain that he must have a cast-iron stomach as well.

"How's your other investigation going?" he asked in between bites. I noticed that his eyes had begun to water a little, and he was taking big gulps of the cold beer.

"It's progressing," I answered between my own bites. "And that reminds me. The girl in the picture, I think her name is Angie."

George thought for a minute. "Angie," he finally said before taking another bite of food and thinking some more while he was chewing. He screwed up his face in intense concentration, and some juice from the steak dribbled down the side of his mouth. "Angie," he repeated after he had swallowed that bite and wiped his mouth with the back of his hand. He was trying hard, but it just wasn't coming.

"That name kind of rings a bell, but I still can't place her." He shrugged his shoulders and said, "Don't worry, it'll eventually come to me," and we both continued on with our meals.

With a deep feeling of satisfaction and pride, I finished my last bottle of beer as I took the last bite of dinner, only to watch helplessly as Pancho immediately set two more beers in front of us. "On the house," he said.

In return, and in keeping with the spirit of the place, both George and I bought the entire bar another round. I now had three beers sitting in front of me again, and I was certain that I would not be able to finish all of them. Why did a dinner at Pancho's inevitably always turn into a beer-drinking marathon?

"So what are you going to do tomorrow besides go looking for Frankie?" George asked. His eyes had begun to glaze over, and he was beginning to show the effects of all the beer he had consumed.

"I've got a funeral to attend in the morning at the National Cemetery over in West LA. Liam Sullivan, a Vietnam buddy. What are you going to do?"

"Go to work, of course." He had finished one of the three new beers that had been set in front of him and had already started in on the second.

"Christ, George, tomorrow's Sunday. And it's Christmas Eve."

"Doesn't mean that crime's going to stop and celebrate the holiday, now, does it?" George pulled a wooden toothpick out of his pocket and began picking his teeth.

"Guess you're right about that," I conceded.

He was quiet for awhile, and then he admitted, "We're pretty pathetic, you know. Two guys who have no idea at all how to spend Christmas."

"Yeah," was all I could think of to say to that, because, truth be told, I was forced to agree with him.

We drank our beers in silence for awhile. Maybe we'd run out of things to say to each other. There are two things that we would no longer discuss—religion and politics. We don't discuss religion because neither of us is particularly interested in that particular subject.

Even when we were kids, we referred to organized religion as organized superstition, and since we both subscribed to the same basic theory, there was little for us to talk about there.

When it comes to politics, George is a diehard conservative, and that makes him a Republican, and I'm more or less a liberal, and this means, I suppose, that I'm a Democrat even though I really don't think of myself as belonging to any particular political party. And of course, as the old saying goes, never the twain shall meet.

So rather than waste our time by becoming belligerent in defending our respective views and ending up in a pointless argument in which nothing is ever resolved, that subject is no longer even discussed. If anything, our motto with regard to these two things was simply 'Live and let live.' Everyone had a right to their own respective beliefs and opinions.

George finally broke the silence with a loud burp before he turned to me and said, "I think you've reached your limit."

"I think you're right," I said as I looked at the half-full beer in my hand. It was starting to become a chore for me to polish it off, and somehow he had sensed that. George reached over and helped himself to my last two beers. He handed one over to Mundo, and he drank the other. I finished my beer and sighed.

George looked over at me and asked, "You good to drive?"

"I think so," I answered.

"I can give you a ride."

"No, I'm cool."

"Are you sure?"

"I'm sure."

"I can't help you if you get busted for DUI."

"I'll be very careful," I said as I got up and staggered toward the door.

Outside, the cool night air was refreshing, and I began to feel invigorated. It was late, and the streets were almost deserted, but I still drove slowly and cautiously. I had the feeling that tonight I was finally going to get a good night's uninterrupted sleep.

Chapter Twenty-One

Sunday, December 24, 1972
The dream had come again in the night, and I woke up with a start in the pitch-black darkness of three in the morning, shivering and bathed in a cold sweat and with a sick feeling in my stomach and a splitting headache from all the drinking I had done the night before. I had not expected the dream because it had been over a year since it last visited me. I guess somehow I had hoped that it had been buried, never to surface again. But it had come once more, and it was still the same terrifying nightmare—the very one that had haunted me in my sleep for years.

In my dream, I was back in Vietnam once again. My throat and lungs were burning with the thick smell of cordite that hung in the air, and my ears were deafened by booming barrages of artillery and the constant chatter of machinegun fire. I had snuck up behind a Viet Cong machinegun nest and had my rifle pointed at the lone machine gunner.

But I couldn't pull the trigger. What the fuck's the matter with me, I'm thinking. That guy is mercilessly killing our own men, and here you can't bring yourself to pull the goddamn trigger.

The machine gunner must have sensed my presence because he wheels around and points a semi-automatic pistol straight at me. But it isn't a he; it's a girl, and she can't be more than sixteen years old.

The expression of surprise on her face is the same as the one on mine, but she doesn't hesitate to pull the trigger on her pistol, just as I no longer hesitate to pull the trigger on my rifle. I see her face explode in a mass of blood, brains, and bone just before I myself am plunged into the dark black void of eternal nothingness, from which I know I will never return.

Nuala was at the funeral dressed in black and sitting beneath the shaded canopy beside her parents, who had come up from San Diego, where they now live. The sun was out and shining down on the large National Military Cemetery off Sepulveda Boulevard in Westwood on Sunday, the day before Christmas. Here in this huge garden of stone lie buried veterans from as far back as the Civil War. Perhaps a day will come when I will be buried here as well.

Staff Sergeant Liam Sullivan was buried on this day with full military honors, and I couldn't hold back the tears in my eyes when the flag that had covered his casket was snapped off by the three-man guard unit before being folded into a perfect triangle and presented by the Corporal of the Guard to Liam's grieving mother.

Afterwards, I stood in line with the others to offer my condolences, and when I reached Nuala, she smiled, gripped my hand, and said, "Thanks for coming, John," before I hugged her and kissed her on the cheek.

She held onto my hand for a moment and told me that the family and friends were getting together at her aunt's house in Sherman Oaks, but I told her that I had a lot of work to do. She nodded understandingly, and we parted. I knew that later she would want to go and stand beside the grave of her husband, Denny Doyle, who was buried here in the same cemetery.

Sunset Boulevard was the long but scenic route to Chinatown. It was a beautiful day to enjoy the comfortable warmth of the California sun and the sights and smells of the road that wound through the tree-shaded curves of Westwood before straightening out in Beverly Hills.

I stopped at the Tower Records on the Strip and bought the Pink Floyd album that I had listened to at Kathy's. As I got back into my car, it occurred to me that my stereo system had been totaled in the explosion and I would have to buy another. That was one more thing to add to the list of things to do, I thought as I tried to ignore a nagging hangover.

The traffic began to get thicker as I drove through Hollywood. You could also feel the temperature change. The Westside was always a few degrees cooler. I took off my coat and put it on the seat beside me.

Holiday decorations were up over the street, and frantic people were impatiently making their way to wherever it was that they were going on this last shopping day before Christmas.

On a normal Sunday, it would have taken about half an hour to make the drive down Sunset Boulevard to Chinatown. I could tell that this Sunday it was going to take considerably longer.

The freeway was apparently not an option. As I approached the Hollywood Freeway overpass, I saw that the lane leading to the on ramp was backed up well over two blocks, and traffic down there was not moving in either direction. A couple cars had even pulled over to the shoulder with smoking radiators. It was not a good sign. At least Sunset Boulevard was not at a standstill, but time-wise, I realized that I was going to be cutting it real close.

Past Western Avenue I began to notice that the Thais had begun to carve out a little district of their own with colorful restaurants and grocery stores that sat alongside the Armenian and Arab restaurants and grocery stores that had settled there not so very long before them.

Further on, past Alvarado Street, the Mexicans and Central Americans seemed to have laid undisputed claim to the area. As I approached the downtown area, a few Chinese restaurants and businesses began to appear, signaling that I was nearing Old Chinatown.

It was five minutes before one when I walked into the Sun Kwong Restaurant. It was even busier than it had been when I was there the last time. The place was packed, and people were sitting and standing around waiting for tables. A quick look around the place informed me that Frankie was not there.

Amid the noise and confusion of the place, I tried to grab the attention of one of the harried waiters, but he simply ignored me. I looked around for someone I could ask about Frankie, but the cashier was busy cashing out a long line of customers, and I seriously doubted that she could speak English anyway.

I was about to leave when the front door opened, and Frankie's young Chinese friend locked eyes with me. He made a gesture with his head that told me to follow him. He didn't say a thing as we walked up College Street, crossed Broadway, and headed north.

Two blocks later, my armpits were dripping wet from the muggy temperature as we arrived in front of Alan Lum's New Grand East Restaurant, and he held the door open for me to enter.

Inside, the air conditioning was on full blast, and it was a pleasant change from the afternoon heat outside. Frankie was sitting at the far end of the bar talking to two tough-looking, well-tanned Chinese men wearing brightly colored Hawaiian shirts. When Frankie saw me walking toward him, he held up his hand as an indication for me to stop, so I took the hint, stopped and waited.

He continued talking to the two men in a lowered voice for a minute or so before both of them nodded and turned to leave. As they passed by on the way to the door, they regarded me with cold looks and obvious suspicion. I definitely didn't want to run into those guys in a dark alley. Frankie finally waved me over to him, indicating one of the barstools that had just been vacated.

As I sat down beside him, I could see that he wasn't smiling. You might even think that he was sort of unhappy to see me. He took a sip of his Pernod on the rocks before he turned toward me. "This is an unwanted surprise, Mr. Wadd. To what do I owe the unexpected honor of your unexpected visit?"

"I'm worried about Suzy. I haven't been able to get hold of her. Do you know where she is?"

Frankie took another sip of his drink, before he answered me. "I think that she's out of town on business. I really don't keep track of her comings and goings, you know."

"Yeah, she mentioned that she had some kind of business deal in the works."

"So there you have it." He turned away from me and finished his drink and the bartender immediately brought him another. He put a cigarette between his lips, and the bartender reached over and lit it for him.

I could tell that he felt that our conversation was over, so I decided to skip the preliminaries and get right to the point. "I meant to ask you the last time we talked—what exactly was Suzy's relationship with Sheila Ross?"

Frankie took a deep sip of his fresh drink and followed this with a long drag from his Lucky Strike. His face would not betray what he was thinking about. Finally, he said, "You'd have to ask Suzy about that."

"I really wish I could. I just can't reach her, and she hasn't returned any of my calls."

Just for a very brief moment, a puzzled look came across Frankie's face before it reverted to its normal expressionless mask. "I wish I could help you," he said, "but I don't really know the answer to that question. I've told you all I could tell you. If you must have answers, like I said before—look closer to home."

With that, he finished his drink and snuffed out his cigarette in the ashtray in front of him. "Have whatever you want; they'll put it on my tab." I considered the invitation and decided that since I was still pretty hung over from all the exertions of the night before, a little hair of the dog could certainly do no harm.

Frankie nodded to the bartender before he got up, and as he passed behind me on his way to the door, he whispered, "Watch your back, Mr. Wadd. At all times, make sure to watch your back." I watched him walk out the door and felt an involuntary shiver come over me. The frigid air conditioning was beginning to feel chilly now, and I began to wish that I hadn't left my coat in the car.

The bartender came over, and without hesitation, I ordered bourbon on the rocks for myself. He looked at my haggard expression and nodded knowingly, and I watched him pick up a bottle of Jack Daniels and, without using a shot glass, pour me a generous double.

When he put the drink in front of me, I reached into my pocket, pulled out a five-spot and placed it on the bar. He lifted up his hand to show me that it was not necessary, but I left it there anyway. I couldn't help but think that somehow that bartender looked familiar. Late sixties, long, sad-looking face with a pencil-thin mustache. I'd seen that face before. I just couldn't remember where.

The bourbon burned nicely going down, and I could feel the pleasant warmth engulfing me. I took another sip, feeling the glow grow inside even more as I thought about what Frankie had said. And then I wondered about what he had not said. I was beginning to feel that I had made a wasted trip.

It was the day before Christmas, and here I was, still chasing shadows. What the hell did he mean by looking closer to home for the answers to my questions? And what did he mean by warning me to watch my back—as if I wasn't watching it already?

Before I realized it, I had finished my drink, and the bartender silently came over unasked and poured me another. I wondered if he was going to light my cigarette too, so I pulled the pack from my pocket and put one between my lips. He reached over and tossed me a book of matches. So much for that thought. I looked carefully at his face again, still trying to place him. He had a very distinctive face.

As I began to light my cigarette, it suddenly came to me where I had seen the bartender before. "Have Gun Will Travel," I blurted out before I could even think to stop myself. The cigarette had dropped out of my mouth and fallen onto the bar next to my drink. I picked it up and put it back into my mouth.

He looked up from the glass he was drying and smiled. "That was a long time ago," he said as he went back to drying the glass. "I'm surprised that you even remember."

"I must have seen you in about a hundred movies or TV episodes over the years. You've been in movies just about forever." He simply nodded. But it was true. During and after World War II, he had played Jap villains or Chinese patriots in dozens of war movies I had watched at the old Aero Theatre in Santa Monica when I was a kid. And he was a familiar face from small parts in episodes of various television shows as well.

"Well, I'll be darned," was all I could think to say. I fumbled with the book of matches and lit my cigarette. "What's your name?" I asked him as I blew a long trail of smoke across the bar.

"Beal," was all he answered as he picked up another glass and began drying it.

"I'm Johnny," I offered, feeling friendly and extending my hand. He smiled, put down the glass, and came over and shook it. I noticed that we were all alone in the frigid room. "Looks like business is sort of slow," I said in a lame but earnest attempt at making conversation.

"It'll pick up with the dinner crowd. That's when the boss shows up."

Although I'd never met Alan Lum, I'd heard a lot about him. He used to own a restaurant on Alameda Street called Lum's, where all the Los Angeles city cops used to hang out. Apparently, he was a real character who not only enjoyed drinking along with his guests but also loved to entertain them with his bawdy wit and uniquely clownish personality.

As I contemplated these thoughts, Beal asked, "You want another drink?"

I downed what was left in my glass. I was beginning to feel good. "Why not," I replied, pushing the glass toward him. He took my glass, put it into the sink, and brought me a fresh one. While he poured my drink, he said, "You seem like a nice guy. What are you doing hanging around with Frankie?"

"He's the friend of a friend," I answered. "You know Suzy Huang?" He nodded, so I continued. "Have you seen her lately?"

He shook his head. "She doesn't come here often. She has her own place, you know. Big restaurant called the Golden Lotus in Monterey Park."

The city of Monterey Park is in the western part of the San Gabriel Valley, not far from downtown Los Angeles. It has a large Asian population, mostly Chinese, who began settling there in ever-increasing numbers around the time when the new immigrants from Southeast Asia began moving into the Los Angeles Chinatown.

More recently, big-money people from Taiwan and Hong Kong began opening upscale businesses and restaurants there. Suzy Huang's Golden Lotus Restaurant was one of these. It was an imposing structure that occupied a good fourth of a city block.

I was greeted by an elaborately ornate doorway that was framed by twin vermilion pillars encircled by artfully carved twin golden dragons. At the top of the doorway, the long flames shooting out from the dragons' mouths met at a point just below the stunning wooden carving of a golden lotus. It was a suitable entrance for the unexpected opulence that awaited me inside.

The entryway inside the Golden Lotus Restaurant was flanked by two large fish tanks that were well stocked with live seafood, unconcernedly swimming around while waiting to be chosen to become a delectably steamed, fried, or sautéed menu item. A host station constructed of polished dark wood stood in the center of the wide doorway leading to the dining room.

No one stood at the host station, but I could hear voices streaming from the direction of the dining room. A quick look at my watch told me that it was a little after three, the quiet in between time that separated lunch and dinner.

I walked up to the host station and peered into the vast, high-ceilinged main dining room. It was a fancy affair that appeared to lead off into another large dining area as well as a whole series of exclusive glassed-off private banquet rooms. The interior décor was in keeping with the ornate entryway—large carved dragon columns reaching heavenward to the ceiling and dark polished wood dining tables covered with red tablecloths.

The restaurant employees were grouped together around a large, circular banquet table in front of the swinging doors leading to the kitchen. They had apparently just sat down to have their lunch. Seeing me standing there, a thin, attractive Chinese girl dressed in a tight-fitting but demure black and white uniform got up and quickly walked over to me.

She reached over and retrieved a large, faux-leather-bound menu from behind the station. "Table for one?" she asked politely and with a pleasant smile.

"Actually, I'd like to talk to the manager," I replied. "It's sort of important."

She hesitated for a moment before looking over at the table she had left and made a slight motion with her head. A middle-aged man dressed in a suit got up and came over. He had a serious but expressionless face, and he looked me over quickly and said, "Yes, can I help you?" He spoke English with a thick accent.

I told him my name, pulled out my business card, and then explained why I was there. He carefully considered what I had said before replying, "Boss has gone away on business. She be back maybe Monday, maybe Tuesday, for sure. You come back then."

"When was the last time that you saw her?"

He thought for a moment before answering, "Friday. She pick up the money for deposit."

"Was it daytime or nighttime?"

"Daytime," he replied, "after lunchtime."

I couldn't think of anything else to ask him. I looked over at the dozen or so restaurant employees eagerly filling their chopsticks with what appeared to be over a dozen or so heaping plates of various exotic Chinese dishes placed on the revolving center of the table, and I suddenly realized how hungry I was.

The three drinks I'd had earlier had awakened a long-dormant appetite, and my stomach suddenly responded with a loud growl. The manager, who was standing right beside me, couldn't help hearing it. He smiled and said, "You a friend of the boss, right?"

"A very good friend," I replied hopefully.

"Have you eaten?"

I shrugged my shoulders and said sadly, "I have not."

"Then come," he invited, leading me over to the table. Along the way, he picked up a plate and pair of chopsticks from the place setting at one of the empty tables and placed them on the table at the empty place next to him.

The restaurant employees didn't stop eating but greeted me with either a nod or a smile as I sat down next to the manager, who spooned some white rice into a bowl and handed it to me.

"Go ahead," he said, indicating all the food on the table with a sweep of his hand. "Eat."

I didn't need a second invitation, so I picked up my chopsticks and fervently hoped that I wouldn't embarrass myself while using them. I couldn't help but marvel at the sheer variety of the delicacies set out for their regular lunch. I've heard it said that the employees of Chinese restaurants were fed very well, and here was proof of it. To say that I was dazzled by the array of dishes set out before me is an understatement. The subtle aromas of the various foods assailed my nostrils and made my mouth water.

Seeing me hesitate, the manager reached over and skillfully deboned the large, whole steamed Red Snapper fish that was the centerpiece of this spectacular feast, extracting a juicy fillet of the delicate white meat topped with shredded ginger and green onion and put it on my plate. I was thankful that he didn't serve me the head, which I knew was usually reserved for honored guests.

I aimed my chopsticks toward their intended target and gingerly placed a morsel of the fish in my mouth. It was delicious. I ravenously attacked the rest of the succulent fillet, eating it with the steamed white rice. The rest of the table nodded their approval, and following their lead, I reached over with my chopsticks and helped myself to the other dishes on the table.

There were scallops sautéed with snow peas and water chestnuts, oysters with ginger and scallions, Chinese broccoli with cured Chinese bacon, golden-skinned deep-fried chicken sprinkled with a spicy pepper and salt mixture, bean cake cooked with roasted pork, squid with pickled mustard greens, oyster sauce beef, sweet and sour pork, Singapore-style rice noodles with shrimp, clams in black bean sauce, spare ribs with bitter melon—everything was delicious, even the thin, white, crunchy slices of boiled beef tripe that had been drizzled with a potent and flavorful hot chili-pepper oil.

I noticed that conversation in English at the table was kept to a bare minimum and occurred only in an occasional courteous phrase directed toward me. Otherwise, the informality at the table was boisterous and infectious, as people kidded around with and talked to each other in Chinese.

Two of the workers at the table were Mexican—probably kitchen help—but I was surprised to find that they not only handled the chopsticks like experts but also joined the conversation speaking in Chinese.

Seeing the expression on my face, the cute, tiny, peroxide-blonde Chinese girl sitting next to me said, "Miguel and Carlos, we teach Chinese; they teach us Spanish." As if to prove her point, she said something to them in almost fluent Spanish. It must have been funny because they both turned to look at me and laughed.

For the rest of the meal, that same cute girl next to me, who told me that her name was Ling, kept filling my plate with choice morsels of the various dishes, laughing childishly as she explained to me in detail what each of them was. She looked as if she couldn't have been more than twelve or thirteen, although in reality, she was probably older than that.

It goes against Chinese tradition to allow anyone to go away hungry, so I left the restaurant filled with food, almost to the bursting point, but happy and strangely content. The food had relegated my hangover to be a quickly forgotten thing of the past.

The trip had not been a total loss, but I realized that I probably wouldn't be able to see Suzy until Monday or Tuesday. And Monday was only tomorrow, but there were so many things that I had to ask her, so many things that I had to get clear on. Beyond that, I had the uneasy realization that I truly did miss her and could hardly wait to see her again.

To me, love has always only been just another word. Sure there's attraction. Sometimes there's very strong attraction, but usually it's just a physical attraction, which—don't get me wrong—can be really intense and good while it lasts. But somehow, my feelings for Suzy seemed to go beyond that. I wasn't going to use the L-word to describe them, but it would be close. Too damn close, I was thinking. And then I thought, what the hell am I thinking? I wouldn't know the L-word if it came up to me and bit me on the ass. With that in mind, I decided to give George Lee a call to find out how his day was going.

Chapter Twenty-Two

After locating the nearest phone booth, I dialed George Lee's direct line on the off chance that he would still be behind his desk at the Santa Monica Police Station. He was, and he told me to get my sorry ass over there right away. He hung up before I could ask him why, so I anxiously pondered this puzzle as my car sped along at ten miles per hour over the speed limit on the Santa Monica Freeway on the way to take my sorry ass to its ultimate destination.

It was just like him to be all mysterious like that. Hopefully he'd made some kind of progress in the case because, at this point, we could sure use a major breakthrough. Aside from scoring some free drinks at one place and a gut full of fine Chinese food at another, I certainly hadn't accomplished much of anything to speak of.

George was seated behind his desk, twiddling his thumbs, when I arrived at the station. When he saw me, he immediately got up, walked over, grabbed his coat, and said, "Come on," leading the way as I followed him out of the station and over to his car.

"What's going on?" I asked after climbing into the passenger seat and closing the door.

He looked over at me and smiled. "That woman you're looking for, the woman in the picture—Angie. I remember who she is now."

On our way to a coffee shop on Lincoln Boulevard called the Penguin, he told me the story of a nine-year-old kid named Walter Harvey who had fallen in with a bad crowd of older boys who had taken him for a ride one day in a stolen car.

George had been on patrol at that time, and when he pulled the car over, the rest of the gang abandoned the car and split the scene, deserting the kid in the back seat and leaving him to take the heat.

The kid was intimidated and scared, but he refused to cry, and he refused to rat out his so-called friends. Since he was so young, George felt kind of sorry for him, and he ended up taking him to his mother, Angie, who worked as a waitress at the coffee shop we were now on our way to.

Angie, who had to struggle to support herself and her son as a single mom, had assured George that her son would never associate with those other kids again. That was six years ago. I knew that George was a sucker for single moms because he had been raised by one. His father had died when he was just a baby.

"You think that she still works there?"

"Probably," he replied, knowing that I hadn't expected him to call and check, therefore giving her a warning.

It was the beginning of the dinner rush, and the Penguin was starting to get crowded. We both looked around but could not see anyone who looked like Angie. George went up to the hostess and talked to her while I walked around the corner to check out another area of the restaurant. She wasn't there either. When I made my way back to the front of the place, George was waiting for me.

"Her shift ended at four," he informed me. "She's scheduled to work the same shift tomorrow, Christmas day, in case we can't find her—but I have her address if she's still living at the same place."

Angela Harvey's address led us to a shabby old two-story apartment building on the west side of 15th Street, about a half-block south of Colorado Avenue. As we pulled up and parked on the street in front of it, we saw her and her fifteen-year-old son struggling up the stairs with a large, bushy, six-foot Christmas tree.

We caught up with them just as they had reached the top and had stopped for a moment to rest and catch their breath. They had both carried the tree on foot from the commercial Christmas tree lot, some six blocks away.

We helped them get the cumbersome tree through the front door and into their small apartment. "Every year I always wait until Christmas Eve to get our tree," she said, "because by then they're almost ready to give them away. This year, that's exactly what they did." She seemed to be very proud of the fact that she had managed to score a free Christmas tree. When you don't have a lot, every little bit that you can save is important.

The tree took up a good deal of the tiny front room, filling it with a pleasant piney scent. There was a tattered sofa bed, which I later learned was where Angie slept, a small kitchenette with an old avocado green fridge, one of those cheap dining tables with those easily bent brown tubular metal legs, and two matching cheap chairs with even thinner and more easily bent brown tubular metal legs.

The sole wall decoration was a dinged-up framed printed reproduction of a colorful Rousseau painting that looked as if it had probably been bought at a yard sale. A small hallway led off to the bathroom, a storage closet, and the single small bedroom that was occupied by her son. In spite of the obvious poverty of their circumstances, everything appeared to be orderly, neat, and clean.

Angela looked a little older than her thirty-odd years, but she was obviously the same woman as the one in the picture, and she was still a very attractive woman. Apparently she recognized George because after she and her son had secured the tree into the already-waiting Christmas tree stand, she turned to him and said, "I'm sure you're not here about Walter because I know he's been a good boy." She looked at her son as if to confirm this, and he didn't look away. "He doesn't have anything to do with gangs or anything like that, and he's making straight A's in school. In three more years, he'll be going to college."

"Mom," Walter said, drawing out the word in exasperation as if he didn't seem convinced.

"You will," she stated with fierce determination. "One way or another, you're going to college—you'll see." Then she turned to George. "Now what is it that you wanted to see me about, officer?"

"Well, it wasn't me that wanted to see you," George replied, nodding his head in my direction.

I took the cue, introduced myself, and explained, with as much detail as I thought prudent, the reason why I was looking for her. She listened impassively but with interest, occasionally looking at her son, who seemed to be listening with interest as well.

I showed her the photograph that Sol's wife had given to me. She looked at it quickly and handed it back. She was wearing a delicate and very pleasant plumeria-scented perfume that somehow reminded me of Hawaii.

"So you think that I'm the woman in that picture."

"Yes, I do."

Walter had moved over beside me and was looking at the photograph that I still held in my hand. I handed it over to him, and he looked at it very carefully, and a sudden look of realization dawned on his face.

"I remember when that was taken!" he exclaimed. He looked up at his mother. "I always wondered what happened to Uncle Solly."

Angela sighed. "He wasn't your uncle, Walter. He was your father."

For a moment, Walter looked at her, puzzled. "So the man you were talking about," he said, looking at me, "the one that died in the car accident…"

His mother had already said it, so I simply confirmed the fact. "Yes, Sol Steinman was your father."

A stunned look came across his face, and he sat down on the sofa, still holding the picture. His mother went over and sat next to him. "I was going to wait until you were older to tell you, but I suppose it's high time you found out about it now anyway," Angela began as she recounted the story of a shy young eighteen-year-old waitress from a broken home who became infatuated with one of her customers, a man who was both kind and considerate to her and who cared for her quite unlike the father who abandoned her as a baby—the father she had never known.

Every day he would come for lunch, where she worked at the small lunch counter on the top floor of Grand Central Market, and every day when her shift as a waitress ended, she would come to his shop to visit him, and after awhile, he gave her a part-time job sorting and cataloging his vast stock of postage stamps.

This provided her with a little extra income, and while doing this, she learned about all the various countries of the world, past and present. He also told her fascinating stories about these foreign places and inspired her to read books to increase her knowledge.

Gradually, they became attracted to each other. They made a strange couple—a middle-aged Jewish man and an attractive young black girl—but they ignored the stares of the anonymous people, and they didn't care about such things anyway, because when they were together, they were happy.

The two of them visited museums, art galleries, and places like Griffith Park and the La Brea Tar Pits together, and she learned about history, anthropology, and many other things she had never known or even thought of before. She had never even finished high school because she had to join the work force to support herself after the untimely death by overdose of her heroin-addicted mother when she was in the tenth grade.

After that, she had lived for awhile with her grandmother, who had been both too poor and too preoccupied to take care of her. Aside from that, her grandmother had been a fanatically religious woman, and they had just never gotten along.

"Solly told me that he was married, but I still fell in love with him, and I think that in a way he probably really loved me too. But I never had any illusions about the two of us. He also told me early on that he could never leave his wife because he knew that she needed him and would be totally lost without him." She wiped a tear that had begun to stream down from her eye. "He said that he loved his wife but was not in love with her. He told me that he was in love with me."

George had lit a cigarette and, unable to find an ashtray, had been looking around desperately for something to do about his ashes until finally deciding to go over and dump them into the kitchen sink.

"Sorry," Angela said, noticing his situation. "Neither of us are smokers. You can use one of those small coffee cup saucers," she said, pointing to the plastic dish drainer. Then she continued on with her story.

"Eventually, I thought it would be better for everyone all around if we just stopped seeing each other. Sol was unhappy about my decision at first, but since I was adamant about it and it was what I truly wanted, he respected my wishes and stopped coming around. I think he thought that I had found someone else and that ending relationship would be best for everyone concerned. I didn't let him think otherwise. And then I discovered that I was pregnant." She paused for a moment as we let this all sink in.

"I decided not to tell Sol about it, and when the pregnancy became too obvious, I left my waitress job at Grand Central Market. I'd managed to save a little money—not a whole lot, but enough to get by on. I had always wanted to live near the beach, so I moved to Santa Monica. Everything seemed so clean and fresh here, so unlike downtown, and I thought it would be a good place for my baby to grow up, you know. But I also had to get another job, and that proved to be a really tough thing to do. I didn't finish high school, but I'm not a totally ignorant person. Still, that doesn't really help in getting a good job."

She looked over at Walter. "And that's why you're going to college, young man." Walter just looked down and studied the tips of his shoes.

Angela continued, "I got a job as a house cleaner for awhile, and after the baby came, I started working as a waitress at the coffee shop. I was lucky. There's a Mexican family that lives in one of the larger apartments downstairs, and the wife and I became really good friends. They have five kids of their own, and she stays home to take care of them, so she also let Walter stay with them when he was little while I was at work. Everything managed to work itself out. So now you know the story of my life."

"Not quite all of it," I said.

She looked at me questioningly for a moment. And then it dawned on her. "Oh, you mean the photograph?"

"Yeah, what's the story behind that?"

"Walter and I had decided to go to the beach one Saturday, and we were waiting at the bus stop when Sol happened to drive by and recognize me. I hadn't been in contact with him for years, and seeing him once again was a total surprise, not to mention quite a shock since Walter was with me.

"He gave us a ride to the beach, and he kept looking at Walter, and I knew that he knew, but when he asked, I lied to him and told him no, Walter wasn't his son. And then I lied to him again and told him that I was already married. But I don't think he believed me because he still persisted, and he even told me, at one point, that he would leave his wife if there was the possibility that we could get back together again."

Her eyes had begun to tear up again, but I had nothing to hand her. I looked over at George and saw that he had sensed the same thing, and he handed her a surprisingly clean white handkerchief. She thanked him, dabbed the tears from her eyes, and continued on with the story. "Of course I couldn't let that happen, so I told Sol that I was very happy the way things were and that I didn't want or need him to be a part of my life.

"Finally, he said all right; if that's what I truly want, he'll respect my wishes, but he wanted to have my address so that he could at least do something to help take care of us. I flatly refused and told him that the past is the past and there's nothing anybody can do to change that, but Walter and I were nobody's burden. I can take care of me and my own."

She stopped for a moment, collecting her thoughts, before continuing. "Then he asked for me to at least give him that one day. That's the day we went to the pier, and the picture was taken. The day that we spent there was the only time that we were all together, ever. That was around ten years ago, because Walter was five at the time. We haven't been in touch since then because I tried to make sure that he wouldn't be able to find us."

After she said this, there was a long silence in the room. Finally, she broke it by saying, "I don't think I should meet with this woman."

George finally said something. "Come on, Angie, meet with her. Who knows, this may be your lucky day."

"I don't believe in luck, Mr. Lee. You see, I do remember your name. I only believe in hard work." She thought for a moment before adding, "No, sorry, but I'm not going to meet with her."

"I think that she would like very much to meet with you," I said.

"Please, if I can do anything, I can certainly spare this woman from suffering any more heartache than she may have already suffered. I can't see what it would accomplish if she were to see me and be reminded of her husband's infidelity."

Of course, I was disappointed, but I could also see her side of it. Still, I had to warn her, "I'm going to have to tell her that I've found you. That's what she hired me for."

"You go and do what you have to do. We all have to make a living."

"Would you give me your phone number in case I have to contact you?"

She laughed. "I have no phone. If I need to call someone, there's the pay telephone outside the Mexican grocery store on the corner."

I looked at George, and he looked at me. At this point, there seemed to be nothing else for us to do than to take our leave. We thanked Angela and Walter for their time, and Angela thanked us for helping them with the Christmas tree.

Walter saw us at the door, and as we left, I noticed that Angela had gone over to a large box of Christmas tree decorations that lay waiting on the floor. She had retrieved and was delicately holding a fragile, brightly painted angel—the kind of decoration that went onto the top of the Christmas tree.

Darkness had fallen and the night air had grown cold as George and I left Angela Harvey's apartment. As George and I drove back to the station, I mused, "You ever think that there's something more meaningful that could be going on in our lives other than what's happening to us here from day to day?"

George gave me a look like I had just brought that one out from left field, and perhaps I had. Then, after a little thought, he replied, "John, I'm just far too busy to go around looking for meaning in my life. Isn't that something we used to do in college?"

"Yeah, I suppose so."

After George dropped me off at my car, I decided that it was still not too late to pay Sophie Steinman a visit. I was certain that she would want to know about the turn of events, regardless of the time. Fortunately for Sophie, I had been able to find the solution to her case, with George Lee's invaluable help, for only a minimum of billable hours. All in all, this was very good for her and very bad for me, but then again, perhaps best for everyone all around. With that out of the way, I'd now be able to devote full time toward getting to the bottom of the murders of Sheila and Billie Rae.

When I parked in front of her house, I saw that the lights in her living room were still on, so I took that as a good sign. I rang the doorbell and a minute later the porch light went on, and Sophie invited me in as if she had already been expecting me.

"Now what do you have to report to me, Mr. Wadd?" she asked after I had taken a seat on the sofa.

"I've located them, Mrs. Steinman," I began. "They're living in Santa Monica. The woman's name is Angela Harvey, and her son's name is Walter."

Her eyes lit up at the news, and when she spoke, it was with barely controllable excitement. "Please tell me about them, Mr. Wadd! Please tell me everything!"

I told her the story pretty much the way Angela had told us the story, with the exception of leaving out a few details here and there that I didn't consider relevant and omitting things that had been said, which might only end up hurting her feelings. Sophie listened to my partially edited version intently, dry-eyed, and with an avid interest that seemed to go beyond the ordinary.

When I finished, she said, "So she doesn't want to meet with me."

It was a statement and not a question, but I still decided to respond. "She thought it might not be a good idea to do so, if only to spare your feelings."

Sophie thought about this for awhile, and then she looked up at me as if suddenly she had made a decision. "I want you to do one more thing for me, Mr. Wadd."

"And what would that be?"

"I would like for you to take me to see her and the boy at her place tomorrow."

I'll admit that I was taken aback by the request, but I'll also admit that somehow I was expecting it. Angela Harvey probably would not be very happy about a forthcoming meeting with Sophie, but after all, it was the latter who was signing my paycheck. I thought briefly about what to say, and unable to come up with anything else, I told her, "It'll have to be later in the afternoon. She'll be at work until four o'clock."

Sophie smiled. "Later in the afternoon will be fine. We can see her after she gets off from work. What time will you pick me up here?"

"If I'm here at four o'clock, that should give us plenty of time to get there and enough time for her to get home," I replied.

"Then it's settled," she said. "I'll expect you here at four o'clock tomorrow."

Chapter Twenty-Three

Monday, December 25, 1972 – Christmas Day
The first mistake I made upon waking up was thinking that this Christmas day would just be a day like any other. I'd finally managed to have a good night's sleep—no terrifying war dreams and no guilty conscience-waking episodes. I actually awoke bright and early, ready to face the day head-on. I was also ravenously hungry, having skipped dinner last night after having enjoyed that monster of a late lunch.

I thought about cooking up some breakfast before deciding that I was feeling too lazy. Besides, today I felt like I wanted some pancakes and maple syrup along with my ham and eggs, and pancakes just happen to be something that have always eluded my very limited cooking repertoire.

I wondered if any place was open today, and then I remembered that Angela was going to be working the early-day shift at the Penguin Coffee Shop. That decided it for me. Before I left the house, I dialed Suzy's number, and there was still no answer. But it was pretty early in the day, and it was also possible that she wouldn't be coming back until tomorrow.

Outside, it was sunny with just a slight hint of winter in the air. It was also relatively quiet. People tended to sleep in when a holiday came around. Later, most of the single people would be heading for the homes of friends or relatives.

Most families would be ensconced in their warm and comfortable living rooms while the ham, turkey, or Christmas goose roasted in the oven and the children sitting next to a tree overloaded with ornaments, unwrapping their presents and squealing in delight as something long-wanted or unexpected came into view.

But this was not the case for my neighbor, Chuck Carter. He

was busy loading his surfboard onto the top of his station wagon as a prelude to going out and catching some Christmas Day waves. When he saw me, he motioned for me to come on over.

"Merry Christmas," I said with as much holiday spirit as I could muster.

"The same to you," he said as we shook hands. Then he got right down to business. "I've been keeping a lookout for strangers hanging around since you asked me to, and I've noticed someone. There's been this Asian guy who's been parking his car a couple of blocks away and sitting in it. I think he was watching your place. I saw him there the day before yesterday, and he was there again yesterday."

"What kind of car does he have?"

"Dark-colored Mercury Cougar, looked like last year's model. It was almost black, but I think it's actually more like a real dark green color or something."

"Is the Asian guy, like, in his middle to late thirties, round-faced?"

"No, more like in his twenties. Thin face, and he has sort of longish hair. That's all I can tell you. I don't see him there today," he said, looking down the block.

"Thanks, man. I really appreciate it."

"Not a problem."

As my car made its way to the coffee shop, I glanced around to see if I'd picked up any tails, but it appeared that no one was interested in following me today. I contemplated what Chuck had told me. At first, I had thought the Asian guy who he had seen keeping an eye on my house was that slimy BNDD agent, Conrad Yama, but from the description Chuck had given me, he sounded more like Frankie's young friend.

When I arrived at the Penguin, I was surprised to see that there were more people there for breakfast than I had expected there would be. I actually had to wait about ten minutes before I was finally seated by a harried hostess at the counter.

The harried hostess had put me next to a big, somewhat overweight young Jewish guy wearing a yarmulke who was in the process of intently working his way through three side orders of bacon. I watched him as he delicately picked up the thick slices with his fingers and blissfully savored each and every one of them. It was proof positive that the forbidden fruit would always be the sweetest.

Angela was one of the waitresses who were taking care of the tables and booths in the dining room, and I caught a couple of glimpses of her when she walked up to the cook's window to put in the new orders and pick up the plates full of food for her earlier orders.

She did her job with the efficiency and consummate ease born from years of hard experience. I think she saw me looking at her, but if she did, she didn't acknowledge me.

When I finished my breakfast, I sensed the pleasant scent of her plumeria perfume and felt the sudden warmth of her presence behind me. I turned to face Angela, and she smiled and said, "You got nothing better to do on Christmas Day?"

"I suppose I don't," I replied. And then, thinking that it was only fair to warn her about Sophie Steinman's impending visit that evening, I warned her. Of course, this somewhat unwelcome news quickly wiped away her pleasant smile.

She stood there, thinking about what I'd told her for a moment and looking none too happy about it. Then she shrugged her shoulders, turned around, and continued on with her work.

After breakfast, I drove over to the Santa Monica Police Station and found George exactly where I expected him to be, sitting behind his desk in deep concentration, typing up some kind of report. He was struggling through it, typing with one finger, which was the same way that I typed. Neither of us had ever seen the inside of a typing class.

"I figured I'd find you here," I said as he looked up briefly to see who had come in.

"Where else would I be," he answered as he looked back down at the typewriter and continued on with his one-fingered pecking on the keys. Occasionally, he would fuck up and let out a curse as he got out the small bottle of white-out and brushed it onto the misspelled word on the paper to make his correction.

I took the seat across from him and waited patiently for him to finish. Finally, he finished the report, drew the paper out of the typewriter with a relieved sigh and a flourish, and turned to look over at me. "So, what's up?" he asked.

I told him about the Asian guy that my neighbor Chuck Carter had seen who had been watching my house. I also told him that the description seemed to match that of Frankie's young friend and that

I was wondering why in the world he might be watching me.

"You don't know that guy's name?"

"No. It never came up."

George scratched his head and absent-mindedly examined what had come off beneath his fingernails. "Fucking Frankie Funai," he muttered. "So you think he may have someone keeping an eye on you?"

"I don't know why he would. I didn't see anyone following me around today."

"Those damn Chinese in Chinatown are always so fucking mysterious. Who knows what in the hell they're ever thinking or why they do whatever they do?"

Then something suddenly occurred to me. "Come to think of it, that car that was following me the other night was a dark-colored car. It could be the same guy."

"It could be," he agreed. "So have you managed to get hold of Suzy?"

With everything that happened yesterday evening, it occurred to me that I hadn't had a chance to fill George in on what had happened with my visits to Chinatown and Monterey Park, so I proceeded to do so.

He had me repeat the descriptions of all of the dishes I had eaten at lunch in great detail, and then he wrote down the name of Suzy's restaurant and filed it away in his overstuffed wallet so he wouldn't forget. I could tell he was going to ask me to take him there one of these days. Hell, I owed him one anyway because he'd found Angela for me.

While I was thinking of it, I tried calling Suzy again but still received no answer. George had left the room to deliver the report he had typed up, and when he returned, I asked, "Did they come up with anything on that partial print from the cigarette lighter?"

"Nothing so far," he replied glumly. "They're still working on it."

"It's been, what, five days?"

"These things take time, John. And what with the holidays and all, you know." He seemed as frustrated as I was about the lack of progress on the case.

"Yeah, I understand."

It had been a week since the discovery of Sheila's body, and probably a good two weeks since she had been killed. The untimely intervention of the holidays and my inability to locate Suzy seemed to have brought things to a virtual standstill. The case was growing cold fast.

A ringing phone broke the strained silence. George answered it. "Lee here—yeah…" There was a long pause, then, "Are you sure it's him?" Another pause followed by, "Ok, I'm on my way." He hung up the phone. "Sorry, John, I'd like to hang around and shoot the shit with you, but it looks like I got myself a Christmas homicide." George stood up and headed over to the coat rack.

"So, who's the victim?"

"Suspected dope dealer we've been keeping our eye on. His name's Bartholomew Cronin. He owns a small art gallery and framing shop over on Wilshire Boulevard, near Bundy. We think he's been supplying the Brentwood crowd," he informed me as he put on his coat. "Not a great loss to the world, in any case."

"Sounds interesting," I said hopefully.

"You want to come with?" he asked as he headed toward the door. "I don't have a partner today. Maybe we could do lunch afterward."

"I got nothing else to do right now," I replied, following after him.

We turned off the Pacific Coast Highway at Entrada Road and pulled up in front of a small house that was already blocked off by two cop cars. It was not a very large house, but it obviously was a somewhat expensive one owing to the area and its relatively close proximity to the beach. There was a black, late-model BMW sedan and a red Alfa Romeo sports car parked in the driveway.

The crime scene investigators had put their yellow crime scene tape up across the porch, and two of them were standing in the yard along with a uniformed officer, questioning an attractive raven-haired young lady and taking notes. As we crossed under the tape, George asked the young cop posted at the entrance, "Has the Medical Examiner shown up here yet?"

"Not yet," was the reply.

George looked cautiously inside from the front door, then looked at me and said, "We'd better wait," and we backed off and lit up cigarettes. As he exhaled a long stream of smoke, he said, "When we go inside, be sure to walk behind me and be sure that you don't touch anything." I nodded in agreement, even though it had been an unnecessary warning.

Then he turned to the young cop standing by the door and pointed to the pretty young woman with the long legs and the shapely ass that was being questioned: "Who's she?"

"The victim's sister," he replied. "She came here to check on him when he didn't answer the phone. They were supposed to go to their parents' place for lunch today."

"So she's the one who found the body."

He nodded. "She has a key to the place, but when she got here, she said the house was unlocked. When she saw him dead in there on the floor, she phoned the station and reported it."

"And you're the officer who responded to the call?"

"Yeah, me and my partner over there with her," he said, indicating the uniformed female officer that was questioning the sister.

Five minutes later, the medical examiner showed up, went into the house and officially declared the dead man dead. We then proceeded to cover our shoes with the paper booties the crime scene people gave us before we carefully made our way inside the house in step behind the two crime scene investigators and the photographer.

The small living room was in an alarmingly untidy mess, and since no one had bothered to open the windows, the stale air inside stank of decomp and death. The mutilated corpse was lying sprawled in a large dark pool of dried blood that had now turned from red to a more brownish color, somewhat like the color of rust, irreparably staining what appeared to be either a real or imitation white bearskin rug that lay on the highly polished pale hardwood living room floor.

"Guess there's no doubt as to how he died," the photographer said as he rapidly snapped the photographs to document the crime scene.

We moved in to get a closer look. The victim had once been a tall, tanned, good-looking young man in his very late twenties or early to mid-thirties. He'd obviously spent a lot of time at the beach and living the good life. His curly, black hair sported a stylish and expensive cut, and somehow this reminded me that my own hair was starting to get a little longish.

What was now left of Bartholomew Cronin was dressed in faded stone-washed designer jeans and a formerly expensive but now totally worthless blood-soaked multi-colored vintage Hawaiian silk aloha shirt.

His wide-open, deep blue eyes were now clouded over by death, but they still reflected the unspeakable pain and pure horror of his final moments. Most disconcerting of all was his face, which had been contorted into a frightening death mask of sheer terror.

But the thing that had immediately grabbed my attention was the chilling sight that had become only too familiar lately. His throat had been slit from ear to ear, almost severing his head, which leaned off to the right at a precariously grotesque angle from the rest of his body, and he had apparently bled out on the rug on the floor where he had fallen.

"Remind you of anything?" George asked as he carefully bent over the body. I almost replied that it was obvious that it did, but then I realized what he meant when he traced a path through the air with his index finger to indicate the man's arm and hands.

There were the unmistakable torture marks of fresh cigarette burns on both of his arms, and it appeared as if all of the fingers on his right hand had been deliberately broken.

"Yeah," I said as I turned away and looked around the room. I could see now that the place was a mess because it had been thoroughly ransacked, as if whoever had been there was desperately looking for something. My thought processes were spinning at a hundred miles a minute, trying to digest everything that had been happening.

It seemed as if the similarity of this murder might well be a coincidence, but then again, I really didn't put much stock in coincidences. In my mind, there was little doubt that this death was somehow linked to the murders of Sheila and Billie Rae. And the recurring thread that seemed to weave through all three cases was drugs.

George gave the living room a quick once-over, and I followed behind him as he walked down the small hallway and took a brief look at the small bedroom, which also appeared to have been hastily searched. There were a few expensive designer-label suits and a lot of high-end casual clothes in the closet. Strangely, these appeared to have been untouched.

We looked into the adjacent bathroom. After carefully examining the sink in the bathroom, George pointed out the faint traces of blood around the drain. Then we moved back into the living room, and he gave a quick motion with his head to indicate that we should move back outside and leave the scene to the investigators so they could get on with their job.

Outside, I took a deep, welcome breath of fresh air, and I puzzled over what could possibly be the connection between this homicide victim and the similarly brutal murders of Sheila and Billie Rae as we made our way over to where the Medical Examiner was standing. He looked up from the notes he was writing as we approached.

"So, what do you think?" George asked him.

"From the state of the remains, looks like he's been dead for at least a day or so," the Medical Examiner replied. "Cause of death appears to be pretty obvious; we'll know more when we do the autopsy. Did you notice his arms and hands?"

George nodded. "Just like our corpse that washed in from the sea and a homicide that West Hollywood has. I think we may be dealing with a serial killer here."

"It would appear so," the Medical Examiner agreed.

George looked over and saw that the interview with the sister appeared to be on its way to being concluded. He gestured for me to follow, and then he walked over and introduced himself before offering his condolences.

Up close, the sister was even more attractive than she had appeared from the distance. Her shoulder-length raven hair framed an almost classically sculpted angular face, like the face of a high-fashion model.

In startling contrast to her dark hair, her eyes, like her brother's, were a deep blue. It seemed strange and somewhat macabre at the same time to realize how much she actually looked like her dead brother. She introduced herself as Heather Cronin.

"You bear a striking resemblance to your brother," George said to start the conversation and gauge her reaction to the situation.

"We're twins," she stated matter-of-factly. She seemed to be remarkably composed in spite of the horror of what she had recently stumbled upon and seen.

"I know it must have been a terrible shock for you—finding him like that."

She nodded. "I just don't think it's all really sunk in yet. I'm afraid when it does…" She left the sentence unfinished.

"Did your brother have any enemies that you know of?"

"No—I already told that to the other officer who asked me the same question."

"I'm sorry—maybe there was a jealous girlfriend he recently broke up with, someone like that?"

She hesitated for a moment and then said, "Bart is—was, gay," and then she added, "So am I, if you must know. But to answer your question, as far as I'm aware, he hasn't been in a relationship for some time now—ever since he got back from Vietnam."

I could read George's thought processes kicking into gear when she said that. "He's a veteran, then?"

"He was in the Army Quartermaster Corps over there."

George nodded his head understandingly. "Do you happen to have a key to your brother's gallery?" George asked.

"Yes, I do," she replied. George told her that it would help the investigation if he could take a quick look around the shop, and she agreed to meet us there.

As we got into his car, George said with evident relief, "That's a big break. I can just imagine how tough it would have been to find a judge and get a search warrant today."

"Do you feel that there's something really strange about all this?" I asked.

"I think there's something extremely strange about all this," he replied, "but I just can't quite figure out what it is yet."

The wide boulevard was unusually quiet and uncongested for a weekday or even a holiday weekday as we headed down Wilshire toward the Bartholomew Cronin Art Gallery. Since it was a major holiday, there was plenty of street parking in front of the shop.

Heather was already there waiting for us when we pulled up and parked behind her red Alfa-Romeo sports car. As she got out of the car, I couldn't help but admire her thin but shapely figure, made even more alluring by the revealing, form-fitting dress that she was wearing. It was an expensive dress. This woman obviously had style.

"You think there's a chance that she swings both ways?" I asked George.

"I don't think she would have specifically mentioned that she was gay if she did," he replied perceptively.

That was really not the answer I wanted to hear. "Yeah, too bad," I said, and I truly meant it.

We followed her to the front door of the gallery, which she unlocked with one of the many keys on her large brass key ring. As we started to walk in, she suddenly stopped in mid-stride, and the keychain fell from her hand and landed on the tiled floor with a loud clunk. We peered in and saw what had startled her.

Inside, the show room of the gallery was in total disarray, just like the living room at the murder scene we had just left had been. The place looked like a tornado had passed through without stopping. It had been torn apart and, more than likely, thoroughly searched.

"Who would do something like this?" she asked in total bewilderment.

We entered the gallery, and George carefully examined the alarm wires at the top of the front door. "The burglar alarm has been disabled," he concluded, "by someone who really knew what they were doing."

We looked around the place and then began sifting through the scattered mass of debris, not really knowing at this point what we actually expected to find. Heather came across a small cash box that had been broken open and apparently looted. "Do you think it could have been a robbery?" Heather asked.

"I don't know," George answered honestly, although I could tell that he had his suspicions. We were both looking at the walls, at the large, framed vintage European advertising posters, and the mostly modern oil paintings done in the abstract expressionistic style somewhat reminiscent of Arshile Gorky. Most of these appeared to have been left pretty much untouched.

The paintings that lined the showroom walls were colorful but relatively uninteresting imitations. It was more than obvious that the gallery was simply a front for his more lucrative drug business.

A few of the framed posters that had been stacked on the floor in the space below the paintings had been turned around and examined, and the glass that had covered them had been brutally shattered.

"Is that his office over there?" George asked as he pointed toward the back room.

Heather nodded. "It's his stock room and workshop—where he does the framing, and he also has his desk in there too."

The workshop and stock room in the back were a small space, about a quarter of the depth of the main gallery. It had been tossed as well. All sorts of things had been carelessly strewn around the room in an apparently violent fashion. Whoever it was that had been looking around had not been happy with what had been found or not found.

Against the wall next to the door, there was an old Queen-Anne-style wooden desk, and papers from the desk and an opened filing cabinet nearby littered the floor, along with the contents of a smashed and broken bottle of India ink, which had dried and left an unsightly stain on the expensive-looking Oriental carpet.

Somebody was definitely looking for something, and from the appearance of things, they obviously were looking real hard. The question is, did they find it?

We looked around and slowly picked through the chaotic mess, finding nothing of particular interest ourselves, until suddenly George gave off a grunt of satisfaction as he retrieved a thick leather-bound combination day-planner address book that had somehow fallen behind the opened top drawer of the desk, where it had remained hidden.

"I'm going to have to take this," he told Heather, who simply nodded. "And I'm also going to have the crime scene investigators go over this place," he added as he placed the book in an oversized plastic evidence baggie he had retrieved from his coat pocket.

"May I call my parents?" Heather asked, pointing to the phone on the desk. "I'm going to have to tell them—about Bart, I mean."

"Of course." George looked over at me, and we both quietly walked out of the office to give her some privacy.

When we were out of earshot, I asked George, "So what do you think that we really have going here—some kind of psychopath serial killer or three cold and deliberate professional hits?

He considered the question for a long moment before he replied, "Perhaps a little of both, John, perhaps a little of both."

It was obvious that George had his work cut out of him for the rest of the day. As for me, well, I had to face up to my obligations too. Neither of us was particularly hungry after everything we had just been through, so we decided to skip lunch and get together later this evening to compare notes and have some drinks and dinner at Dear John's in Culver City, a place that we both knew would be open for business tonight. Then George dropped me off at my car so I could keep my four o'clock appointment with Sophie Steinman.

Chapter Twenty-Four

At four o'clock sharp, I picked up Sophie Steinman, who was already waiting on the porch outside the front door of her house. She was nicely dressed in the most fashionable dress I had ever seen her wearing, and she had even taken the pains to conservatively apply a little make-up. Along with her purse, she carried a small gift bag that contained two tiny, colorfully wrapped Christmas presents.

"Right on time, Mr. Wadd," she said as I opened the door for her like a gentleman, and she carefully eased her way into my little sports car. I have no idea how it was that she knew I was right on time because I could plainly see that she didn't even wear a watch. She had apparently been waiting outside in the afternoon heat for awhile because a thin line of sweat had begun to form on her upper lip.

Fifteen minutes later, we were walking up the stairs to Angela Harvey's apartment. A long minute or so after I had knocked on the door, it was cautiously opened by a suspicious and hesitant Walter Harvey.

"My mother's not home," he quickly said. I introduced Sophie to him and informed him that I had already told his mother that we were coming. He reluctantly let us in and stood looking at us awkwardly, uncertain about what he should do next.

Sophie looked curiously around the apartment before walking over and taking a seat at the small kitchen table. She picked up the well-worn library book that lay open on the table and examined it. "All Quiet on the Western Front by Erich Maria Remarque," she read off the title while looking at Walter. "Are you reading this?"

"For my English class," he replied.

"Did you know that your grandfather fought in that war, World

War I? He was in the German army, just like the soldiers in this book." Walter looked at her in wide-eyed amazement. He obviously had not known.

"His name was Solomon Steinman, just like your father's," she went on.

"But wasn't he…" Walter stammered.

"Yes, he was Jewish, but at that time it didn't matter, you see. In fact, over a hundred thousand Jews served in the German army during that war because they simply felt it was their duty to do so. They fought for a country that would later turn around and betray them."

At that moment, there was the sound of a key unlocking the front door, and Angela entered wearing her waitress uniform, looking tired and careworn, and carrying a bag full of groceries. Seeing me and then Sophie, she said, "Oh," and put the bag down on the floor before closing the door and walking over and putting her arms protectively around Walter.

There was a long, awkward moment before Sophie stood up and walked over to Angela, extending her hand as she said, "I am the woman that Sol loved—you are the woman that Sol was in love with."

I was stunned. I had not mentioned that part of Angela's story to Sophie because I had thought that it might hurt her.

"So you did know about me," Angela said.

"One day many years ago, Sol said that to me because he thought that I should know this and be aware of the fact that he might possibly have a son. It was the one and only time he ever mentioned it, but I have the feeling that in spite of everything, he never stopped searching for you, if only to find out how you and your son were getting along. I wasn't actually certain about anything until I found the photograph, but over the years, I have thought about you often, you and your son. I know that you really didn't want to see me, but I wanted so very much to meet you both."

There was another long, uncomfortable pause before she continued, "I know your name is Angela, and you must call me Sophie." And then they suddenly embraced like long-lost sisters, and I saw tears in both their eyes and even felt them beginning to well up in mine. I turned away, slightly embarrassed by this and, at the same time, not quite knowing what to do about it. I took some solace in the fact that Walter seemed to be just as uncomfortable as I was.

"You've met Walter?" Angela asked.

"We were talking before you came. I was telling him about his grandfather," she said, looking at Walter. "I think he's a fine young man."

"He is. He's in the 9th grade, a freshman in high school now, you know."

Sophie turned to Walter. "So you'll be going to college soon."

"Yes, he will," Angela answered for him. Walter shifted around uneasily. "He'll be going to UCLA."

"Tell me, Angela," Sophie began, somewhat hesitantly. "Do you like living here—in this small apartment?"

"It's what I can afford," Angela answered defensively, "and it's close to where I work, so it works for me."

"I only ask," Sophie continued, "because I have an apartment building in Mar Vista that has a beautiful large ground-floor two bedroom, and it's more than twice the size of this place."

Angela shook her head. "I couldn't afford that. There's no way I could afford something like that."

"I don't want to rent it to you, Angela. I want to give it to you."

"You want to give me an apartment?"

"No, dear, not just the apartment," she said. "I want you to have the whole building. Of course you'll have to manage and take care of it, you know. It would be a full-time job, and I suppose Walter would have to help too."

"You can't be serious about this."

"I'm very serious, Angela. That's one of the main reasons why I came to see you."

"No, no." She shook her head. "You just can't give away something like that."

"Of course I can. We all deserve to have something. I have more than what I'll ever need. You deserve to have something too." Angela still looked unconvinced as she stood there, shaking her head in silence.

"Look, Angela," Sophie continued. "I'm far too old to handle the responsibility of that apartment building now. All of the tenants have been living there for years, and they're very dependable and pay on time. Don't get me wrong. Taking care of the place will be a lot of work. In fact, it's a big headache you'll be relieving me of, but of course all the rent you collect would be yours."

Angela thought about this for a minute before she said, "Thank you for your kindness, but I really couldn't accept it, Sophie."

"Yes, you will, and I insist that you do," she said, taking the younger woman's hand and holding it in her own. "Angela, since Sol died, I really don't have anyone anymore. I have no family here, no one to share my life with."

"We'll be your family, Sophie—Walter and I, so you don't have anything to worry about. I mean it."

"So it's settled then. I already have made an appointment with our attorney to take care of everything the day after tomorrow. As far as I'm concerned, that apartment building and the property that goes with it belongs to you and your son. You're going to find that you both will really need it someday. And it's certainly a lot closer to UCLA than this place is."

There was a pregnant silence. Then Angela broke it as she softly said, "I don't know what to say."

"There's no need to say anything. I only wish that I could do more for you and Walter. Now let's put away those groceries that you brought home. I'm sure that you have some perishables in that bag."

Sophie helped Angela put away the groceries, and then she presented them both with the Christmas presents that she'd brought. Walter unwrapped his present first to find an old original watch box that contained a vintage eighteen-carat gold TAG Heuer chronograph. "It belonged to your father," Sophie told him. "Although he seldom wore it, he treasured it, and it still works beautifully. I'm sure that he would want you to have it."

The wrapping paper came off of Angela's present to reveal a small red jeweler's ring box that contained a diamond wedding ring. "And I want you to have this," Sophie continued. "I wore it for many, many years, but now it no longer fits my finger." Angela started to protest, but Sophie took the ring and slipped it onto her finger before she could stop her. "See, it fits you perfectly, dear."

It was already dark when I pulled into the driveway of Sophie's little tract home. I opened the passenger door for her and helped her out of the car. Like a gentleman, I walked her to the front door, waited until she put the key in, and was starting to leave when she said, "Please come in for a minute, Mr. Wadd. I'd like to settle my account with you."

"I'll send you a bill, Sophie."

"No, I insist. I hate having loose ends, so please indulge me and let me pay you right now."

I shrugged my shoulders and followed her into the house. She went over to the large business-size checkbook that already lay open, waiting on the dining room table. "How much shall I make the check out for?"

"Well," I began as I gathered my thoughts. "Fortunately, I didn't have to spend all that much time tracking them down. And as I told you before, I was working on another case at the same time. And come to think of it, the expenses don't really amount to much of anything."

She regarded me sternly, "How much, Mr. Wadd?"

"Two hundred will cover it," I replied.

She began writing in her checkbook, and when she finished, she carefully tore out the check, saying, as she handed it to me, "I want to thank you sincerely, Mr. Wadd, for making an old woman very happy."

"It's been my pleasure, Mrs. Steinman," I said, taking a quick look at the check as if folded it, but I stopped in mid-fold. She had made the check out for two thousand dollars. "I think you've made a mistake here, Sophie," I said, handing the check back to her.

"Put it in your pocket, Johnny. I haven't made a mistake."

"But two thousand is way too much for…"

"For bringing a little happiness into the world on Christmas day?" she interrupted. "That's just what you did, you know. I may be an old lady, but I'm not a fool. I know that Angela and Walter weren't so easy to…track down, as you say." She shook her head. "We didn't even know their names to start out with. You really did do a remarkable job, you know."

"Still…"

"Look, we both know that you can use the money, and believe me, I can afford it. So stop being so stubborn and go before I become very upset with you."

And with that, Sophie Steinman showed me to the door.

When I walked into the near total darkness of Dear John's on Culver Boulevard and my eyes could begin to make out things once again, I saw that George was sitting in one of the plush black leather booths instead of his usual accustomed place at the bar—which was probably just as well because the bar was standing room only tonight and filled with a bunch of boisterous regulars.

I nodded at John, who was behind the bar tonight, and made my way over to join George. He was nursing the last two swallows of what looked like a tall gin and tonic.

"I figured it would be better to sit and talk here than at the bar," George explained needlessly.

"At least we'll be able to hear ourselves think here," I added. The bar regulars at Dear John's could be a little noisy at times because this dark 1950's-era cocktail lounge and steak house served generous drinks as well as great food. If you were to walk into the place for the first time, you'd probably get the impression that it was some kind of Mafia hangout. Which it may well have been at one time.

"Place looks the same as it always did," I observed, looking nostalgically around the room. George and I hadn't been here together in years. In fact, he's the one who first brought me here on the occasion of celebrating my twenty-first birthday. It was the first time we were able to get legally drunk together. He's about three months older than me, so he'd already been there once before. And as I recall, we got really wasted on gin and tonics that night. So George is somewhat of a sentimental fool after all.

The waitress came over, and I told her, "I'll have what he's having," and George ordered another. After she brought our drinks, I told her to bring us a couple of menus, and she nodded. When she left, I raised my glass in a toast and told George, "Tonight dinner and drinks are on me."

We both took a deep gulp of the refreshing liquid, and the waitress efficiently returned with a couple of menus, and George, being the clever detective that he is—homicide or otherwise—said, "So I guess you got paid a little more than you expected."

"She gave me a generous Christmas bonus."

"Good for you."

"Well, I couldn't have done it without you."

"You could have—it would just have taken you longer."

"I'll drink to that." I raised my glass.

We both drained our gin and tonics and held up our glasses to signal the waitress for another round. Dear old John, being the perceptive bartender that he is, had already made us two more. He knew just exactly how to make them for us—very light on the tonic while still serving a tall cocktail glass that was filled to the top with a good grade of gin. "Couple more of these," I admitted, "and I'll be three sheets to the wind."

"Ah, you're a lightweight, Wadd."

I shrugged my shoulders. "Maybe I am," I agreed, but we both knew different, and the gin was beginning to make me feel much more relaxed after an unusually tense day.

"So everything worked out well at the family reunion?"

"Everything worked out well. And how was the rest of your day?"

He took a long swallow of the fresh drink that the waitress had delivered. "It really sort of sucked. You don't know how hard it is to come up with anything even remotely helpful to solving a homicide on Christmas day."

"I can imagine."

"I went through Cronin's day planner. He had lots of meetings with lots of people, but he wrote down very few names. There were lots of initials and stuff like that—like some kind of code. His address book wasn't much more help, although there may be some of his drug customers in there."

"I sort of figured he wouldn't leave anything real incriminating at his place of business to be readily found."

"Or if he did, somebody else already beat us to it. But I did manage to come up with something." He took a cigarette out of his pocket and lit it before thinking to offer me one. "You were over there in Vietnam, John," he continued, and I could tell he was leading up to something.

"That I was," I regretfully admitted as I lit the cigarette he had given me. I knew that George had been released from service because his father had been killed during World War II and he had sole surviving son status, which had exempted him. I remember thinking how lucky he was back then. But then, I suppose, losing a father doesn't really make you very lucky at all.

But George thought he had been lucky, and I guess that's really what counts. Once, a long time ago, he had told me, "Hell, if I end up getting sent over there—the way I look, I'd probably end up getting shot at from both sides."

George took another healthy swig of his drink and looked over at me. His eyes were fixed on mine, and they were dead serious. "Tan

Son Nhut—does that name mean anything to you?"

I hadn't heard or even thought about those words for a long time, but of course if you'd been over there, and unfortunately I had, they were words that you were not likely to easily forget.

"It's a place," I told him. "It's the place where the army mortuary was—where they'd gather the remains of the dead servicemen and prepare them to be shipped back to the States."

George processed this information for a moment before asking the next question. "And the Quartermaster Corps was in charge of that?"

"They were."

George nodded, and then he said, "Tan Son Nhut was where Bartholomew Cronin was stationed in Vietnam."

Before I could even react to this new bit of news, we were suddenly interrupted by the reappearance of the waitress, who casually asked, "Are you guys going to be eating something?"

I'd almost forgotten that I hadn't eaten since breakfast. The drinks had awakened my appetite somewhat, and I began to realize that I was actually kind of hungry. "Yes, we are," I answered. I hadn't even bothered to look at the menu yet, so I asked, "What's the fish today?"

"Mahi Mahi, and it's fresh and delicious. I had it for dinner myself."

"Sounds good to me, and I'll have blue cheese dressing on the salad."

"You want rice pilaf or the baked potato with that?"

"I'll go with the rice pilaf, please. No, wait a minute—could I have fries instead?"

"I'll bring you both, honey."

She smiled and turned to George, who said, "Since he's buying, I'll have the prime rib medium rare and a baked potato with butter and sour cream and chives, thousand-island dressing on the salad. And you can also bring us a couple more drinks."

"Coming up," she chirped as she walked off to put in our orders with the bartender and the cook.

After she left, I picked up my drink and finished it to keep up with George and asked, "Where were we?"

"We were contemplating Bartholomew Cronin and Tan Son Nhut."

"Yeah," I said, and suddenly I was a lot less hungry as the unforgettable image of Cronin's blood-soaked body made an unwelcome flash through my mind. And I also remembered that I had once been to the grisly charnel house at Tan Son Nhut and had seen the rows upon rows of the dead servicemen lined up, some whole and some only in pieces, waiting to be matched up and assembled before being put into those gleaming white caskets to be sent back to the States.

That's why I had been sent there—to try and help identify the body pieces of one of my buddies. It had been one of the most horrifying and terrible experiences of my life—one that I only wished I would somehow be able to forget.

"Damn it!" George exclaimed. "I feel like this murder has supplied us with another piece of the puzzle, and a key piece at that, but I still can't figure out how it all fits together."

By the time I staggered through the new door of my house, I actually was three sheets to the wind and so enshrouded in my gin-based alcoholic fog that I was truly feeling no pain. We had downed many more than a couple more of those dangerously potent drinks. I only hoped that I would be able to make it as far as my bed. Somehow, and I really couldn't tell you how, I managed to do that.

As I lay there, waiting to be embraced by the welcoming arms of sleep, I tried to put all thoughts of corpses and mortuaries, death and dying, and the terrible things that human beings can do to each other out of my mind.

I gathered all my concentration and willed myself to think instead of Sophie, Angela, and Walter, trying to truly believe that there are some good things still happening in this fucked-up world. I'm not really sure, but I have the strange feeling that I finally dropped off to sleep with something resembling a smile on my face.

It had been a Christmas day, totally unlike any other.

Chapter Twenty-Five

Tuesday, December 26, 1972

The next morning, however, was another story altogether. Since the friendship with George had been rekindled, my being hung over was starting to become a regular and somewhat unwelcome condition. He was definitely a bad influence, and I resolved to watch myself much more carefully in the future. The key to good health is moderation, especially when it comes to booze, I thought as I carefully made myself a Bloody Mary.

As I sipped my breakfast, I told myself that today was Tuesday, and it was the day that Suzie was supposed to definitely be back. I dialed her number to hear the same old answering machine greeting. I'd stopped leaving her messages about a dozen calls ago.

My wristwatch told me it was eight o'clock—still early—so I decided to go over to the police station and see how George was putting together the puzzle of the new homicide case. It was obviously somehow linked to Sheila's death and Billie Rae's violent murder, and, like George, I had no doubt that it was the key to the whole situation. All we had to do now was to find the door that this key opened.

When I got to the Police Station, George wasn't at his desk, so I sat down next to it and calmly waited for him, resisting a strong impulse to nose around the papers and reports that lay there. I didn't have to wait long. George entered carrying a handful of thin thermal-fax paper, which he proceeded to fold and tear into individual pages after he sat himself down behind his desk.

"There's coffee in the squad room," George motioned with his head. "Bring me a cup too—black."

I found the coffee maker in the next room and was not surprised to find that it had probably not been cleaned in months, or more likely, even years. Being the fastidious person that I sometimes am, I carefully picked out two of the cleanest-looking of the chipped and stained coffee mugs beside it to pour the suspicious-looking black liquid sludge into. As I suspected, the coffee was thick and foul, but it was also strong and hot.

When I got back to his office, George was still reading over his report, so I handed him his cup, and as he took it, he nodded his head as a substitute for not saying, "Thanks."

I bravely took a small sip of the hot coffee and winced. I think I would have much rather swallowed gasoline instead. Still, it seemed to be doing the job of waking me up. To distract myself, I asked, "Anything new on the Cronin homicide?"

George nodded. "This just came in," he answered without looking up, shaking the thin fax pages. "He'd been dead for about a day when we got there, and they're now sure that all three of our victims were killed by the same guy."

"How did they manage to arrive at that conclusion?"

"Well, the broken fingers and cigarette burns were pretty obvious to us, but the coroner compared the depth and style of the cuts and concluded that the same person made them. We're obviously dealing with some kind of really over-the-top psychopath here. One of the people in the medical examiner's office is an expert on knives, and he thinks the killer used a SOG S-1, a knife that was commonly used by the MACV-SOG Special Forces units in Vietnam."

"You know what those initials stand for?" I couldn't resist asking.

"They stand for Military Assistance Command Vietnam – Studies and Observation Group. I'm not a total idiot, John. I've been known to do my homework now and again."

"So the cigarette lighter with the Special Forces insignia must belong to the killer," I said as I smelled the toxic fumes that were steaming up toward my nostrils from the coffee cup I held shakily in my hand.

"Sure looks like it. Now if we can only get a match on that partial print that was on it." He continued scanning through the fax pages. "The crime scene investigators found some footprints at the murder scene that matched some footprints also found at the art gallery, size ten shoes." He looked up at me. "There weren't any footprints at Billie Rae's. You know something? I think our killer is starting to get a little careless."

"Maybe time's running out and he's beginning to get a little desperate."

"Time's running out on what?" George asked as he put down the papers.

"Grace London said that Sheila and someone else—probably Suzy—were trying to set up some kind of sting operation to take down a big-time drug dealer."

"So far, that's only a supposition—we don't have any hard facts."

"But it all makes sense, George," I explained, still trying to put two and two together to come up with four. "You have Sheila buying the tape recorder from Kathy Heller, then Sheila turning up dead, and then her former roommate, Billie Rae, is killed in the same way."

"For all we know, Billie Rae could have been that other person who was in with Sheila on this harebrained scheme."

"I don't think so. I talked to Billie Rae, and she really didn't know anything about it. She was scared, but I'm pretty sure she was telling me the truth."

"What makes you so sure that Suzie's not the big drug dealer that they were going after?"

"All my instincts tell me that she's not."

"All your instincts may just be located in that big dick of yours."

George may have a point there, I thought. Maybe I was cutting Suzie too much slack. "So then where do you think that Bartholomew Cronin fits into all of this?"

"When we find that out, I think we'll have the answer to the whole thing."

"Well, I think you're right about that."

George mulled this mystery over while I struggled to finish my cup of coffee by holding my breath and swallowing it down quickly before the gag-reflex could kick in. I felt a sudden electrifying jolt in my brain as all that concentrated caffeine violently kicked into my system, disrupting my entire body organism in the process. There's no doubt about it. That stuff is really and truly dangerous.

My pulse was logging in at a thousand beats per second, and my heart was beating like a Tahitian drum. My eyes were wide as saucers, and I watched in wonder while George sat back and leisurely sipped at his own cup of coffee, as if he were slowly savoring each delightful mouthful.

I had started to feel a cold sweat, and it seemed as if my ears had begun to ring. I almost didn't realize that it was the phone I was hearing until George picked it up and the ringing abruptly stopped.

From the way his eyes lit up as he listened to the person on the other end, I could tell that what he was hearing was very important. And whoever it was that was talking to him talked to him for what seemed like a very long time. George appeared unusually anxious when he finally said, "All right, I'll come right on over," and then hung up the phone.

"Finally," I said, reading his expression, "a break in the case?"

"A big break," he confirmed. "You're coming with me. I've got to go downtown and talk with the Vice boys."

"What's up?"

"They got a match on the print on that cigarette lighter, but things appear to be a little more involved than we had expected. They can't discuss it over the phone, they said—something about some kind of ongoing investigation."

Two vice cops wearing almost but not quite matching suits and ties were waiting for us when we arrived at Parker Center, which is the downtown hub of the Los Angeles Police Department. It also houses one of the largest crime laboratories in the world—a crime lab that occupies an entire floor of the eight,story building.

One of the vice cops was somebody I already knew but wished I didn't. His name was Holtzer. He was the one who looked at George and asked him, "What the hell is he doing here?"

"He's helping out on this case. You have a problem with that?"

Holtzer looked at me suspiciously and grimaced like he did have a problem with that before he turned back to George and said, "Well, from what I understand, you don't really have any case. You're the guy from Santa Monica PD who found the piece of evidence for the West Hollywood boys, right?"

"Right," George sighed.

"Well, then it's their case, isn't it?"

"It links up directly with one of my homicide cases in Santa Monica," George continued, unfazed.

"Yeah, the dead floater with her throat cut. But it seems like you don't remember that you were taken off that case, am I right, pal?" Holtzer smiled.

"But I haven't been taken off this one," George smiled back. Being of Oriental ancestry, George didn't smile often, but when he did, he positively beamed. This time, he was beaming like the cat that ate the canary. With a flourish, he pulled the pages of a folded-up copy of a police report from inside of his coat pocket and handed it to Holtzer. "It also links up directly to a homicide case that I'm currently investigating—the murder of a Santa Monica art dealer named Bartholomew Cronin."

Holtzer's jaw dropped as he slowly examined the report he had just been handed. Then he handed the report to the other vice cop, who looked it over carefully. "This happened yesterday?" Holtzer asked.

"The body was discovered yesterday."

"We haven't heard anything about it."

"Well, you're hearing about it now. So let's get down to business. I've been given to understand that our fine crime lab on the fourth floor has made an ID of the partial print found on that cigarette lighter I turned in for the West Hollywood homicide?"

"They have," Holtzer said as he went over to his desk and picked up a report. "But you can't do anything about it."

"Who says I can't?"

The other vice cop, who had been silent all this time, finally spoke up. "The print belongs to someone that's currently being investigated by the FBI, the CIA, and the BNDD."

"It belongs to a drug dealer?"

"No, it belongs to an FBI agent," the other vice cop, who now appeared to be obviously the one in charge, continued.

George, who was still trying to take this all in, said, "Wait a minute—what are you saying here?"

"What I'm saying is they've been setting up a sting to catch this rogue agent who's been using his position and connections to smuggle heroin into the country from Southeast Asia. Our narcotics division has been cooperating with them every step of the way."

"And what's this crooked FBI agent's name?" George asked.

"I can't tell you that," the vice cop replied smugly.

I finally decided to break my silence to see if I could hit them with a bomb. "It's Mark Ulrich, isn't it?"

The vice cop looked over at me as if I'd just hit him with a major bomb blast. "Just who the hell are you?"

"My name is Johnny Wadd."

"He's not a cop," Holtzer added with a smirk. "He's a private dick."

The vice cop looked over at George. "You know he has no business being here, don't you?"

"I know," George said. "So answer his question."

The vice cop was not about to answer my question, so I did the only other thing I could do under the circumstances and continued dropping bombs, hoping that somehow they might hit a target. "And what can you tell me about his buddy, Conrad Yama?"

Holtzer and the other vice cop looked at each other, and their expressions clearly confirmed my suspicions. I'd managed to land bulls eyes on both targets.

The vice cop looked at me with deep suspicion before he asked, "How do you know so much about all this?"

"It's not hard to put two and two together," I replied. "Now I've got another question for you, and please think this one over carefully before you answer. Where does Suzy Huang fit into all this?"

After I dropped Suzy's name, both Holtzer and the other vice cop looked at each other again, and then the other vice cop got on the phone, and ten minutes later we were all sitting in a big, important-looking office on another floor of the building.

The important-looking man that came with the important-looking office stared at George and me from across his large mahogany desk. He was a big man physically as well, over six feet tall with silvery gray hair that sported a short military-style crew-cut. He was dressed in a very expensive, dark suit. He was the Chief.

"It seems like you two boys have stumbled into the middle of what we consider to be a very important investigation," the Chief began with a soft and quiet voice that was totally at odds with his gruff exterior. "In fact, the sting operation—and it is a large one with federal, state, and local co-departmental collaboration— set to go down tomorrow, so you see—we have ourselves somewhat of an awkward situation here. We've been coordinating this thing for a long time."

"But we now have evidence that Mark Ulrich committed three atrocious homicides," George protested.

"We only have circumstantial evidence, Mr. Lee. And in all likelihood he probably committed many more than those three. There's no doubt that we're dealing with a very disturbed person here. The FBI has been suspicious of him for some time now, especially after he fell under the radar of the BNDD, which is in the process of rooting out some of their own corrupt agents. It seems that he and the BNDD agent Conrad Yama have had their own thing going for quite some time now."

"What do you know about Conrad Yama?" George asked.

"He's another strange one. Actually, he used to be a Marine. He's got a violent temper, and he's been in trouble from time to time, but there's nothing much on his record other than a few reprimands."

"And Ulrich was a Green Beret?

"He was with the 5th Special Forces Group, and he saw a lot of action around the Cambodia border area. As you might know, it's pretty wild and wooly in that neck of the jungle, and we don't know what he was really into there, but whatever it was, I have a feeling that it wasn't very pleasant." The Chief had obviously done his homework.

"Are they aware that they're being investigated?" George continued.

"Both of the agencies have been very secretive about it. In fact, they were both assigned on a collaborative investigation that was set up just to see what they would do," the Chief replied.

"So they actually think that they themselves are the investigators—very clever," I added.

The Chief nodded and then turned to George and sighed. "I know that you want to close your cases and believe me, I really want you to, but let me tell you what's at stake here. We've known that heroin has been coming in from Southeast Asia for several years here on the West Coast, and now we've finally been able to link the traffic to Ulrich and Yama, but we've never been able to pinpoint just exactly how they were bringing it in."

"How did you link it with these two rogue agents?" I inquired.

The Chief finally turned his attention to me. "Mr. Wadd, you asked about Suzy Huang's involvement in all this. Well, she was our link. She has been with the operation from the very beginning."

"She's actually been working with you guys on all this?"

"Of course normally we wouldn't allow a civilian, but she's a friend of the Mayor, the DA, and even the Governor, for Christ's sake. And it's something she insisted on doing—I don't know why—I guess she has her reasons. Anyway, she allowed us the use of her companies as a front to set up the buy for the largest shipment to be brought into the country yet. And since she refused to deal with middlemen, she managed to lead us directly to Ulrich and Yama. Delivery of the shipment is scheduled for tomorrow."

"So she's one of the good guys."

"She's one of the good guys," he confirmed.

I was relieved now that Suzy was exonerated. I turned and flashed George a smile, which he pointedly ignored.

"So what do you want us to do?" George asked.

"I don't want you to do anything for at least twenty-four hours. I want you to give us enough time to complete the operation."

Something suddenly occurred to me, and I couldn't stop myself from blurting out, "I think I know how they're getting that stuff in the country."

All eyes suddenly turned on me.

Chapter Twenty-Six

Like I said, it's easy to put two and two together and come up with four—especially when you have the key piece to the puzzle. And in this case, the key piece to the puzzle was a corpse named Bartholomew Cronin.

After I explained my theory, which by now was backed by some irrefutably solid circumstantial evidence, we all proceeded to an even larger office on the same floor that was populated by three teams of people that seemed to be busily coordinating the operation that had been the subject of our previous discussion.

Introductions were made, my theory was discussed, and the FBI team went right to work tracking down any recent flights that had originated from the Da Nang Air Base in Vietnam. They hit pay dirt almost immediately. A flight carrying a cargo of caskets containing deceased servicemen that had originated from the Tan Son Nhut Mortuary had arrived three days ago.

Within thirty minutes, they learned that twelve of the caskets had been delivered to the Los Angeles National Cemetery in West LA, where they were awaiting burial; three went to the San Francisco area cemetery in San Bruno; and the rest had already been trans-shipped to Arlington National Cemetery.

By a fortunate coincidence, the Los Angeles office of the FBI is located in the Federal Building on Wilshire Boulevard in West LA, right across the street from the cemetery. Within the hour, the agents that were sent over to examine the caskets reported back that all twelve contained hidden compartments that had been used to smuggle the heroin. Of course, by now the bags of drugs were long gone, but the residue found in the compartments had confirmed my theory.

Nobody was questioning my presence there any longer. There was still a question that was bugging me, so I asked George, "Why do you think they killed Cronin?"

George shrugged his shoulders. "Maybe they found they didn't need him anymore. Maybe since this was such a big score, they got greedy."

I nodded. "Greed is probably as good a motive as any."

George looked at his watch. "It's going on eleven. Since we're already in the area, what say we pop on over to Chinatown for some lunch?"

"Sounds good to me," I answered. "Just let me make a quick call to try and retrieve my messages," I said as I picked up the phone at a nearby unoccupied desk.

I breathed a sigh of relief when my call went through successfully, and I was informed that I had two unheard messages. The first was from Wilma, thanking me for the lovely tea set and inviting me to stop by whenever I was in the area so she could put it to some good use. My heart skipped a beat when I heard the voice on the second message. It was Suzy.

"Hi Johnny," the message began. "It's Suzy, and I'm back in town now. I'll be finished with all this business I'm involved with by tomorrow afternoon, and perhaps we can get together tomorrow evening at my place for dinner. If you'd like to…"

There was the sudden sound of a distant crash, and Suzy's voice said, "What…" and then the sound of the phone being put down on the table. After a moment, Suzy's voice is heard shouting, "What are you doing here?" Then silence, followed by a click as the receiver is replaced on the cradle.

"George!" I shouted as I ran over to him, almost in a panic. "Something happened at Suzy's! We've got to get over there right away."

George gave me a puzzled look, but seeing the urgency of my expression didn't say a thing. We ignored the stares and surprised expressions as we ran through the building to get to George's car.

The lunch hour traffic on the Hollywood Freeway was infuriating, but it gave me a chance to tell George what I had heard Suzy say over the phone. George listened to what I said, then, after a moment of strained silence, got on his car radio and called for backup from the West Hollywood division.

We arrived at Suzy's apartment building just as two squad cars pulled up. The neighborhood seemed undisturbed and serene, except for the sound of the chainsaw trimming an overgrown tree across the street. I looked over and saw Chris' truck. I looked up and saw Chris perched precariously on a ladder beneath one of the branches. He waved at me before continuing on with his work.

One of the West Hollywood cops had gone over to the front door to find it locked. "Security building," he said. He joined George and me as we walked over toward the underground garage, where the gate lay wide open. "Why's the gate open?" the same cop asked.

When we reached the garage gate, we saw why. The lock had been blasted away by a single gunshot. We walked cautiously through the garage and took the elevator to the penthouse suite. The door to the penthouse had also been blasted open. Again, we entered cautiously, but it soon was obvious that there was no one in the apartment.

Inside, we found the living room to be only in slight disarray. The office, however, was another story. It looked like it had been hastily turned over and that there had perhaps been some kind of struggle. The wall safe was open and had been emptied, and there were a few bundles of documents with Chinese writing that lay dumped on the floor beneath it.

"What the hell happened here?" one of the cops asked, but no one answered him.

The silence in the room magnified the sudden sound of a loud click. "What was that?" the same cop asked in a more startled tone. George looked around, and his eyes rested on the cassette recorder lying beneath the desk on the carpeted floor. He picked it up, and we heard footsteps approaching, and two of the FBI agents and two of the BNDD agents that we had seen in the office at Parker Center walked in.

"How did you guys get here so quick?" George asked.

"Siren going full blast," one of them answered. "We left right after you did." He looked over at me. "The call that you made from the office and the call that you picked up from your answering machine was monitored and recorded, you know."

"Yeah," the other agent said. "You really have to be careful which phones you use around the FBI."

George had pulled the tape out of the portable recorder he had found beneath Suzy's desk. "Ninety-minute cassette," George said, examining the tape.

"Rewind it," I said with anticipation. "I think Suzy recorded what happened."

George put the tape back into the recorder and rewound it. He had to fast forward through a brief one-sided conversation in Mandarin Chinese, and then we heard Suzy's voice begin talking in English.

"There!" I exclaimed. Everyone gathered around and listened to the tinny voices coming out of the tiny speaker of the small machine.

SUZY: What are you doing here?

[There is a long silence followed by the click of the phone being hung up.]

SUZY: You can't just break into my apartment like this!

ULRICH: It seems like we already have.

SUZY: What is it that you want?

ULRICH: The deal's going to have to go down today.

SUZY: That's impossible. I won't have all the money together until tomorrow.

ULRICH: How much cash do you have here?

SUZY: *(After a pause)* Not much—about thirty-five, maybe fifty thousand.

ULRICH: Get it.

[There is some movement about the room.]

SUZY: Why does the deal have to happen today?

ULRICH: It just has to, that's all.

SUZY: Let me make some calls; I'll see…

ULRICH: *(Interrupting)* No, you're not making any calls. I don't trust you.

SUZY: Why not? We've always been aboveboard with each other.

ULRICH: Have we?

[Another long silence, followed by some shuffling of feet]

ULRICH: All right, there's fifty thousand here. Now Conrad here tells me that big restaurant of yours was real busy over the holiday weekend, right, Conrad?

YAMA: Yeah, there were at least five really large wedding parties.

ULRICH: And all those usually pay in cash, if I'm not mistaken. So you must have something like maybe a quarter of a million sitting there waiting for you to pick up, am I right?

SUZY: It's possible.

ULRICH: So it looks like we'll be able to conclude our transaction after all. What time does the restaurant open?

YAMA: At noon on weekdays.

ULRICH: So we have time to get there and take care of everything before you open.

[There are sounds of a struggle.]

SUZY: Let go of me!

[This is followed by sounds of things crashing around, feet shuffling, and other unidentifiable noises—then only silence.]

The silence on the tape carries over to the room. It is as if everyone is so shocked by what they have heard that no one knows quite what to say.

"How long ago did this happen?" one of the FBI agents asks.

"Can't be much more than ninety minutes," George replied. "The recorder automatically shut off just before you arrived."

"Let's get going!" I exclaim.

Outside, Chris was loading his truck. I quickly run over to him and ask, "Chris, did you see the Chinese lady?"

"The one that owns the building. She left in her silver Mercedes when I started working on that tree."

"Was she alone?"

"There was one guy with her, and another guy following in a white Chevy panel truck—a 1970, I think."

"How long ago was this?"

He thought before saying, "'About an hour and a half, maybe longer."

"'Thanks, Chris," I shout back while not breaking my stride as I run to get into George's car. He'd already pulled out the flashing light and attached it to the top of the roof.

We arrived at the Golden Lotus Restaurant only five minutes after the first responders, but a lifetime too late for Suzy. The yellow crime scene tape was already up and attracting the interest of the curious few as well as a small lunchtime crowd that had gathered and were wondering why they were being kept out of their favorite restaurant.

I could tell that it was going to be bad inside after we pulled up, and I saw a big, burly cop walk out of the building and throw up in the parking lot.

Inside the restaurant, they were all dead, even Ling, the cute little peroxide-blonde China doll who had been so nice to me at lunch that day. She lay small and quiet beneath the body of Suzy, who, it appeared, had thrown herself over her to try and protect her. Ling had been shot in the heart. Suzie had been shot in the back, and her throat had been slit. The manager lay in a large pool of blood not far from them. He was dressed in the same suit that he had worn the last time I was there.

The rest, including the two Mexican busboys, Miguel and Carlos, had been lined up against the wall and shot execution-style in the head. There was no rhyme or reason for all this wanton carnage other than the fact that it just happened to happen. Everyone there is thoroughly appalled by the senselessness of it all.

I walk around in a daze, taking in the still-fresh scene of blood and death that stretches out before me. I feel a hand on my shoulder and look around to see the sympathetic eyes of George lock onto mine, and only then do I realize that tears are streaming uncontrollably down my face and that I've been crying.

In all, nine people had been murdered simply because two psychotic misfits just plain enjoyed killing. We were all suddenly startled by a scream that came from the direction of the entryway.

A pretty young Chinese girl that I immediately recognized as the hostess stood there with her eyes wide open and her hands covering her mouth. She had come to work late because of a dental appointment. That dental appointment had saved her life.

We spent an hour at the restaurant with the crime scene investigators and afterward returned to Parker Center to sit in on an emergency meeting that the Chief had called. After an exhaustive search, no drugs had been found at the restaurant, so it was apparent that Ulrich and Yama had intended not only to collect the money but to keep the drugs as well.

It was obvious that something had gone terribly wrong with the supposedly well-coordinated inter-agency, inter-departmental sting operation, and everyone was desperately trying to figure out what exactly had happened. Later, it would be discovered that there had been a leak from a source somewhere in the CIA that had alerted both Ulrich and Yama about Suzy, forcing them to switch to a hastily improvised 'Plan B.'

As it stood now, the operation was blown, and Ulrich and Yama were nowhere to be found. They had cleared out everything from their respective apartments, and it was just as if they had simply disappeared. I told the team about the white 1970 Chevy panel truck that Chris had seen, and an APB was put out on it.

Flyers bearing pictures of Ulrich and Yama were immediately printed and circulated. They had gone to ground, but we all knew that they would eventually resurface. They still had a lot of heroin to sell.

Eventually, George and I went back to his office at the Santa Monica Police Station. Not really knowing what to do at this point, he just sat quietly behind his desk, and I sat quietly in the chair across from him. We seemed to be looking everywhere but at each other.

George finally broke the long silence. "We're going to get those guys, John." I could tell he really believed what he had just said.

"Yes, we will," I said, just as determined as he was.

There was another long silence. "So what do you want to do?" George finally asked.

"Go home and get very drunk," I replied.

"You mind having some company?"

"Of course not," I answered. I could tell that he was concerned about me. Or maybe he just wanted to get drunk too.

As soon as we got inside my house, I was surprised to see that my new furniture had been delivered. I had completely forgotten that the furniture was scheduled to be delivered this morning.

I also noticed that all the walls were now completely painted, and the living room now looked as new as the furniture. I guess the landlord had been over to finish painting the walls in time to let the delivery guys in. The smell of fresh paint and new furniture permeated the living room.

"I like your new stuff," George said admiringly as he patted my brand new white sofa sectional set. I walked over to the bar and picked out one of the bottles of single malt I had bought the other day, filling two water glasses with the Scotch.

I handed one to George, and we clinked our glasses in an unspoken toast, and George went over and turned on the television before plopping himself down on the sofa. It was a little after six o'clock, and the news was on.

All over the world, they were condemning President Nixon's Christmas Day bombing of North Vietnam, but I couldn't work up any interest over the subject. Neither could George, I thought as I watched him stare glassy-eyed at the appalling images that flashed seemingly non-stop across the television screen.

One thing we both knew from experience was that violence can only beget violence. How many more monsters with damaged souls will return from the battlefield to wreak havoc on our society?

George must have been thinking about pretty much the same thing because after he took a long, deep swallow of Scotch, he turned to me and asked, "What's happening to the world, John? Why can't it be like it was before?"

"Like when we were kids," I answered, but it wasn't an answer. Or maybe it was. Like when we were kids and we were young and innocent. But we had to grow older, and now we were no longer young—and we were no longer innocent. Innocence had only become a distant memory.

There are so many ways to lose your innocence, and once it's lost—like a girl's virginity—it stays lost. Now all that remains for us is the harsh reality of a cruel, uncompromising world. There's simply no going back to a past that's now long gone.

"You want something to eat?" I asked. "We haven't eaten anything all day."

"Nah, I'm not hungry."

I knew how he was feeling because I wasn't feeling hungry either. I was just empty inside, but I also somehow knew that no amount of food and no amount of drink would ever fill that painful emptiness that was now eating away inside of me, eating away not only at my heart but at my soul as well.

All day I had been trying to keep Suzy out of my mind, but now it was no longer possible. The memories came like a flood, relentlessly flowing and unstoppable, and before I could smother them, an anguished sob pushed itself up from deep within me. I just couldn't help myself, even though I felt embarrassed for losing my self-control.

George came over and embraced me, hugging me hard as he said, "You really loved her, didn't you, John?"

There was no way I could have answered him, so I didn't. After what could have been a minute or an eternity, I reached up and dried my eyes with the back of my hand and said, "I'm all right now."

I looked down to see that my hand was shaking and the Scotch in my glass was almost gone, so I downed the rest of it and poured myself another. George came over and did the same. I'd finally managed to settle down, so when we raised our glasses this time, I said, "To Suzie."

Our glasses clinked and George repeated the toast, "To Suzie," and both of us drained a good half a glass before coming up for air.

"This is sipping Scotch," George slurred, "and here we are chugging it."

"But it burns so smooth." I was beginning to slur myself. "And it makes my mind feel all warm and fuzzy."

There was a long silence, and the mood started getting more serious all of a sudden.

"So what are we going to do, George?"

"What are we going to do about what?"

"What are we going to do about life?"

"I don't know," George said. "I don't have the answers. I used to think I did, but now I know that I really don't."

We both proceeded to get drunk as skunks until George passed out on my brand new sofa, and somehow I managed to find a blanket to throw over him before staggering into my bedroom, finding my bed, and passing out on it still fully clothed.

Chapter Twenty-Seven

Wednesday, December 27, 1972
A sharp, unrelenting pain in my arm startled me, not quite awake but to a sufficient state of consciousness to realize that my head was killing me, and my mouth tasted like something had crawled up into it and died. I tried to open my eyes, but it was far too painful, and suddenly I had the sensation of being tossed up into the air, only to immediately land back down painfully onto some kind of hard, unyielding surface.

I felt like throwing up, but since I hadn't eaten in such a long time, all I could manage was something like an approximation of the dry heaves. I suddenly felt another jab of pain in my arm, and I opened my eyes to see that I was being kicked by a hard-toed leather shoe, and I moaned, "Stop."

I heard George's voice come from somewhere next to me as he said, "Sorry, just wanted to see if you were still alive."

As I was once again jarred violently into the air, I realized that my arms were bound behind my back, as were George's, and we were both lying crammed in with a cargo of boxes on the floor at the back of a moving panel truck. And the truck was, at that very moment, moving over what seemed like a very rough road.

I tried to sit up, but my body was so sore and my headache was so bad that it didn't seem to be worth the effort. "What happened?" I asked.

"You tell me. I just woke up a few minutes before you did."

As I took in our surroundings, my head started to clear and the situation was becoming obvious. "I think we're getting a ride in a white 1970 Chevy panel truck that could certainly use a good set of shock absorbers."

"Well, lucky us," George grunted. I could see that he had been trying to work on the ropes that were tied tightly around his hands. I could also see that he had not made any progress; they were just too well tied.

"Trying to get some circulation back in those hands?"

"Trying, but it's not working. It looks like we're fucked."

I was going to say 'Yeah' but decided not to. The game wasn't over yet, even though, at this point, it sure looked like it was. So instead, I said, "Why do you think they came after us? I mean, like, at this point, what good could it possibly do them?"

"Your guess is as good as mine."

We wouldn't have to guess for long. After a few more bone-jarring bumps, the truck came to an abrupt stop that threatened to send several of the boxes flying onto us, but fortunately, whatever was in the boxes—and we had a pretty good idea about what that was—proved to be too heavy.

After we heard the front doors of the truck slam shut, we waited in silent anticipation of what was to come next. What was to come came a long minute later when the back door of the truck squeaked open, and along with the overly bright early morning light of day, a fresh sea breeze gusted in, rustling through our hair and cooling our sweating faces. I could hear the sound of waves crashing against rocks, and the loud and familiar screeching of seagulls confirmed that we were somewhere near the ocean.

The irises of my eyes quickly adjusted to make out the smiling ferret face of Mark Ulrich as he stood hovering over me. "Well, well, awake now, are we?" he said as he looked down at our prostrate forms. Conrad Yama stood in his accustomed place, just behind and to the left of him.

"So what is this?" I asked. "Are you taking us on some kind of picnic?"

This brought out one of Ferret Face's obnoxious laughs. "Yeah, we're going on a picnic. You really crack me up, Wadd."

"Let's get to it," Yama said impatiently.

"Oh, let's have ourselves a little fun first." Ferret Face smiled. "There ain't no one for miles and miles around to hear us all having ourselves a little fun."

"I'd rather just get it over with," Yama insisted.

Ferret Face sighed. "I suppose you're right. We still have a lot of shit to do, now, don't we? So we'll do them one at a time. Ok, Wadd, sit up."

I didn't like the sound of this at all, and deciding that I wasn't going to make his job any easier for him, I said, "You know, I've sort of grown accustomed to the position that I'm in."

"The position that you're in is a shit one, pal," he said as he reached in and pulled me up to a sitting position, which proved to be just as painful as my reclining position but with the added effect of a sudden unpleasant feeling of dizziness and nausea.

"I think I'm going to barf," I said quite truthfully.

Ferret Face took a step back while I was racked with the dry heaves, and when it was over, he took a large gold ring off of his left middle finger and reached over and put it on mine. "Don't say I never gave you anything," he said.

"What are we, now, engaged?" I asked, trying to maintain at least a semblance of cool.

"Yeah, we're engaged. And I hope you like the wedding," he muttered as he pulled his ID wallet and badge out of his coat pocket and stuffed them into the back pocket of my pants.

So that was the plan. George and I were destined to be two corpses—a tall Caucasian one and a short Asian-American one, complete with the personal jewelry and IDs that indicated our names were Mark Ulrich and Conrad Yama.

"This isn't going to work, you know. They're still going to compare our dental records."

"What makes you think there's going to be a head along with the body to compare? Besides, by the time you guys wash back to shore, there won't be all that much of you left anyway."

I looked over at George, whose eyes told me that he thought that this was as much of a revolting development as I did. I began to realize, with more than a little desperation, that we were actually truly fucked.

"All right, Wadd," Ferret Face continued. "Show time, and that means get your ass up and off the truck." He was clearly enjoying himself, and I was resenting him for it.

"I'm just now starting to feel a little better, so I think I'll remain sitting here if you don't mind."

He motioned to Yama, who pulled out his Colt Gold Cup .45 Autoloader and pointed it at me. "You ever been shot in the nuts, Wadd?"

"No, I've been waiting all my life to have that particular experience."

Ferret Face pulled me roughly out of the van, and I fell out onto the hard, pebbly ground on my knees. The pain was excruciating, forcing me to utter a long string of expletives.

Conrad slammed the back door of the truck shut to keep George in before giving me a hard kick in the ribs. "Get up if you don't want another one," he warned.

I tried to get up, but it was extremely difficult with my hands tied behind my back. And aside from that, both my legs seemed to want to buckle and cave in. Ferret Face pulled me up and tried to steady me.

Even though the wind was blowing my unruly hair into my eyes, I could see now that we were in one of those deserted areas along the Pacific Coast, probably somewhere between Los Angeles and San Francisco. I could see the narrow dirt road in the distance that led to the outcropping where we were now standing. The highway was probably miles and miles away.

Conrad's gun was prodding my back, moving me toward the direction of the edge of a cliff about thirty feet away. I had noticed that the sleeve of the blue blazer that he wore was missing one of its brass buttons.

When we reached the precipice, I looked down to see the waves crashing violently against the jagged black rocks some fifty feet or so below.

"Just in time for the high tide," Conrad said with some satisfaction. "It'll float you out to sea, and the fish will be able to make a good long meal of you before you float back in, probably sometime next week."

"It'll be a regular wedding banquet," Ferret Face laughed.

I tried to think of an appropriate retort, but at this point, one wouldn't come to mind. I watched Ulrich as he suddenly got serious and pulled his SOG S-1 combat knife out of the custom leather sheath attached to his right ankle. He lovingly passed his finger over the well-sharpened blade, then looked over at me and smiled.

"So do you have any last words, Wadd?"

The wind had died down somewhat, and I felt the warmth of the sun on my skin. I took a deep breath of the fresh sea air because I knew it would probably be one of my last, and I said, "Yeah."

"Say them," he said as he lifted his knife to my throat.

"You're one sick puppy, Ulrich."

Then, just as he began giggling that ridiculously nutty laugh of his, there was a loud, echoing boom, and his head exploded into a mist of red—blood and brains splattered and sprayed across my face and hair.

I turned to see that Yama had turned to see where the shot had come from. His eyes showed panic, and he was holding Ulrich's semi-headless corpse as a shield in front of him, and for the moment he appeared to have forgotten all about me.

I took that opportunity to slowly back away from the precipice and drop belly to the ground, eyes facing Yama, who was still standing there behind Ferret Face's dead body, looking furtively around.

The wind had begun to kick up again, blowing thin swirls of dust into my eyes. There was another loud, booming shot, and Yama turned and returned fire in the direction of the dirt road.

The wind suddenly died down once again, and I watched Yama out of the corner of my eye and wondered if he had been able to nail whoever had been shooting. The answer came with another loud, booming shot, and this time the bullet blasted into the center of Ulrich's chest with a force of impact that sent both of them toppling over the edge of the cliff.

I remained breathing dirt on the hard, stony ground while waiting for another shot to come, but thankfully none came. It seemed like half an hour, but it was probably only five minutes before I heard the sound of a car pulling up and stopping nearby and the sound of the car door opening and then slamming shut.

I strained to turn around to see who had arrived as leather soled shoes beneath khaki pants crunched on the ground and leisurely approached where I lay, then walked past me and on over to stand at the very precipice of the jagged cliff.

After a few moments, the shoes and khaki pants walked back toward me and stopped as whoever was wearing them bent over me, and I heard the faint click of a stiletto switchblade knife flipping open. After a moment, I felt a slight pulling at my arms and at my hands before I realized that my hands had been cut free from the tight binding of the ropes and I could now use my arms once again.

I turned around and allowed my aching hands to push myself up to something like a sitting position, only to come face to face with the now familiar unsmiling face of Frankie Funai, who was squatting next to me slowly and carefully closing his switchblade knife.

He was probably the last guy I had expected to be my savior, but I certainly wasn't going to look a gift horse in the mouth, and I would have been happy to admit that I was glad he had come to this particular little picnic.

I tried to think of something appropriate to say, but all I could think of to say was, "So you were following me."

"Suzy wanted me to look after you," he said. Then he jerked his head toward the cliff and looked thoughtfully out at the ocean as the wind blew his hair and quietly informed me, "But this one was only for Suzy."

There was a silence, and I felt perhaps the same deep sadness that he was feeling, but I really didn't want to show it, so I said, "You know, you're pretty damn good with that rifle."

He shrugged his shoulders, but there was no way he was going to be modest about it at this stage of the game. "From two hundred yards, you just better believe it."

"So what happened with the second shot?"

"It must've been the wind."

I was still thinking of Suzie, and I was still trying not to let my emotions get the better of me, so I asked him, "What kind of rifle did you use?"

He looked over at me. "You're full of questions, aren't you, Wadd?" Then he saw how my eyes were struggling to keep back the tears, and he looked away and said, "It was a Weatherby 300 Magnum."

"Shit, you could kill an elephant with that." I tried to laugh.

"What makes you think I haven't?" He rubbed his right shoulder with his left hand. "Anyway, my shoulder's going to be sore as hell for a few days, even though I only used 130 grain loads."

"Remind me not to mess with you."

"I don't think I'll have to remind you."

Suddenly, there was the sound of frantic banging and shouting coming from the panel truck. Frankie looked up. "Who's that?"

"George Lee."

"George Lee, the cop?"

"That would be one and the same."

"I think it's time for me to take my leave." He got up and started toward his car. "I hate having to talk to cops."

"That truck is full of heroin, you know."

He turned around, stopped, looked at me, and said, "I told you, I didn't come for the heroin. I came for Suzy." Then he reached into his pocket and pulled out his switchblade knife and tossed it to me before saying, "Just one more thing, Mr. Wadd."

"My friends call me Johnny."

"Johnny," he said before giving a dramatic pause, then continuing, "I have one thing to ask of you."

"Yes?"

"Please don't cut him loose until after I've gone."

I let myself ignore George's kicking and screaming as I watched Frankie get into his dark-colored Mercury Cougar and drive away. I turned back toward the ocean, and I thought about Suzie and about all of the life and death I had encountered in my past. As I listened to the familiar sounds of the screeching sea gulls and crashing waves and felt the comforting warmth of the sun and the cool caress of the wind across my face, I contemplatively wondered about all of the life and death that was still to come.

Afterword

Although this is first and foremost a work of fiction, I have tried to be as historically accurate as possible with regard to the time period and the background details. For example, as I recall, the month of December in winter of 1972 was a particularly cold one for Southern California, and while I may not be spot on in my descriptions of the day-to-day weather conditions, I believe that they were somewhat similar to what I have depicted.

It has been quite an experience, this attempt at going back in time to life in Los Angeles in the early 1970s. It made me realize that this really was an interesting period in our nation's history and a truly amazing one to have lived through.

By 1972, the senseless and misguided military conflict in Southeast Asia known as the Vietnam War had been going on for over thirteen years and would continue to go on for almost another three before the Fall of Saigon would finally signify its inglorious end.

Unfortunately, there was to be no peace with honor. There was only the unmitigated disaster of defeat and withdrawal as our troops came home, not to a hero's welcome but to a country anxious to forget the lost cause to which these men and women had risked and offered up their lives.

They returned home broken and disillusioned, and the sad tragedy of this war is that a good many of them returned addicted to the drugs that had proliferated over there with easy availability and abundance.

Their return opened up such a great demand for these drugs that it would usher in a new era of violent and deadly criminal activity in this country. And as the recreational use of illegal drugs and controlled substances started to become the norm rather than the exception, it threatened to undermine the very fabric of our society.

It's ironic that what began ostensibly as a paranoid attempt to halt the spread of Communism and its perceived threat to this country would ultimately end up destroying it from within.

The BNDD, or Bureau of Narcotics and Dangerous Drugs, was an actual government agency that had been formed to stamp out the menace of the rapidly growing international traffic of illegal drugs. It was the precursor of the current DEA, or Drug Enforcement Administration, with which it merged when the latter was formed in 1973. 1972, the BNDD had something like 1,500 agents throughout the country and around the world.

Most of them were good agents who were seriously concerned about the growing drug problem in this country. They tried to conscientiously do their job to the best of their ability. Some of them, however, turned out to be opportunists who used their job to further their own agendas.

To his credit, John Ingersoll, the head of the BNDD, was aware of this and had become so concerned about the corruption within the agency that he eventually enlisted the aid of the CIA to assist in his determined campaign to root out the corrupt agents.

Various sting operations were put into place that resulted in a number of arrests. The agency was trying to clean house and send a determined message, but the message was falling on deaf ears. The highly profitable drug business could not be wiped out so easily.

Of course, it really did not help when you take into consideration that the CIA itself was supposedly directly involved in transporting the opium from the Golden Triangle to Taiwan, where it was processed into heroin and then ferried back to Vietnam to be sold to our own troops.

It only confirmed the old sayings, which stated that "money is power" and "money corrupts." The one thing that the drug lords had plenty of was money. All this provided me with the background for the story of Flesh of the Lotus.

The science of forensic technology has evolved considerably since 1972. Such things as computational forensics and DNA profiling simply did not exist at that time. In fact, DNA profiling as a technique was not readily available until 1987. So the medical examiner had to work very hard with whatever means he had on hand at that particular time to build a case on the basis of scientific evidence.

There were no extensive automated fingerprint databases such as we have now, and making fingerprint comparisons was still a rather slow and painstaking process. I have attempted to keep whatever evidence that has been presented in this book within the bounds of the technology of the time.

Many of you who are familiar with the Los Angeles area will find that I have used places that either still exist or used to exist to give this novel a sense of authenticity. Some of the people as well as the places described may even seem familiar, but please bear in mind that they are all being used in a totally fictitious context that has no actual bearing on reality. I hope that I have not offended anyone by doing this, and if I have, I apologize.

Most of all, I sincerely hope that I have been able to provide the reader with an entertaining work of fiction.

—Bob Chinn

ABOUT THE AUTHOR

Bob Chinn is the creator and porn auteur of the nine-part Johnny Wadd adult film series that, in 1970, launched the career of legendary porn icon, John Curtis Holmes. After graduating from UCLA film school, Chinn had aspirations of becoming a mainstream Hollywood director but began to accept work opportunities in the erotic movie genre in order to support his young family.

Printed in Great Britain
by Amazon

42825674R10151